CH00869597

The Last Defender

38059 10081349 4

The Last Defender

Derek Keen

Copyright © 2011 Derek Keen

The moral right of the author has been asserted.

Apart from any fair dealing for the purposes of research or private study,
or criticism or review, as permitted under the Copyright, Designs and Patents
Act 1988, this publication may only be reproduced, stored or transmitted, in
any form or by any means, with the prior permission in writing of the
publishers, or in the case of reprographic reproduction in accordance with
the terms of licences issued by the Copyright Licensing Agency. Enquiries
concerning reproduction outside those terms should be sent to the publishers.

Matador
5 Weir Road
Kibworth Beauchamp
Leicester LE8 0LQ, UK
Tel: (+44) 116 279 2299
Fax: (+44) 116 279 2277
Email: books@troubador.co.uk
Web: www.troubador.co.uk/matador

ISBN 978 1848765 245

British Library Cataloguing in Publication Data.
A catalogue record for this book is available from the British Library.

BARNSLEY LIBRARY SERVICE	
10081349	
Bertrams	29/03/2011
GEN	£8.99

To my only son

'Faith is not a possession of all people'
(2Thess 3 v2)

- 4 MAY 2011

"Kick it! Just kick it!"
In a split second he heard the shouts ringing out above the sudden buzz of the crowd. With every progressive dribble he felt them pounding into his ears, but paid no heed as he prodded the ball further into the space ahead of him. Not yet. A despairing lunge arrived too late, as he spun away to his right, where the goal loomed nearer into focus. The big centre-half was closing in, so a quick decision was needed to throw him off. A stepover or a shimmy. Jiggle wide to make him lose his balance, as he hesitates. Yes. He spotted the gap which the unsighted goalie had given him. Now. An infinitesimal dip of the left shoulder announced the lightning speed of a shot. As though a missile had been launched from the hammer of his right foot the ball swerved almost effortlessly, curling its way past groping fingers, and fizzed into the top corner of the net. The winner! A tumultuous roar whooshed in his ears like a blast of a high wind as the scorer skipped away, the vibrating ground lifting him to float deliriously towards the corner flag. Then, overcome, he fell to his knees, as team mates arrived in leaps and bounds to add their delight to the mix: "Ol-ly! Ol-ly!" The chants were coming thick and fast …

He looked up, his whiskers tingling and the end of his tail twitching, as, all too quickly, that magical moment began to fade. Though the mid-morning rim of the sky was powder-blue, the dark stones beneath it towered over him in a starker, granite relief. Flat on his back, even as the dream dissolved, the sight of a familiar face jinking in and out of a half-open upper window jerked him back to alarming reality. Two pointy ears and a pointier nose began to appear, then disappear, in a wild effort to grab some kind of firm footing. A long, scrawny paw was squeezed against the window, as the other began to jab away freely toward Olly's prostrate figure below. All at once the sharp, slitty eyes looked up and narrowed as they caught sight of an unexpected and hopeful ally drawing near. Then came a voice, hoarse as a rattle.

"Hey! You down there!"

An altogether more prepossessing figure, cool and cream, with flecks of pale brown flanking his haunches like beads of moist sand, stopped and took his time isolating the origin of the sound from the surrounding silences. Dappled by the sunlit branches that overhung a larch-lined pathway, a muscular, tufted foreleg flicked playfully at a yellowy carpet of leaves and made them dance and twirl merrily in the sun. The figure continued on, carefree and regardless of the vocal interruption. So, the voice from above hissed once again in a fiercely insistent undertone. Then louder still, this time with added directions.

"*You!* Over there! Look! About ten paces this way."

The owner of the equally lean and scrawny body stretched himself further, repeatedly pointing with such crazed abandon that he was in danger of slipping

2

entirely over the sill. With his reverie broken, the cream cat below posted an annoyed upward glance to the direction of the urgent cries.

"Do you see it! A rat! A skulking rat!" hissed the voice, barely able to contain its mounting agitation.

"Do your natural duty. You must!"

The last words were emphasised so forcefully that he banged his head against the stone lintel in extreme frustration. The cream cat edged forward slowly, checked his stride and began to peer intently into the honeysuckle ranged in clusters along the wall. Having already wriggled out of the direct glare, Olly was desperately trying to inch himself back as far as possible into the still deeper shadows of the doorway's stone portal. In a moment there would be nowhere to run, nowhere to hide. His heart accelerated as he felt each beat boom into his head and pulse hotly through his ears. All at once the thought came to him: that he was never going capture that scoring feeling for real. Only in his dreams. Never to get that gloriously awaited goal, here in this wide world outside. But, then, this wasn't his world. It had never quite become his world. The familiar feeling of guilt crept up over him. Was one moment of glory really more important than your life? Than the family you would leave behind? ... your friends? ... the rest of the team? ... Death's door brought you down to earth in quite a different way, it seemed.

He screwed up his eyes in shame and shook his head rapidly as if to extricate all such negative, self-centred thoughts from his mind. A kaleidoscope of evolving cogwheel patterns commingled with stars churned their way across unseeing eyes, as pure fear finally took over and blotted out everything else. And now … the final end … was coming. But nothing happened. Nothing changed. In his dread of expectation he slowly opened one uncertain eye ... to behold the vision of a large, white and wavy cat sitting nonchalantly before him, every thick curl in his mane shining regally in the glare of the light. Olly pressed hard against the wall, wishing the dark stones could absorb him, render him invisible, do anything to make the large, lowering head move away. A strange spluttering from the window above soon broke the surreal spell of the silence once more.

"You've got cats' eyes, for goodness sake! Why are you squinting like that? You see it, surely? There! Right there! Grab it, before it decides to make a run for it! Get it! Get it now!"

The 'its' spattered like pellets from an air gun as the rat-spotter raised his voice to a manic screech and tilted further from his already precarious position. The cream cat narrowed his gaze, right paw tilted over gemmed eyes, almost in a mock salute; as though he was having great difficulty in determining whether there was actually anything worthy of his discovery. Then, in a coarse, though not unfriendly whisper, he nodded downward.

"G'day t' yer, mate! Down't you be warryin' abowt owld scraggy up theyre. Oi seen dingoes with more meat than he carries. Brayver, too. Better scarper, afore he gets clapperin' down them stairs. Yew shoot

4

off quick end enjoy th' dhay."

With this brief remark earnestly expressed, the cat winked and strolled on jauntily as if nothing could possibly have happened to disturb his morning. An exasperated groan of disgust descended as a postscript to the missed opportunity.

"Useless! Useless! Oh, bothersomely useless!"

But nobody below was listening. The head jerked back inside and wasn't seen again.

A distant church clock began chiming eleven. The rodent heart took almost as long to subside before an involuntary tremble brought its owner to his senses and triggered a rush of adrenalin to act on the suggestion that had just been made. He scrambled nervously over the portal wall and wriggled under a worn corner angle in the great oak door. There was a pause, as his feet came into contact with a withered green carpet which covered most of the hall around the foot of the staircase. The big east windows in the library shone their combined rays of softer light over a large portion of its surface to create an effect which never failed to remind Olly of the conditions best suited to football - a lush, flat, stretch of turf. Without dwelling too long on this he began to listen for the tell-tale sounds coming from upstairs. You might never hear a cat's movements, but the continual mutterings of annoyance and low-spoken grievances made by Arturo as he roamed about the house made it somewhat easier to avoid a chance meeting. The other rats, too, had quickly worked this out to their advantage. There was a scuffle, followed by a few squeals from the room directly above, then a quick slam of a door and a harsh clack of footsteps. Olly tensed and, juggling the options over in his mind, thought perhaps the west wing as his best bet for escape. Astonished to still to be in one piece, he didn't relish the thought of pushing his luck again so soon.

Getting back by this route would involve navigating a convoluted trail of bending pipes and twisted cables, choking dirt and darkness. Par for the course. But at least you couldn't swing a cat in it. The west wing was always a deserted place; where the skeletal lamp stands and massive mahogany furniture, forever draped in great folds of hideous white sheets, never failed to lend the room a consistently spooky appearance. From previous observations he knew Arturo would steer well clear of this part of the house whenever possible. Olly shrugged and offered up a quick smile of fake bravado to the great clock as his sole witness. Fine. He would take whatever fate had in store for him, although just smiling through was not his way of dealing with the consequences.

But fortune, it seemed, was still prepared to smile on him, and it turned up, literally, with the intercepting suddenness of a click. Beneath the staircase in front of him an ancient, arched door swung open to reveal the equally gnarled and knotty fingers of old Pale the gardener. With head bent, and fumbling absent-mindedly for a ring of keys caught in his apron pocket. It was but the work of a moment for Olly to sprint past unseen into a grimy stairwell, whose dry and dusty steps seemed quenched only by a moist and reeking darkness. Although the floor at the bottom of the cellar was as stone-cold as the ceiling was low, he breathed easily now, moving in familiar territory.

Whether ancestral ghosts still roamed the labyrinthine bolt-holes, bore holes, pipelines and tortuous tunnels of renown that mapped their way about the house, mattered little to him as he picked his way through the gloom. Any footfall or whisper, however slight, would surely mean only one thing - the presence of that freakishly slant-eyed creature known as a cat, egged on by his equally insufferable and interfering mistress. Looking out for blood. The blood of any rat stupid enough to stumble into their path. *He* wasn't any rat, and certainly not so stupid to fall for their traps. If daydreams ever proved to be the instruments of his downfall, without quite knowing how it came to him, the spontaneous thought that a live rat was infinitely better off than a dead lion offered him an immediate and immense reassurance. The more secret (perhaps sacred) paths were unknown to most of the rat community he sought to rejoin. They were hidden away, well concealed behind and below creaking floorboards; warped timbers that had at one time clattered regularly like a ship's deck with the bold and sturdy feet of now long-departed voyagers. A few, however, had stood the test of time and remained shored up in good repair for any emergency which might arise. Not that their descendants ever imagined a time when they would be needed. Caution was ever a watchword, but the manor was their heritage, their history, and their freedom had never been challenged as far back as anyone could remember. Freedom. Now that was a word he'd been questioning repeatedly in his mind of late.

As he reached the far end of the cellar all worries about cats and dying began to ebb away into the enduring silence of a darkness where natural light stood no chance of penetrating. He blinked rapidly, fine-tuning night vision eyes to the shapes that suddenly seemed to reach out and surround him. Etched out ahead in an inkier relief rose two colossal figures, gaunt and forbidding, and so closely touching that they seemed to be locked in a dance of death. The structures were surmounted by two ragged, forward-leaning heads with faceless, invisible eyes that seemed to stare a warning to all intruders: that to advance would indeed be a very dangerous move. Olly went on briskly however, confident that such warnings didn't apply to him. With his own eyes on the ground and head tucked low in respectful awe, he scuttled carefully through the gaps formed between a mass of spread-eagled limbs. The figures did not stir, but remained monstrously poised, the flow of their locks fantastic in a motionless slipstream of tangled ferocity. He firmly believed that if an enemy ever did approach, they would instantly come cranking to life with frightening results. A clash of steel, perhaps; for they appeared to have long swords and javelins slung about them. Lief said they had been standing there for centuries. Like the pyramids. Whatever they were. As guardians to an inner sanctum, albeit in a way perhaps not originally intended, they partially obscured a great curtain immediately behind them. Made from a heavy, velvety material, which had grown gauzier through years of dust and decay, its thick folds were crocheted and intertwined with beards of cobwebs to complete a near perfect camouflage; a more than opaque window to whatever world it was that existed beyond. Olly slipped silently beneath one of the folds and vanished like a conjuring trick.

If, in another world, conflicting thoughts could be skimmed off like dross and good intentions refined to a purer resolve, who would ever wish to stray from such a place? However, standing inside the boundary of this other world, he experienced no such noble feelings to console or soothe his troubled spirit. Even beyond the curtain darkness still dominated, and some portion of it, having got sucked into his brain, was swirling about and filling it with all sorts of nagging uncertainty. The golden goal of his dreams had nearly been the last one he ever scored in all his short life. Though admitting as much, the urge frustratingly remained. With a see-sawing sense of determination and depression racking his mind, he descended a passage the existence of which even the most cunning of smugglers would have been proud to acknowledge or set foot in.

Almost at once he detected the familiar earthy smell that hung in the deadening air. Absence made the heart grow fonder, it was said. But not for him. He flicked his tail and shivered once as he touched the cloying dampness of the rough plaster walls which descended, narrowed, then levelled, at a sudden turn. A sickly yellowish glare began to creep over the them, giving the tunnel the vague appearance of some god-forsaken and long-forgotten mineshaft roofed with the folded arms and squatting legs of dead men's bones. Perhaps, like the probing of those resilient grave robbers, the sun's rays might finally have wormed their way through to its depths and were about to dig a big spadeful of dazzling light into what was left of a crumbling vault. *If only.*

He mouthed the words resignedly under his breath, guessing all too well the source of the light which was evidently growing more feeble with each passing moment. His mind broke away once again. He was tired of the endless repetition of training, playing, grubbing, then yet more training. Not the beautiful game. No, he had never yet lost his love of the game; but the cold, unchanging Arena, the centre of the only life he knew, was no longer an inspirational place. It seemed to have reduced his natural exuberance to a joyless indifference over which he felt he had little or no control. It wasn't that he saw himself as an entirely solitary figure in those goal-getting dreams of his. After all, his fellow players were there too, as sharers in his glory. Taking centre stage was, he readily believed, just a concession to vanity which any of the others would likely imitate in any similar state of downheartedness. Or so he had convinced himself. Increasingly though, he found himself drifting out of a match as it wore on, staying clear of involvement, out of position, merely a peripheral figure to all the furious confrontations being fought back and forth around him. And if anybody noticed, well, they weren't saying too much. Except for the Whisperer.

That mysterious whisperer of words, whose exotic presence came and went like an unuttered *cri de coeur,* though always bringing much needed temporal comfort to his spirit. Inspirational and sometimes poetic, they were words spoken from the heart of cold dawn's earth: echoing up into the heights to soar away beyond the blue-perforated crowns of green and distant trees. The rising and falling of an euphoric symphony: of an endless sky swooping with the wind to carry him along in the visionary delights of a sweet and summery embrace. Ah, all very desirable, to be sure. But hold on. Could such distilled words of hope really stoop to one so low? Reach out to the lowest of the low? How far would freedom extend its hand? Beyond all dreams naturally human? Let its yes be yes, or such hopes meant nothing to him. Nothing.

An ache panged dully again throughout his limbs, as the words melted away almost as quickly as they had come. There was a ruffling sigh within the rafters, where a pocket of air eddied down from an unseen ventilation hole - a whispering, unsubstantial token to his own abject condition. Like a chink of daylight bored through a rock cave, a tiny sliver of flame finally came into view. He continued at a snail's pace, while his thoughts quickened again.

Now take the Twins, for example. They felt a bit like himself, he felt sure. But, then, they were really onto something, mind you. Of all the rats, they were currently the most beguiling, adventurous pair around. It was they who had secretly sat up in the Master's tower and watched the World Cup unfold. Once they had found out about the tournament there had been no stopping them. He had a peculiar notion that the dear fellow had even encouraged them, or at least tolerated their presence. His old bloodhound was as much indifferent, so they said. Never alerted by any scent of theirs and more than content to fall asleep before an ever-burning log fire. Most nights they came flying down, full of what they called 'useful tricks'. You couldn't do everything a man could do, but you'd make a few adjustments, scale them down a little. No one had done that for years, down here. Some tricks a rat could actually perform better. Improve on 'em, so they claimed. A bit star-struck, both. But one or the other were capable of getting you a goal out of nothing. And laugh all the way back to the centre circle. High tails and high-fives every time. Captain didn't find it so amusing though, calling it a mockery, a dereliction of duty which would only sidetrack the younger players. Olly recalled the words well, for they were often repeated for his own benefit. Anyway, these two were definitely a breath of fresh air where it was needed, as far as he was concerned. Nothing, surely, stood still forever. Improvements were, well, improvements, if they really made life better. He shaped his mouth into another wry smile as if to defy its present woeful expression and trudged on.

The tunnel began to taper off as though all the energies and resources in its construction had been simultaneously spent, and its builders had determined to cut their losses on the spot. It finished at a dead-end of a wall, where Olly estimated a man might just be able to stand if he kept his knees bent a good deal. Like the candle flame ahead (for such it was), his strength seemed to drain away with every leaden step, in a display of body language which any keen observer might have correctly interpreted as being a rather perverse or quite irregular form of home-sickness. The stump of candle had been plugged at the foot of a large, solitary, well-rusted ring firmly bolted midway into a low wall of solid stone. The flame was spitting fitfully, almost at the point of extinction. The candle had been left to show his absence had been noted, and it was now in the final throes of its lonely vigil. Olly groaned inwardly, barely able to contain his annoyance at being regarded as a species of some wayward child whose proneness to misadventure was now to be taken for granted. To be given up on as a lost cause! Was that it? Huh! His own answer to this charitable act was to blow it out with a force of due contempt. A wisp of its invisible smoke rose thinly into the low-ceilinged darkness.

Without need of any such light, he felt his way further along the wall till he touched a smoother upright stone, one vertically sandwiched at ground level between two slimmer oblongs. He rapped against it impatiently and waited. If he was expecting something to happen, it didn't. Then he thumped it with the heel of his foot three times, before shaking his benighted head wearily. He waited again. Suddenly the stone began to judder and screak as it was drawn from the wall. Staring out from the space created, a pair of eyes began to blink steadily.

"Who is it?"

"Who do you think it is?" came the thoroughly fed-up reply.

Surrounded by the subdued glow of some inner light, the silhouette of a small head nodded in nervous recognition.

"Sorry, the Captain - er - we thought you would be late," whispered the correspondingly timid voice.

Olly eased his sturdy frame through the space without saying a word. With that, the stone was carefully pushed back to its former position and wedged in firmly from the rear. Followed by the dutiful attendant, Olly silently retraced the worn, pitted steps of the place he had had no real wish to return to, once more to confront the glimmering enclave of his youth: the hallowed ground which had ever measured and bewitched their very existence.

One of the scouts had been on a ship (so he had said) and, in listening to his recollections of life on it, Olly had found the obvious and most perfect of dismal comparisons. Their habitation was a place that was called the bilge. The lowest of the low in the ship. Bilge? Were they known only as bilge rats, he had wondered? It was the darkest, bottommost portion of life on a rolling sea, where, according to him, you could almost hear the big fish roaming and nosing

14

about with their big snouts outside. Vivid imagination, had Lief. There were plenty of men and a cat or two on board as well. The ocean was a hostile world around them, and to escape a sinking ship you would have to find a boat and throw yourself to the mercy of the sailors – or the sea. Till its restlessness was no more ... no more ... or you were no more.

His eyes adjusted themselves again to the present. The Arena: smooth, cold, grey stones surrounding a finely-honed floor of whinstone flags. Iron sconces hung midway between each wall, each having a chunk of whitish candle wedged into their cone-shaped, iron grilles. Three of them were already delivering their graceful, vertical flames, while the fourth was in the process of being ignited by some adept and acrobatic volunteers with a taper. The unmistakable figure of Captain Greybands stood at the half-way point on the side where the paltry steps jutted down, as several of the younger volunteers, scattered here and there, busied themselves in remarking all the faded lines, including the centre circle, using broken sticks of chalk. He was aware of Olly's presence, but pretended at first not to notice. He surveyed both sides of the playing area where still others were meticulously redrawing the goalposts and crossbars, according to their statutory size, with more pieces of the chalk. While it may not have been a ploy to get the young renegade to make the first move, it did, however, have that necessary effect. With his head slightly lowered Olly sidled over almost indifferently to the Captain's side. He began clearing his throat.

"Getting everything ship-shape then, sir?" he ventured, almost chirpily, in the hope of gaining his superior's attention.

"Ah, Oliver. Good of you to come. And since when were *you* ever a rat of the high seas?"

Greybands, head unturned, remained intent on the business going on in front of him. Olly cleared the dryness of his throat a second time.

"They're good boys. Reliable for the dirty work, eh sir?"

"Dirty? A little, perhaps. But work? I prefer to call it plying their trade. Our speciality in this house, remember. Our calling. A learning curve to develop an affection for the game."

Here he looked Olly up and down from the corner of his eye.

Good for enthusiasm, future prospects. Teamwork. As he, of all people, should well know, he rounded off. He waved an order to one of the trainees, then turned, as though to invite a positive reaction to such tried and tested concepts. But Olly could only equate prospects with these unrelenting, never-changing routines in this bleak, one-dimensional playground: something he presently found hard to accept, much less get ecstatic about. Prospects where nothing ever changed. He resisted a shrug, though.

"That Jed is looking ok, sir. Neat and incisive when he takes care. Just needs to grow an inch or so more, I think," he replied in a carefully restrained tone.

"Ah, yes. How observant you are. While we're touching on the matter of care, Oliver, you really

16

ought to take a good deal more care, yourself."

Olly straightened suddenly, wondering how the captain could already know about his brush with the cats. His mind faltered as he searched for an excuse.

"Well, sir, if you mean - "

"I mean you really must take care to inform someone if you're intent on going off. Especially when there's a training stint arranged for the same day. Time and place are of the essence."

The relief was palpable.

"I just like to put myself about, sir. It gives me hope, if you know what I mean."

"Well, putting yourself about may dash your hopes sooner or later, if you know what *I* mean," came the concerned reply.

Some smaller trainees, each holding a stiff broom hair, were scuffing out the irregularities in the flagstones by one of the goalmouths. One of them patted a dab of chalk dust from his nose, grinning. Captain Greybands smiled at Olly reassuringly, his large brown eyes at once authoritative, yet kindly, in a fatherly sort of way. As well as the furrows fanning out from his forehead over his broad back, which gave him an undeniably distinguished air, he also bore a few other marks of triumph and defeat. More impressive still was this ability of his to maintain and co-ordinate all the strands of the rats' communal affairs. The central cord around which everything else was wound was, needless to say, the football - as philosophy as well as family. The Captain was, quite simply, manager, head coach, occasional player and counsellor - all rolled into one. And, as Olly knew to his cost, he possessed the uncanny ability to know what his charges were often thinking.

Olly shifted his feet uncomfortably as two of the most unlikely characters of those so far observed breezed onto the Arena. Their fresh faces and long, loose limbs exuded a slick, cocky confidence that belied the casualness of their approach. A bewildering exchange of short passes were flicked between them, before one of them took up his position out near the touch line with the rubber ball at his nifty feet. Another group of trainees huddled about the goal area, unsure as to whether they were to be spectators or unwilling victims of this situation. Olly looked on with keen interest, sensing what was about to happen. With a 'Ready Nobs?' the ball was deftly raised as though poised on a seal's nose and instantaneously lofted with supreme accuracy onto the chest of his companion in the middle. Nobs it was, who then juggled the ball with both knees before swivelling round as it dropped, to crack a venomous right foot shot past gaping defenders and an even more hapless and gaping goalie.

"Benchwarts and duffers!" shouted Hobs, as the ball thwacked with precision inside the newly made upright before bouncing back into the midst of the trainees. Both crosser and finisher then raced together and began hugging each other, hopping up and down, giggling with unbounded joy. The customary high-five followed immediately thereafter. Olly allowed himself a wide smile, whereas quite a few of the younger rats clapped and cheered their immediate and unbounded appreciation for the virtuoso skill of the set-piece. A group of more seasoned players who had been stretching out in the shadow of a shallow recess at the opposite end nodded and gave the thumbs up, but did not speak.

Greybands gestured generously with his arms and murmured, "Quite good, quite good," following it up with a "Cleverly done Herbert", and a "Well put away, Norbert", to each as a verbal pat on the head. Then his arms came down and went into a smartly folded position. He became serious again.

"But do you both honestly believe that could be executed in a real match?"

The eponymous Hobs and Nobs stood side by side, somewhat crestfallen and dismayed by this question.

"Why not, sir?" cried Hobs, now finding his voice.

"We put in the crosses - ," he chortled.

"And then they suffer the losses," added his twin gleefully.

Both laughed together at this self-evidently wacky quip, while the others chuckled in the background. The Captain raised a hand to hush all the noise and continued his appraisal: "If you both indulged less and spend more time on the needs of the team, supplying others with much easier opportunities, you will be better served. William, here, can explain for the umpteenth time what I despair of saying any more to either of you."

The twins looked first at each others feet in a state of confusion, before raising their knowing heads with an upward swoon to the rafters high above them. Everyone seemed to be shifting uncomfortably on their own feet in the ensuing silence.

William, or Billy Battle, as he was better known, was a wiry rat, toughened by resolution and past experience, a follower of the old school of thinking and who adhered rigidly to the rules of play propounded by his leader. The tactics were simple, and, to monosyllabic Billy, did the job. Standing next to the Captain he grunted no little reluctance to speak up on these matters. Yet he pointed a fist at the twins, and, with teeth slightly clenched, asserted: "Mainly, you don't track back. You goal hang an' allow too much space 'tween you an' them full backs. Support th' defence an' put in more tackles. Get th' ball movin' like with less fancy stuff. Hump th' ball up to me an' Cedric. We c'n finish the job. Quicker."

The twins looked on aghast for a few seconds. This was a big and unbroken speech coming from Billy, but they had heard its substance all before.

"Yeah, yeah," was all they could reply, taking little heed of his blunt and uninspiring analysis. Once more the Captain waved down the hum of chatter that had begun to stir all around him.

"We have every reason to keep together at this time, more so than ever, I fear."

He paused and cast a swift glance, not only at Olly, but over everyone of the footballing fraternity now assembled.

"Our movements are being watched, as some of us can testify. Therefore more due watchfulness, that is to say vigilance, on our part is needed while we wait to see what is going on. I can only add that -"

The Captain got no further in rounding off his thoughts, as a minor commotion of flurrying feet came bouncing down the steps behind him.

"Just back from the kitchen, sir," panted a high-pitched voice excitedly. "Grandstand view of it all we had, too. Sir, she's bin threatenin' for days, and now she's finally done it."

"Who has done what exactly?" asked the Captain calmly, though already sensing the seriousness of the breathlessly inexplicit message.

"She has, sir. The lady upstairs. Blown her top clean off," answered the second of the two scouts. "Reckon we're in for it. Big time. Real big time"

Their commander deplored the use of these sensationalist phrases coined from modern-age lingo, the kind of nonsense too many people obviously acquired from listening to too much radio up in the kitchen and other places. But their usage appeared to be mitigating in this instance. Greybands looked at Billy and frowned.

"Remember fifty-seven," said Billy, again through his teeth, "one of the greatest - probably *the* greatest ever - finals played down here."

Handed down by word of mouth, it was a game that lived in the memories of some of the older rats, embedded in their psyche, to be recalled and passed on in times of adversity. Now was such a time. Greybands knew the details of that never-to-be-forgotten match: 19-18 after several counted-down periods of added on extra-time - calculated in the traditional way. The winners had been 11-3 down at one stage. They were the comeback kids who overcame the odds. Yet statistics from the past, however well remembered, could not alone guarantee the survival of the present gathering.

The general hubbub had descended into silence as the rats of a different generation awaited further winsome words from their Captain. Their elongated shadows, distorted by the angles of the Arena, were darkly captured in the flaring fusion of its glimmering moons: those perpetual enigmas to its children's children. A children of the forever changing, yet never-changing, sands of historical time. The Arena was indeed the mysterious and inviolable keeper of their numerous souls.

Their present leader said no more, but turned aside, deep in thought, in the realisation that their lives may be about to suffer a change. A change more unimaginable than they would ever have believed possible. For a certainty, they were going to have to think on their feet - but in many more ways than one.

With all its infinite variables, it is a calculation to leave even the most eminent of volcanologists scratching his head in uncertainty. The final inch of an ultimate downward slide that tips the balance and presses the unpredictable tectonic trigger - to release those pent-up, angry convulsions that lie seething, churning deep within earth's crust. So likewise, all the bubbling and burbling cheerfully simmering away in a low-beamed kitchen were but a mere side-show, a deceptive prelude, to the explosive spew of molten bile about to erupt from a pressure of similar proportions. And the ashes raining down from a darkening sky would leave its survivors in no doubt that, once blown, the result to their particular landscape was going to be one of undeniable change.

Without laying any special claims to such scientific knowledge, Edward Brimble, resident master of Brokehill Manor, had a nevertheless reasonable excuse for being in the right place at the right time (or wrong time, depending on your view of volcanoes) as he sat in his favourite chair pouring himself his usual mid-morning cup of tea. The hiss of a saucepan or two and the staccato clucking of lids were a reassuring backdrop to Cook's garrulous small-talk, as the preparations for a traditional and splendid meat pie came on nicely. But it wasn't so long before he became acutely aware of another quite unrelated rhythm, one seemingly set to drown out these pleasanter ones, as it neared ominously.

"D - do you hear 'em, sir? Footsteps a-comin'," said Cook, taking equal note and flustering in alarm.

A pin could not have popped and deflated the atmosphere any faster as she stood back and tried to reassert a measure of her composure. It was, indeed, the lull before the storm. The kitchen door presently swung forward in a full one hundred and eighty degrees of violence, with enough force to leave its hinges humming from the rebound like a tuning fork in aftershock. There was a gusty whirl of a voluminous skirt as a tall, angular-faced woman swept inside with all the ferocity her very prominent disdain could muster. Edward Brimble smiled collectedly, as the disruptive figure wheeled round the table behind the chair opposite and fixed him with a glare.

"Good morning to you Euradice," was his only remark, as he sipped what little remained of the tea, most of which now floated like a moat in the saucer.

The woman ignored the greeting and slammed a well-thumbed magazine entitled *Health Spas of Europe* next to the teapot, momentarily disturbing its steady drift of steam.

"Peo-ple must think me mad," she said with measured deliberation, putting great emphasis on the last word by clamping her bony fingers against the sides of her finely-coiffed hair. The irony of this display was not lost on her brother, although he had very much the air of the proverbial man who, having recently allowed his patients a free run of the asylum, was as yet unwilling to admit the gravity of the mistake. To be figuratively tarred and feathered would be a step too far, though He shook his head slightly.

"I cannot imagine anyone thinking that of you, Euradice," he replied in all sincerity.

Such intimidating mood swings were nothing new to him, and he was quite prepared to see this one out. He poured more of the tea and went on sipping.

"Any-one would go mad spending one single day in such a house. And to think I've been here nearly three weeks!"

Her anger had barely subsided as she eyed the refilled cup: "Hah! And didn't I just know I'd find you here. As always, drinking tea."

"If you have anything to say to me, I am always available, either here or up top," said Mr Brimble, calmly tilting the remaining liquid in the saucer back into its rightful place.

His sister rolled her eyes in disbelief with a slight lift of her head before fixing them on the pot.

"Much purpose that serves. You may as well beg an anchorite to come down and re-join the real world. My friends would simply be as-tounded by the sheer lack of vision, the for-gone opportunities, the great po-tential to-tally and ut-terly unrealised!"

The list was an appalling one, and with each failure she pressed her fist into the magazine to show the ex-tent of her incredulous wrath. This was no storm in a teacup.

"Well, we agree to disagree on your proposals, I will admit," came the meek reply, all quite passive to the aggressive. His sister, again ignoring the remark, determined to continue on in her same fiercely-toned vein.

"From the minute I arrived, I felt this un-worldly atmosphere hanging over me. An in-difference, no, rather a re-calcitrance, to change. No-thing replaced when it needs replacing. I find nearly every casement loose and draughty, rooms belonging to the Ice Age, doors that either creak or re-fuse to shut properly. And this morning what do I find? My window pushed wide open, with papers flying here, there and ev-erywhere about my a-partment! No-thing should surprise me, though - but for the rats. Ugh! These rats! They are slinking ev-erywhere in this wasteland of a house. My Arty does not sleep, bothered ter-ribly by their sneaky antics." Here her voice deepened portentously. "But we know their moves, and we shall find them out, you can rely on that."

Edward looked on bemused by these latter imprecations, while waiting for the next barrage. At that very moment, as though having heard his name called from a guest list, Arturo's pointy head peeped nervously through the unclosed door. He tip-toed beneath the table before squirming the rest of his leanness between the chairs and up onto an adjacent dresser. He looked down, scanning the floor furtively, while the spillage of his mistress's bile continued without letup.

"I have come with a perfectly sen-sible plan to ra-dically transform the lower floors of the manor into something that will only enhance its - er – parochial structure, lift it from out of the past. This house can become a centre of renown and distinction. Stanmore's Spa Centre. The 'Heart of the Country'. Cos-mopolitan in its dedication to health, vigour and - and - beauty, - naturally."

The ludicrous epithets were rolled off as though Brokehill's eventual destiny was a forgone conclusion. Then came the punchline.

"Not to mention the *money* it will make for you, Edward".

Her voice became more controlled at this point, though some of its balefulness lingered. With the carrot sufficiently dangled, and having run out of any more words to say, she leaned over the table and began drumming the fingers of her right hand impatiently on it. The pots on the stove clucked and chuckled away rhythmically, as though privately digesting these proposals amongst themselves. Mr Brimble meanwhile compressed his lips into a large O and sucked in air slowly.

"No. I cannot be a party to these foolishly grandiose ideas, Euradice. In heaven's name, the costs would prove astronomical! And, in any case, it would not be appropriate for the manor to be subject to change for such a foolhardy purpose. To ignore its past, its ancient history, in the certainty of destroying its character, is, as I have said before, not on, simply not on at all."

He shook his greying head gravely before drawing comfort from another generous sip of the stimulating tea.

"Pah!" Euradice spluttered, momentarily digging her nails into the glossy magazine. "Don't you dare 'my dear' me! All you know or appreciate about renovation and modernisation could be written on the back of a postage stamp! Look! There are *manoirs* in here which have been simply trans-formed! But I know you too well to think you will im-pliment sensible changes of any kind."

She picked up a spoon and waved it accusingly in front of her brother's nose. Cook darted between them to remove a cake knife out of harm's way, just in case. Another visitor who had, meanwhile, entered unnoticed from the outhouse end of the kitchen, now joined the fray by loping imperturbably towards the table. Without a sound or bat of an eyelid the cream-coated cat side-stepped the opposition and leapt up onto a chair by his master to sit, statuesque and spectral, weighing up the dourness of the opposition. The old man cheered at the sight of an ally and ruffled the cat's neck good-naturedly.

"Hello, Prince, my fine fellow," he said quietly.

Prince noticed the respective position of Arturo just behind his mistress, but did not change his sphinx-like expression. Euradice gave him a contemptuous glance before grinding out her stream of invective to a completion.

"You sit up there," she cried, bringing the spoon to a higher position, "with just a men-agerie to relieve your solitude. Another world where you live in the past - a past with no future."

"You're forgetting Harriet," her brother replied

abruptly, but getting no further.

"Oh, the grand-daughter doesn't count. A mere child whose head you fill with all sorts of nonsense. Perhaps you'd like her to be the next lady of the manor, one day!"

His sister brushed away the thought with an imperious gesture. Arturo bobbed his head in delight at this, trying to catch the cream cat's impassive stare and sneering anyway. She glared, then folded her arms in quick succession, endeavouring to quash such an idea in case it should germinate into an attractive option.

"You once said I could always be assured of a home here, if and when I became a widow," she reminded him. Her snake eyes reverted to his, softening ever so slightly as she waited intently for any sign of weakness they might reveal. Sentimental feelings of brotherly obligation were not, though, in evidence as he scooped up crumbs from a slice of Madeira cake and handed them delicately to the cat at his side. He took a generous bite and munched on thoughtfully.

"I did so. And I trust the lower floors are sufficient for your needs?" he said at last.

"Perfect. For the fulfilment of my heart's desire," she said, clapping her hands together and rubbing them them vigorously, while she endeavoured to maintain the regenerated vision in her mind's eye without it being spoiled by the presence of rats.

Her brother looked weary as he read her face.

"The rooms were put *at* your disposal, Euradice, not for you to dispose *of*," he said, making this distinction very plain.

"I will not be denied," she said resolutely, wagging the spoon at nowhere in particular.

"First things first. Decline and fall. Arty and I are very definitely not for declining. We shall deal with the de-infestation of the rats forthwith, cellar key or no cellar key."

Here she touched on another acutely sore point.

"When they are e-radicated, Brokehill shall very definitely be 'broke' no more."

Uttered in such a magisterial voice the clumsy pun gained an immediate stamp of approval from Arturo as he curled a compliant lip. With this prophetic resolution out of the way, she rubbed her hands with a wiping motion, turned, and, in keeping with her ubiquitous sense of timing, swept from the kitchen as dramatically as she had entered. Arturo offered Prince a final leer before dropping down to follow hotly in her wake. The survivors suddenly found themselves left to recover from the confrontational fallout as best they could. Mr Brimble pushed the teacup to one side and, running his own hands distractedly through what hair he had left to him, exclaimed: "My sister is just absurd. Completely and misguidedly absurd!"

He rose stiffly from his seat to brush away a small remainder of crumbs.

"I'll be over at the stables, if I'm wanted, Mrs Dains," was all he could say as he left via the outhouse.

The good woman looked on with a mixture of confusion and horror, thinking how the master had so woefully misjudged the seriousness of the situation. Beyond the outhouse, thin brushstrokes of cloud skimmed gracefully along a blue expanse of sky that had arrived as a welcome interlude to the overcast sleetiness of late November. Alas for within! Where angry rifts, like a lava-red river, were beginning to carve out some scene-altering divisions which, in the coolness of time, would inevitably harden to obdurate and immoveable rock. Cook had no spirit to finish the dinner preparations and sat down and sighed, wishing she hadn't guessed it might come to this. But she plainly had. All that woman's toin' and froin'. Busy-bodying and steering her prying her eyes into every room she could find. And that bein' well nigh all of 'em. Wanting that awful cat fed and watered at her precise times. She got up again and began to sweep the floor to stop herself from thinking about it. Glancing along the table she realised that a better-looking cat had not yet left the scene of devastation, but was still sitting placidly on the chair. She doled out some cooked bits of chicken to go with some milk that was already poured into a bowl. The handsome Prince jumped down in gratitude and saw off the lunch with great relish. He then left, happily aware that the meal had originally been meant for Arturo. More tit-bits would be coming his way again soon enough, when the master dined later on in the tower.

As he mounted the staircase, he reflected over the morning's unusual events. He had rescued a rat, to be sure. Exceptional for this old residence, for a certainty. Then there was the lady's wild behaviour. That

31

certainly required a clearer bit of thought, what with her views on the rats. Coops was the one to make some sense out of it. Confidential he was, he nodded to himself. In this ebullient mood Prince reached the first floor where he looked around for signs of life. He sniffed the dry, fusty corridor where portraits of stern war heroes and sullen local gentry interspersed the drabness of the flock wallpaper, their accusing eyes following his movements with a distressingly omni-directional awareness. He didn't get too narked by pretty well most areas of the house, but he was always relieved to see these fellas well out of the way.

He soon reached the point where a thickly-carpeted spiral staircase of much smaller dimension beckoned, and, putting on his devil-may-care exterior once more, leapt up two at a time before nosing his head just inside the tower door. He chewed on the remains of some chicken skin which had lodged in his teeth and swallowed easily as he surveyed the curve of the room. A stack of logs in the fireplace looked well advanced in their charred state and the smoky glow they emitted appeared to provide the sole source of light for the chamber. The curtains were fully drawn to deny any portion of the bright afternoon from penetrating the obscurity with a few interstitial gleams prior to the onset of twilight. Before the grating lay sprawled an inert, neutral-coloured mass which had shown no reaction, nor any other obvious sign of life, to Prince's noiseless entry. The cream cat alighted beside this formidable shape like an apparition and sat in an admiring silence. The gradual opening of a watery eye beneath a broad flap of an ear became steadily more recognisable.

"Well? Can't you see I'm sleeping?"

Though the senses were deceptively languid, the voice was hyper-alert.

"Sorry, Coops, awld son. Bin goin' walkabout," came the chippiest of answers.

The bloodhound grimaced as he hoisted himself onto his forelegs. Without looking, he stuck out his right foot and shoved it against a ball of ragged towelling which had been wrapped round the handle of a long poker. The tip of the poker slid between the charcoaled ruin of several logs, chipping away a few smouldering remnants in a shower of heated sparks. After a further prod a tongue of flame flew up to bathe the fireplace and its immediate vicinity in a sombre glow. One more mechanical nudge coaxed additional flames to stutter into life, and, gradually, the overall visibility improved. To show he had not lost his train of thought, the bloodhound, getting comfortable once more, followed up with a mild rebuke.

"Not so much of the old, if it's all the same to you. DH Cooper's the name. DH to you, you know."

Prince, his glistening curls quite unruffled by these terse words, twisted his neck and licked at the warm fur down his chest for half a minute, as he mulled over a suitably choice response. DH seemed to have relapsed into snooze mode and it was difficult to observe whether he was still listening or not. But he probably was. Prince decided to go straight to the issue troubling his mind.

"There's bin a grate bust belaw stairs. Th' laydee was givin' th' merster a real hard toim."

"In keeping with the prevailing wind," returned a matter-of-fact voice. The brief statement was as meaningful as the face was expressionless.

"Been prying around ever since she came here. Governor gives an inch, she wants a yard, so to speak." He had summed it up succinctly, without moving an inch himself..

"Blow me, you're a right un'," exclaimed Prince in genuine admiration.

"That's 'cause I'm DH. As Detective Hound, my job's not to miss much."

"Nor nuthin', Oi reckon. You were with the p'lice one toime, didn't you saiy?"

DH sighed as he recalled it.

"A Private Agency it was. That's where I lost out. Poachers. Jumped too near a rifle as it went off. Caught the stock on recoil. Made my ears ring a bit, but they were fine after. It's the nose what got well and truly walloped. All of a sudden, can't get a whiff of anything. Smell never came back. Not exactly top-notch for a bloodhound, you see."

DH made a symbolic attempt to rub the offending organ, then closed his eye again.

"So merster took you in, then?"

"He said I had good ears and eyes, and that was enough for him. Called me a natural gazehound. One doors closes, another one opens."

Ending on this rather philosophical point, the hound

adjusted his position, the thickset folds of his coat shining ruddily in the flicker of the firelight.

"Come with me and I will show you another world. His exact words," he said after a moment's pause, hoping his listener would catch the sentiment.

"So that's why you sleep all day?" Prince chuckled.

DH gave him another watery eye.

"Ah, very droll."

He shunted a different toe against the poker, allowing new flames to break rank and creep upward to radiate the hearth and chimney face. The pillars surrounding the fireplace were carved in wood that had been darkly polished by age. Plumes of fruit and coiled branches draped in symmetrical swirls shone a rich, grainy jet in the reflections of the dancing light. Prince decided to pursue the nagging issue further.

"He seemed raither shayken. Not the merster Oi naw."

DH looked on into the flames grimly.

"She's a prolific liar from what I've seen. As are all delusionists. A charlatan, if ever there was one. So, what's she here for? That's what I ask myself. So if I'm asking, I hope the governor is, too."

The cream cat mused over this profound piece of information and twirled his considerable tail in an arc around his back and his tufted feet.

"How long've you been here. Two months, or so?" ventured the bloodhound.

Prince assented with a wink of his jade-lit eyes.

"You may've been playing a few of your regular tricks back in - where was it again?"

"Quainsland, Sowth Orstraylia ind," Prince chimed in with a further nostalgic look in the jade eyes.

"Right. But not so many in this charming spot. Neither you, nor the governor have shown each other all your cards yet, I'll wager. See those?"

DH aimed his broad, anosmic nose at various statuettes and framed photos now glinting irresistibly on the mantelpiece.

"You main the football, eh?" said Prince, knowing full well he did.

"The very," insisted DH. "Means as much to him as the house. One and the same, you might say. Go back a long time. He played a bit, before an injury scuppered his hopes. Knows a player when he sees one. What we in the detective line call intuition. Not easily pulled over, his eyes ain't."

"How d' yew mean, 'pulled owver'?"

"The wool, Prince. The wool. Not fooled. Forensic."

DH's own eyes sagged as he gave a yawn. Not altogether sure of this concise term for Mr Brimble, Prince simply murmured "a blinder" and continued to stare at a photo of a team in celebration at lifting a trophy.

"What he saw in me, he may see in you, too. A doggedness. And that's saying something for a cat. You stand your ground. In fact, I've long reckoned there's something of a bulldog in you."

"Not a wolf, perraps?" asked the cat hopefully. "Yer no tom kitten yerself, moind."

"No," considered the wily dog, "more of a crouching tiger, don't you think?"

36

As if to prove the description valid, he got up and moved to the door with surprising agility, listening, head askance, for the slightest sound. Somewhere near the window a clock's pendulum was marking off time with an insistent and metronomic regularity.

"Can't be too careful," he said in a low voice, coming back to a new position beside the cat.

"Ded on th' mark there, Coops," said Prince, "quoite a few of them are gittin' owt an' abowt lately. Owtsoide es well es in."

"Who are?" said DH, starting abruptly at the mention of this unknown quantity and peering about him uncomfortably with a series of reflexive jerks to his large head. Every obscure patch of shadow, from the mantelpiece to the curtain folds, at once became a potentially suspicious hideaway for the enemy. Finally he made a satisfied grunt and resumed his low view of the flames.

"Nothing could be too small or insignificant for me not to know about it. Forgive me for my ignorance though, but who exactly have you been seeing in your dreams?"

"The rets. They're all owver th' playce, so long as yew know jest how end where to spot 'em."

"And you do, of course," said DH, regarding the other with a measure of understated admiration.

"Stends t' reason, Coops. Part of th' furnicher, they are. Our problems are theirs as well, an' naw mistayke."

"Bright as the day is long and honest as driven snow, you are, too," smiled DH. "Point taken. Talking of which, tomorrow's the week-end, and the governor's grand-daughter's staying over again, as I understand it."

Mention of this raised Prince's spirit immeasurably. Since his arrival both he and the young girl in question had been inexplicably drawn together by a shared and secret sense of wonder over Brokehill and all its peculiar enchantment. The bloodhound beside him turned his head and became confidential again.

"The way I see it is this: you stick to Miss Harriet, while I do the same with the governor. Then we may get to spring all the traps and win the game. Rats or no rats."

"Laydee's a goer. It may be a long gayme," suggested his companion, without saying any more concerning the future prospects of the aforementioned rats.

"Indeed, it may," said DH almost in a whisper.

And thus they remained, marking out time within the warming glow of the room's dwindling embers; for the present, seemingly undaunted by any faster-encroaching rings of fire.

Recruitment   Chapter 3

The foundations for the new beginning lay loosely
buried in a morass of orange peel and unread Sunday
supplements strewn across a satin-quilted bed. Many
deleted, undeleted and redeleted sheets of scrunched-
up notepaper were, however, a clear evidence that the
pathway to its realisation had not proved to be an
entirely smooth one. For, as always, the devil was in
the detail. At the press of a repeat button, strains of
Oochie Coochie Man vied once more with the
background scenes of a black and white *film noir* for a
flash of inspiration. But though such slices of
nostalgia were worth little more than a wing and a
prayer, a thousand phantom galleons fleeing outside
across a grey expanse of sky could not have provided a
more cumulative smokescreen for the grand plan
being formulated in this first-floor bedroom. Yet the
midnight oil had long ago burned itself out into
another day of fitful enlightenment - leaving only
vapour trails of perpetual indecision in its wake.
Maybe it was vice versa ... er ... or perhaps not ...
She couldn't make up her mind. Like the weather, it
was all still an unsettled and cheerless blank.

Pzzaff! The portable TV stuttered and blinked
several times before converting to a distracting snow
screen of its own. Damn them! Another trick from
those infernal rats. Probably slowly chawing through
the cable right this minute. Euradice lifted her head

from the latest of the scribbled lined and craned her long neck around the room like an irate ostrich. Confounded creatures! Lovers of dark places. They were the very reason for her being wretchedly taxed in this way. They represented everything that was totally wrong about Brokehill manor, with its whole creepy-crawly past. A past she'd never wanted any part of anyway. Not that she'd ever had one to begin with. Primogeniture, and all that. Better to have two irons in the fire, then, where the deceptive lesser would lead her on to the all-consuming greater. But she was keeping that well down in the recesses of her duplicitous heart for now. And when she had what she wanted, why then, anything was possible, wasn't it? Traipsing throughout the house had been an onerous and painstaking task, although the woeful inertia of its inhabitants had soon concentrated her mind wonderfully. The menagerie had utterly ignored Arturo's spirited advances, and any of her own friendly inducements received similar short shrift. Sometimes she thought that mournful hound of Edward's seemed to know exactly what she was thinking. And as for that preposterously pompous Persian cat he'd dragged in from somewhere, it, too, was equally indifferent in an otherworldly sort of way. No amount of cajoling could bring him over to their side. Yet, having fine-combed just about every nook in every room - including her brother's - to no avail, it was annoying to find that the cellar remained that one crucial, out-of-reach exception. This being the junk room, the grand repository, where almost everything ultimately met its fate, it was therefore now the most likely place to find what she had every intention of finding. And here is where this neat plan of hers came in. When her brother saw the impressive results of the rat catching programme, then he would surely cave in to her very 'reasonable' demands for access. Being a reasonable man, he would not deny her that. Hah! It was an idea which really did look very clever indeed, the more she thought about it. The determination it engendered was only to be matched by the confidence that grew from the certainty of its success.

With a beat of her pen she hummed out the final background strains of the song's coda. As if to compliment a drum roll in the fadeout the attention-seeking TV came up with another untimely crackle of its own, leaving its lines dissected by the glitziest grin of insatiable sharks teeth imaginable. Irritations! This was becoming more than a blasted nuisance! She rechecked the socket and touched the mini-aerial, lop-sidedly poised over the set like a grossly misshapen paper clip, before deciding the problem was not of their making. Her gaze returned once more to the lumpy old bed, her eyes swivelling intuitively towards a sandbag arrangement of two or three pillows between which a skimpy wedge of belly fur was just about recognisable. It was from this relaxed position (one in which *she* never slept) that Arturo's arrowhead was poked - upwardly aimed in an unconscious state of vertical bliss.

"Is it you, Arty?" snapped his mistress, her suspicions becoming increasingly aroused. With a jerk of his lean frame the toothy zig-zag of a smile was promptly replaced by a frozen page of garbled teletext.

Yesterday had dragged tediously for Arturo, and today felt like another long day after a meagre night's breakfast. Euradice leaned across and snatched away the offending remote wedged beneath his stomach. She put the attention-grabbing telly out of its misery and perused her sheets at a more leisurely pace, though with markedly less concentration than before, crossing out a few more names from the interminable short list. Having scanned its contents haphazardly for a further minute or so, another name, which had been once in favour, then out of favour, too many times before to recount, was frantically scored out for the last time; the force of which tore the sheet in two. She swore. Only two now remained along the upper half.

A cold draught stirred round the room, and although the casements had lately been stuffed with folded strips of newspaper, Euradice tightened her gown and went to the door to note where it was coming from. Could she but have compared it to the icy chill inside her own soul, a place which no collective amount of ruthless zeal would ever begin to warm! She cast another impatient glance in the direction of Arturo's motionless rump locked within a spindly contortion of legs and tail. It was an incontrovertible fact that Arty was no leader of cats. Neither was he, as she had shrewdly foreseen early on, a killer of rats. All his numerous excursions had ended in abject failure, without one single victim to show for his honest, and yet patently inadequate endeavours. His instincts simply weren't up to the job. Poison for the rats had always been out of the question, as her brother would never consent to such methods under any circumstances. The risk to the other animals was maybe a real one, and anyway, she didn't want Arty accidentally dropping dead on her just yet. So, alternative, more natural resources were needed, in order to ex-punge the rats from their sewer-life existence. What was wanted was a few doughty cats, organized to contend with the foe and beat them at their own game. With Arturo you were stabbing at flies, but with an experienced leader strategies could be knocked into shape and, then, well, victory was theirs for the taking. Order and precision had never been Euradice's strong points, although the myth had been peddled long enough. Yet she recognised its virtues. The ideal candidate was to be not so much a feline mobster, but more of a commanding, charismatic figure, a sort of modern-day Ratfinder General, one who could maybe show a bit of gangland nous at the same time. It was a striking CV for a striking line of work. Someone who would create events rather than be led by them was the phrase that came to mind. She had read this somewhere, and had taken rather a fancy to it by writing the words as a superscription to the reduced list which she now tetchily pored over once more. She pondered. It required an *aristocat* who really could ... Yesss! She slapped the notepad down and pressed a trademark, knuckled fist hard against it.

"I've made up my mind," she declared, holding up

the vital slip like some crumpled representation of a signed declaration for peace. Checking the number scrawled at the bottom, she made the call at once. A thin warbling tone repeated itself interminably before a click came at last from the other end.

"I'm calling about the visit I made yesterday. Before noon. If you remember, we talked at length about that mister - er - whatever it was. Squalls, or Squills, was it? Well, I've decided to take *him*."

Euradice stifled a tremble as she collected herself.

"Oh, and the other one that was with him. The ginger tabby, wasn't it?"

There followed a brief pause before a faraway voice crackled with delight.

"So, so glad you 'ave chosen 'im, my dear. As I remarked to you, that Mr Quills is a rallyer, 'e truly is. A rallyer. An' I do b'lieve 'e was quite taken with you. An' as for 'is companion. Cubs is constancy itself to 'im. Like two peas in a pod they be, if I may quote Mrs V."

"I'm sure you're right. I should prefer to pick 'em up right away today," replied Euradice affirmatively, much relieved.

The voice became a touch more deferential at this suggestion.

"Thinkin' on them other boys of 'is, though. After 'is departure, I means. What their futures will come to is too tragic to imagine. 'E is such a rallyin' kind, if you get my meanin'."

To Euradice the voice began to sound haggling and wheedling. She became thoughtful for a moment,

44

then brightened considerably.

"I see where you are leading me. Look, I'll take 'em all, then. Not as we originally bargained, but, hey, there's no gain without pain, as they say. I shall be over in a trice."

With the deal confirmed, she sat up and punched the air over the bed in triumph. All peel, napkins and discarded slips of paper were duly swept into a waste basket - and herself into a long, hooded coat and scarf. "Time to get up - *now!*" she shouted, flinging the notepad in the direction of an oasis of satiny warmth. It clipped an arc of an ear as it rose like a tip of an iceberg above submerged and slumberous depths. Arturo stirred, showed a bleary eye, then tried squeezing the torpor out through the end of his nose. Without any further warning, he found himself scooped up and, in no time at all, dexterously dropped onto a much colder carpet. Euradice side-stepped some empty coffee cups that littered the floor and began hunting for boots. She carefully counted a thick wad of twenty pound notes and slipped them back into a small clasp handbag along with the notepad.

"So. All present and correct. At least, one of us is," she hissed finally, more for her cat's benefit.

Two or three hours sleep was all she had managed, but now the action was moving up a level, the dream getting one step closer to reality, so she couldn't afford to feel tired. Arturo yawned weakly and limped half-heartedly over to the door, where he waited, skulking and shivering, looking decidedly thin-limbed.

"Time to go!, And you're *not* staying in here," his

mistress declared, as a key was produced from the bag with an exaggerated, mechanical motion of her hand, as though in a mime. A key to the abyss.

"So, *out!*"- to the stricken cat, as she levered him unceremoniously over the threshold with the toe of her boot and locked the door - all in one seamless movement. At the staircase landing she stopped, making her escort look up with an uneasy sense of foreboding. Striking up intimidating poses came naturally to Euradice, but between the murkiness of the staircase and the persistent buffeting of the wind against the outside walls, her gaunt stance evoked something more dramatically sinister in this instance. Arturo grew goggle-eyed with a suspenseful fear.

"There's been a slight change of plan. You're staying in this house. Down there to be exact."

Her towering figure pointed an irresistible finger towards the kitchen below.

"Soldiers must share quarters and muck in," she insisted, "in order to bond. Camaraderie and all that sort of thing."

Arturo turned away and tried to feign indifference as he began to grapple with the implications of what was meant. Without giving pause for thought, Euradice marched down to the kitchen in silence, her pitiful subordinate now loping close behind as though held on by an invisible leash. In the outhouse a few blankets had been spartanly laid out in a corner along the back wall, where a small lamp also burned. Euradice waved earnestly at these arrangements in the hope that such an austere example of bivouacking

46

would bolster her trooper's flagging spirits. Yet even for an optimist, a dark lantern would have been a generous description of Arturo's mindset at that very moment. He gulped hard, and wildly considered meowing, before thinking better of what he knew full well would be a futile protest.

His mistress was becoming fairly discomforted with this flip-flop attitude of his and seemed hurried as she wrenched at the stiff, heavy door at the end. It gave way at the second attempt, to send a terrific blast of wind careering into every corner, oohing and aahing like an inquisitive ghost on a whistle-stop tour. As though scalded, Arturo leapt to the window's narrow ledge and vainly tried to shield himself from the worst of it. Euradice, brazenly challenging the forcefulness of the wind, looked out and waited for the synchronous confirmation of a distant bell: her lineaments taut and wan against the matching backdrop of a greyish luminescence. The armada of smoking ships had long since been swept away, sucked into a maelstrom soup of lowering cloud; where only the specks of screaming swifts could be seen, looping and wheeling above a nearby copse, as they skived the drab remains of a canvas sky with their endless tattoos of whirligigs. Inside, the feeble rays of the small lamp were finding it difficult to resist the gloom as it crept on into the dampness of the outhouse like some extended, downward-tending shroud. Euradice made an about turn, and the finger which had been testing the air was now pointed towards Arturo.

"Stop being such a drama puss."

Her voice had to compete with the bluster of the buffeting wind.

"Time to get a grip, Arty. Face it out. The rats won't just run away, you know!" she said scoldingly.

She clutched at a bunch of car keys and shook them in her fist, as a priestess might rattle an amulet or fetish in order to appease some mighty gods of war (or weather). In an afterthought, she raised the point of her hood and tightened it over her, an act which only made the imagined similarity more awful still.

"This mission is going to change the course of our fortunes," she pursued. "A battle we dare not lose has approached. So, man the trenches for your - er - new platoon!"

Rather than stare anywhere else, Arturo stared with unseeing eyes out of the window, thoroughly aggrieved. He was rapidly tiring of these ludicrous military references. Talk about pots and kettles. It was all pure theatre. She had transformed herself from warlord to warrior to wicked witch in nearly as many minutes. And as for anyone running away and vanishing, he wasn't so sure didn't want to himself, the way things were going.

Euradice set her ear against the wailing wind. A bell tolling. Four o' clock. She instantly obeyed and strode out, her face an impervious granite mask, before shutting the door firmly behind her. To leave a house, swept through by storm and silences, bleak and unguarded in its emptiness. To return, and fill it with a multiplying madness of her own making.

Arturo slipped back down into the residual warmth that filtered in from the kitchen and waited for the start-up of an engine with its inevitable rasp of wheels over the gravel. The sounds he dared not look for duly came, as the sleekness of a black BMW roared to life and sped off into the unknown. He kept his ears pricked in case there was a belated change of plan, or a change of heart. But the car was soon out of earshot and remained so. There was no turning back now. Feeling like an alien in an alien place, he closed his eyes.

Nuzzling his chin as low as possible on a flat portion of blanket, he began miserably to recount the recent events that had led up to this - with his frustration mounting at every recollected thought. Saturday had annoyed him intensely. It had started out as fun, racing along high-hedged lanes, testing the bendy b-roads. Like there weren't enough hours in the day. And that truly was the case by the end. Stop after never-ending stop, until the final one, by which time they had got perfectly lost. Going round and round in circles, and with nothing to eat except useless hunks of chocolate. Spat them out the window before he'd got any queasier. The rest just became a blur of unfolded maps, filling station lights and hunger pains in his stomach, as he kept his head down on what turned out to be the homeward leg when the dawn began to break.. And all for what? he asked himself. Wasn't too sure. He was angry not to have been given more time to sort out those bold-faced rats. Even though that traitorous cat from upstairs was no help. Now someone else was coming to share the glory. Take all the glory, more like. Bother! Bother! Enough was enough. All this analysing was starting to give his head the bends. He decided to wedge himself further down between some suitably soft folds and, while fierce gusts pummelled at the door like unruly spirits clamouring to get in, sniffed wearily several times to console himself to sleep.

★　　　　　★　　　　　★

A musty volume swayed crazily, teetered on the brink, and fell to the floor with a thud.

"See. When push comes to shove. Trust me, Hobs."

The undaunted whisper of a small voice revealed its place of concealment to an empty room of gathering gloom. His less adventurous companion looked down uneasily.

"It's all very well for you to talk, just because you know every secret hole ever made in this house for the past four hundred years! But even the scouts have had to cut back until further notice. Captain told them to stick to the kitchen, and on no account use the stairs or passages. Caution is necessary - those were his exact words."

Nobs the Intrepid inhaled deeply, though not from any feeling of exhaustion, and blew through his broadened cheeks. He shook his head in despair.

"Caution. Caution. What exactly does that mean? Tell me, Hobs, are we, for instance, never to watch another match up in the tower? Seems to me nothing's changed since that bit of scaremongering a while back. What's necessary is what's for me. So it ought to be for you."

Nobs hopped down from the low-level shelf to inspect the withered spine of the fallen book. Standing over it like a proud huntsman beside his victim's carcass, he pushed an arm underneath and raised it slightly.

"It's not so heavy as it looks. I think the two of us can prop it up again, no problem."

He leaned on the spine and returned to his grievances with self-justifying conviction.

"Anyway, we were here before her. And I like coming here almost as much as the old ballroom. Look, she was out and about all day yesterday, and now again today. *There's* something for you."

"What, exactly?" replied Hobs, more than puzzled at his partner's mysterious inference.

He squinted at the dim slivers of window pane still partly visible behind the curtain, then hopped down and peered about him anxiously.

"Brr-rr! Hear that wind," was all he could murmur. He looked as though he'd heard enough already without having to throw any more caution to it.

"Like I said," Nobs went on fervently "her and black Art are getting out and about a lot lately. Should be viewed as a positive, I reckon. She don't like it here, that's plain. So she starts looking for somewhere else to live."

He was pleased with the logic of this conclusion.

"And as for those changes she intended to make?" challenged Hobs, alert to the fact that there might be something amiss with this reasoning.

The answer couldn't be more obvious.

"Old man says 'no go', so she's given up."

Nobs began tapping his best foot suavely on the linen hardback, confident of forestalling any further argument.

"Anyway, Hobby, door's locked. We heard it. So they must've gone off out again."

Hobs was lifted somewhat by this, even as another optimistic thought came to his partner.

"Which probably means we'll be ok in here for a while. Not that I admire him any more for it, but you have to say Black Art's kept well and truly on the grind. A nerve-shredder, she is."

The perceived creaks and rustles accompanying the wind now held a little less fear for Hobs, though he kept his voice low.

"The things I get into with you," he said, with a tiny shake of his head.

"The thrill of the chase," grinned the other.

"The thrill of being chased, more like," Hobs corrected him dryly.

Nobs moved noiselessly to the foot of the bed where the basket lay piled up nearly to overflowing.

"Wonder what she's been slinging in here?"

Ever inquisitive, he scaled the wickerwork to its rim and, gaining a wobbly grip, tipped himself head-first into a haphazard pool of paper generously laced with peel and other fibrous strands. The acrid, zesty smell made him sneeze, and sent him jack-knifing backwards, pulling the basket over with him as he gripped its edge. A few tightly screwed-up sheets bobbled aimlessly across the carpet in the manner of poorly-struck snooker balls looking for a pocket. The basket lay on its side like the belly of a gasping whale disgorged of half its contents due to a vomiting fit of unexpected indigestion.

"I hope you'll be leaving this place just as you found it," said Hobs, smiling, as he surveyed the upset waste, with his friend lying stunned in the middle of it all.

"The Arena could do with a few of these. To practice our lobs," said Nobs, picking himself up gingerly from the muddled heap and casually hoofing a suitably-sized paper ball back into the basket's mouth. Hoisting it to its former position took some energy out of both of them, leaving Nobs finally sitting down cross-legged on an extended corner of the bedspread to look around the room with a nostalgic eye. His partner sat above, dropping some of the sheets, one by one, back into the cavernous basket.

"The earliest impressions remain the strongest, you know, Hobs," remarked his friend. "This room is the first I ever visited. Peace and tranquil associations, to be more specific."

"Well, in case you haven't noticed, you're in rather an eye of a storm," came the joky response, "with all that howling and rain out there. I suppose most of mine come from the Arena."

Nobs breathed deeply. "It sometimes feels like we've been around for ages," he said at last.

Hobs chucked in a couple of grubby, stained sheets and reflected on this.

"Well, I remember a phrase Cook said once – that only the good die young."

"Really? Lief says it's not normal. He has a theory about an unknown something or other affecting the co-ordinates in our brains. What Greybands calls our 'sportive adaptations', an' all that. So we get to live longer. Longer than other rats elsewhere, apparently. Being widely travelled, you have to suppose Lief's view should be taken seriously. Mind you, I've never had the urge to travel."

"Not like someone else we know," said Hob darkly..

"Yes, but Olly really only wants to broaden his horizons locally. I don't think he'd do a runner on us. This old place has a hold on all of us like that."

Nobs sighed and was about to offer a further appropriate reflection, when his friend checked him.

"Hey! Look at this!" He handed down a folded sheet that looked unlike any of the others. "The rest have loads of crossed-out lines of words. But this one looks different."

Nobs spread it out in front of him with a blank look of non-recognition and yawned.

"Just odd letters and numbers. Like those football records we've come across in the tower. Stats. Maybe houses she's been eyeing up. Who knows?"
He seemed fairly unimpressed by the enigmatic jottings.

"So what does it say, eh?" Hobs jumped down and grabbed it.

"Who knows? I can't read. After all, I'm only an ignorant goalscorer."

They sniggered at this and punched each other playfully on the chest.

"It's not just those. It's this shape underneath them I find interesting," said Hobs in earnest. "Now where have I seen that before?"

Nobs made a small yawn, hardly aware of its significance. "Don't know. Maybe some early impression it reminds you of. Think its time we went, don't you?"

Hobs complained how, as soon as matters took an interesting turn, he (Nobs) always cooled off. Could he think of at least fifty of the most unforgettable things he'd ever seen on his many travels? Nobs kept a straight face and declared only one: something round and almost the size of his (Hobs') slipshod head - a football to be precise. In that case, Hobs decided that he (Nobs) must be an idiot not to include the goals at each end. His partner was duly miffed over this obvious exclusion.

"Alright, maybe it's cos I don't score so many these days, what with having to shunt it around, flogging myself in midfield *and* supporting the defence more. After all, with a ball at your feet just about anything's possible, isn't it?"

"Yes. But what's possible with *this*?" Hobs wondered, as the intrigue remained.

Nobs yawned again. "That's got me beaten. Sorry. Anyway, since when do we pick up souvenirs?"

Hobs was carefully folding the sheet into quarters,

and showing every intention of taking it with him.

"It is only rubbish, so it won't be missed," he shrugged. "Besides, she knows something I might know, too. So if I look at it now and again, it might eventually come to me."

"I see. Caution to be sacrificed to a memory jogger, is it? It could slow you down. But take it, if you think your brain cells need a poke," said Nobs, as he headed back to the book.

They balanced the volume on its edge between the two others, before Nobs climbed through the gap to cling on to it tenaciously from inside the ledge of the ground-level shelf.

"All aboard, then. And pull away!"

Hobs tossed the keepsake neatly into the recess and jumped up. He waited and listened to the rain's snare drum beat snapping against the glass. Bam-bam-be-bam! There was no mistaking what that meant, he thought, before bidding the room farewell with a symbolic and grateful flick of his tail..

A musty volume swayed crazily, teetered on the brink, and closed like a drawbridge - tight shut.

*   *   *

It had been a strange day, and no mistaking. DH had gone out, which was a rarity these days. Then this storm. A real bowler that kept him moping around longer than usual. Before Miss Harriet decided he was the ideal pantomime cat, that was. Never a dull moment after that. All got up in a cape and a golden

56

crown. A lion king was what she called him. The larks they'd had afterwards, what with the dancing and prancing round the room. Till she sprawled over the bed, read to him, then fell asleep at his feet. He'd stood at the window and watched the larches stretching and straining against the rising wind. Till that black car came reappearing out of nowhere, shooting off down the side path. *She* was another goer and no mistake! What was she about this time? Better to look in upstairs. Mistress looked like she was a guest in a house of dreams, whereas he was a just a restless one in hers. Well, then, let her sleep.

He slipped out into the north wing passage and looked up and down as DH had advised. Although he couldn't say if this made any difference. He had always come to expect the unexpected in here anyway. Though whether the unexpected ever regarded him in the same way was another matter. The wind had now receded to a muffled sound, a moaning concerto to the cymbal shivers of pouring rain. The corridors went back and forth, from deceptive greens to oblivious greys, fed only by morsels of a grim and grimy winter light. They seemed to him depressingly more than a mite shifty in their gloom this late afternoon. Not that such unattractive optical illusions could have too much effect on him for long. He had decided it was high time he reported back for a routine update, and, not feeling in the least majestic, but more like some costumed crusader on the wrong mission, he retraced his slow-paced steps back up to the tower. On arriving at the stairs, he stopped. He thought he could detect sounds quite unconnected with the miserable groaning of the weather. Voices. Twittering voices. Could be heard arguing. There was a sudden start in the shadows, as the air tensed. A small, furtive whisper followed.

"I saw something move. There. See where those spiky bits are sticking up!"

Terror trembled in the smallness of the voice as another one tried its hand at reassurance.

"I can't see anything. Can't be Black Art, and if it's Cream Tart, why, he's really ok."

The cream cat, dressed to kill as it were, broke into a smile as he waited. The little fellas taking liberties again, he thought.

"I told you that thing would bog you down. Still, I have it on good authority, from no less a person than Olly, that he is actually quite - "

Prince shuffled his feet and shook an uncomfortable ear, cocking the crown to an unprecedented angle over his forehead

"Let's go!" struck in the first voice, heedless of the other, as two streaks, darker than the surrounding passage, having concurred, immediately jerked into life and fled skittering down the stairs. Despite the darkness veiling pretty much everything along the landing, Prince quickly picked out a whitish spot where the rats had frozen. He trotted over for a closer analysis, his jade eyes steadily widening in surprise. A square of folded notepaper. Well, well. Since when had they started to acquire a taste for any letters? Been on the scrounge. And at the lady's expense, he'd wager. What kind of a letter would be of interest to them, he wondered? Maybe it was something for DH to mull over. Too scared to come back for it? Keep it bonzer, mateys. He snatched up the mysterious document and headed up the spiral stairs feeling very much more like a lion in winter.

The door was left slightly ajar, and Prince scraped at it three times by way of an agreed signal before entering to the welcoming sight of the fire resplendently shining its familiar warmth upon a wide-backed chestnut leather chair, and where Mr Brimble, insulated, as it were, from any outer disturbance, lay fast asleep. In close proximity a silver replica lampstand of the Jules Rimet trophy glistened benignly, jostling for supremacy with the other statuettes, cups and cherished paraphernalia winking away on the mantelpiece above. Meanwhile, the dimly solitary figure of DH was sitting on a chair at the window, gazing out onto the ravaged landscape, as splinters of rain glanced off the bowed windows like flimsy, toy arrows.

"Been expecting you," said the hound without altering his gaze, as the cream cat made his flamboyant way to the window and silently dropped the folded note at his companion's feet. Whether it was Prince's appearance or the note that startled DH more was hard to say, but after studying both at length he nodded, as though grateful for the interest they provided.

"Very colourful," he said at last, "Don't let the governor see you like that, though. He might prefer it. Maybe you're taking your responsibilities a bit too seriously."

Prince could not tell if he was joking and shifted self-consciously from one foot to the other, with the crown, skewed over one eye, glowing discreetly within the greater ambience of the room.

"Well, thenks muchly, mate," he replied with a vigorous shake of the head. The pitiful crown was showing a marked reluctance to fall off, so he turned his attention to the sparkly cape whose crushed purple had also been refracting the gleams of the fire in a similar manner. His struggle to free himself was equally in vain.

"Just me and the mistress hevin' a bit of fun," he confessed. "At least, thet's more than sum peeple do."

He glanced across to where his master remained asleep, head lolling against his chest and with an open book gradually slipping down his lap. DH followed his look to explain.

"Oh, we've been out with the village team all morning. Some coaching there was to start with. Then he was pacing up and down the touchline during the game, waving instructions and orders. Gave quite a lot of vocal support, too. Shouted himself hoarse. Never seen him like that for ages. Did him good, I think."

"And you?" said Prince.

"Implacable as always. Fourth official, you see."

Prince didn't exactly, but was glad his master had risen to the occasion, to shake off the low spirits which had been weighing him down recently.

"Didja win, then?" he asked hopefully.

"Naw. We lost 3-1. Dodgy lot, really," came the blunt reply.

His interest turned to the note, as Prince dexterously sidled up onto the sill and pushed it right in front of him.

"Guess how I cayme t' foind this?" whispered the cat, the tilt of the crown now giving him the half-baked look of a jolly swagman.

"Something purloined is bad news. Howsoever, let's take a closer dekko, shall we?"

He placed a paw against a bottom edge and skilfully prised the folds apart with the other until the entire note with its code-like scribbles and diagram lay crumpled at the edges, but exposed.

"So, what y' reckon, DH? Anythin' worth readin'?" said Prince eagerly, his voice rising a pitch.

DH hushed him.

"It's the lady's handwriting, I've no doubt about that. Seen her leave Cook grocery lists and suchlike."

Without wishing to appear interrogatory he gave the cat a questioning look

"So, where did you lay your twinkling toes on this? Not dropped by accident, I'll be bound. Not a folded note, she wouldn't."

Prince related how he'd waylaid a couple of rats who'd skidaddled off mighty quick on seeing him.

"In that outfit, it's no wonder they were in a hurry. So, now we get to the forensic bit. Stains near the middle. Orange juice. Smallish scratches where its folded. Not yours, of course."

DH pointed out the give away clues to Prince's great delight.

"Meaning? It was probably binned, and they took it when she weren't around. I take it you noticed her car has gone again?"

Prince nodded.

"Sumthing seems on the cards theyre, an' naw mistayke."

"Problem now is - why?" pondered DH, not to be side-tracked. "Them audacious rat discover something interesting enough for 'em to take into safekeeping. Why?"

"Hes t' be a raison fer doin' it, eh?"

The hound scratched at the several folds under his chin. Prince bowed his head low to inspect the baffling contents of the notc himself. He looked up expectantly, but still baffled.

"Oi think it's roight up your street. Any moment now end you'll hev the answer clear as dhay."

DH took another look.

"Methinks your hopes are premature." he murmured. "Can it be solved? Mebbe. I don't know."

The last three words made Prince wiggle his ears, which brought the crown lightly to the floor. He observed the gaudy object disconsolately.

"Aw. Blowed if it's ownly me agin!"

"But I do have another idea," DH continued, mildly amused. "There is someone better qualified than us to find an answer."

He turned and nodded toward Mr Brimble slumped deep into the chair. The hound took up the note and ambled across to his governor's side. Prince followed as nimbly as the cape would allow and waited to see what he had in mind.

"See here. One of England's finest goal poachers, and the governor's never happier than when relivin' those days."

The book *Greavsie* lay with a small crested bookmark drooped between the master's thumb and forefinger over an open page.

"So we put the paper in here and, bingo, he's sure to give it a good look over. And if it means anything, knowing him, he'll be sure to poach a goal of his own."

The jade eyes lit up as they always did when a good impression had been made.

"Coops, yore Captin Marvel, you are!" was all Prince could say.

For once DH didn't mind the double misnomer.

★   ★   ★

He had no idea how long he'd been sleeping. He never did just lately. He kept his eyes voluntarily closed in the hope that what he had begun to hear was something caused by the distant wind intruding upon an already fractured dream. Which would be something to be preferred. But as the sound of scuffling grew louder and more persistently jarring to his senses, it left him little choice but to do the only obvious thing. One eye opened and peered tentatively into the real world, as though through a smeary

63

spyglass. Emerging from behind a large cardboard box, shaking the bedraggled ends of her hair from a half-hidden face, a larger-than-life outline of Euradice speedily banished his premature dream. Her bony hands were gripped tenaciously at its corners as she pressed forward, heedless of Arturo's dozy presence, before roughly heaving the box into a space beside the lamp in the far corner of the room. The outside gusts had more or less subsided, although rain was still falling in a steady drizzle. Exultant, and unmindful of Arturo's inquisitive look following her every step, she returned to the car which had been parked deliberately closer with its interior light left on. Arturo slipped over to the window and watched her rummaging inside a capacious back seat before the whole process was repeated with another box of similar size. Then she went out again. Beginning to have doubts as to whether he actually was wide awake, he rubbed his eyes vigorously, as though mistrusting all he had just seen. He hopped onto an ancient washtub beneath the window and warily eyed the flaps of both containers which had been partially left asunder. His pupils narrowed like exclamation marks, as the deeper of the two began to bulge and retract horribly. He was going to satisfy his curiosity even if it killed him, which, next to drowning himself in a perpetuity of bad dreams, wouldn't seem to be a much worse option. Yet even as he leapt down, the door was shouldered open once more as Euradice swept inside, this time flushed with a look of supreme self-satisfaction. Following behind her came the aces in her pack. A distinguished and impressively marked tortoiseshell cat strolled forward, throwing a few cursory, bright-eyed nods of approval to his new surroundings. He was closely accompanied by a rather more aloof ginger tabby whose blander markings seemed to match the discreteness of a more formal disposition.

Euradice, seeming to have extended her already considerable height, clapped a mock-ceremonious welcome to both, eventually acknowledging Arturo with a deliberate glare and a mouthed snarl of 'your leader' for his benefit. Such a reminder of his lowered rank not only stung him, but served to increase his perplexity regarding the boxes. He looked from the newly-appointed leader and his sidekick back to the cardboard flaps with increasing desperation. He didn't, however, have to wait long. His mistress rammed the door fast and stood bracing herself, legs astride, surveying her acquisitions as if they were the missing pieces from a long-unfinished jigsaw puzzle.

"May I introduce - er - all of you to your ever trustworthy friend and leader, who in no small way has been instrumental in bringing you to your new abode. I give you - Mr Quills, and - um - his very good adjutant whose - er - own name eludes me at this present time. Though better acquaintance most certainly awaits us."

It was a clunky and pointlessly over-decorous introduction. The unimpressed tabby winced at this description of himself as he idly picked a spot on a blanket next to Arturo. Mr Quills jumped onto the vacated washtub with considerable natural decorum and, puffing out his chest to make the double v-neck markings around a pure white frontispiece look more formidably dashing than ever, brushed away a few drops of rain with a cultured flick of a paw. His purchaser looked on admiringly, mentally applying the fitting words of a familiar song to the little general which certainly 'made him look a little like a military man' in her estimation. Right on cue, three more members of the Honourable Mr Quills Appreciation Society popped their sleepy, feline heads over the larger box as if governed by a strange telekinetic power. Having rid themselves of their restrictive packaging with no little athletic charm, they were soon huddled together again on a vacant blanket to keep warm. To say Arturo was stunned would be an understatement, yet, with his mind working overtime, he quickly regained a sense of composure. She had earlier uttered the word 'platoon', he distinctly recalled. This surely implied a company. And this lot certainly were that.

"Ah, the other two are still asleep, it seems," she said disconcertingly with her arms akimbo, and went on glowering like the Queen of Tartarus.

Hey? Two more? Arturo, ever more stunned, sat rigid, eyeing the other box carefully, while totting up the total under his breath. Seven! There certainly wasn't to be any peace for the wicked. The old cook had spoken those words on another occasion, and, for the moment, he was inclined to agree. Without a wicked thought in her own head, though, Euradice, remembering some leftover scraps in the kitchen, quickly decided on the very fitting idea of gathering her troops for a late meal together. The three fresh-faced cats, huddled together to keep warm and, absorbed as much by one another as by their new surroundings, were soon paying much less attention to their rallying elders. Arturo took one long look at the whole group and judiciously thought over his next move. Successive shocks had unquestionably brought him fully to his senses, and it was now high time to do some careful vetting of his own.

Only a cat could truly understand another cat, and he couldn't help feeling that a few things here were definitely not quite as they should be. He turned to the ginger number two languorously stroking away the moisture that still adhered to his prickly and extensive whiskers.

"And you are?" he said, trying to look friendly.

"Oh. Name's Cubshaw. And this gentleman," raising an immediate and directive eye to the little general, "is my superior, Mr Quills."

The number two continued on with his automatic preening.

"Yes - yes. I've got his name now, thanks," Arturo faltered with a subdued annoyance that he found hard to keep down.

"And yourself?" returned Cubshaw, without so much as a look.

"Eh? Arty - er - Arturo." He compressed his lips.

Mr Quills, who had been observing the preparations in the kitchen with a great deal of interest, paused on catching the name.

"I say, no Venician extraction there, by any chance?"

His handsome almond-shaped eyes blinked affably. Arturo looked up nonplussed.

"Didn't we come across an Italian duke of that name, Cubshaw?" said Mr Quills, casually looking down to seek his inferior's superior recollection.

"I believe it was Alfonso, sir," suggested Cubshaw, all humble reliability.

"Reminds me of those summer picnics we had at her Ladyship's retreat." went on Mr Quills.

"Garden parties," Cubshaw modified with due deference.

Mr Quills eyes became dewy.

"Yes. No expense spared. Exquisite tastes. Hampers of cold beef, ham, pheasant. Oh, I could go on. Remember the cheeses, Cubshaw?"

"How could I forget them, sir," responded the spruced ginger tom graciously, running his tongue along the upper ridges of his teeth.

"Not forgetting, another time, that awesome selection of fish," added Mr Quills, testing the air with another sniff.

"Smorgasbord, sir. Her style was so reminiscent of those grand Victorian families. Such customary treats have, sadly, altogether long departed."

For them at any rate. Cubshaw sighed and scratched his groin as a completion to his ablutions. Arturo found himself looking on amazedly from one to the other. It was begging the inevitable question, the one that had to be asked.

"Ok. You've both had a high time of it. So how come you end up in a cat's home, then?"

Cubshaw coughed, but remained stock still with one eye on Mr Quills.

"Sir, I feel it is only proper that our demotion should be rightfully explained," he began.

His leader huffed his chest, which gave a fresh powder-puff impetus to its surrounding decorative markings of magnificence.

"Really, Cubshaw, I do think we ought not to go into all that - "

"No, no, sir. I feel we must set out our stall plain."

Mr Quills vaulted from the washtub to remonstrate, but his pleadings fell on deaf ears. Except for Arturo's. Cubshaw cleared his throat as he cast a dutiful eye on the bored antics of the nearby threesome.

"Her Ladyship had - humph - a musical son," he began. "Mercurial, it seems. Experimental in the tonic. There was a converted studio, an annexe of the farmhouse where, by all accounts, some ground-breaking sounds were attained."

Mr Quills, still in the radiating pose of a male peacock, took up the tale, trying to sound innovative himself in his relish for all things artistic.

"He harmonised a fiendish combination of notes to make 'em sound like - what were those instruments, Cubshaw?"

"Crumhorns, sir."

"Ah, yes. Twenty or so crumhorns and some odd cellos, as I remember it. And odd they were, too. What was that devilish phrase he came up with?"

69

"Alpine Stockhausen, sir. An atmospheric synthesis utilising modulators and shifters," explained Cubshaw with all the conclusive air of a seasoned electronic lab technician. "Although the sound struck me as more of a cosmic thing."

By this stage of the conversation Arturo felt that something was indeed distinctly amiss, and his alarm bells were beginning to jingle.

"To cut a long story short, we, that is to say, Mr Quills and myself, made an unfortunate and lasting contribution to these proceedings. Obstacles of wires and switches trailing everywhere, you understand. A freak accident, really. A misplaced paw, or claw. I believe. Led to a sort of voltage blow. Anyway, sparks flew and the whole place rapidly caught fire and burned to the ground."

There was a determination on Mr Quill's part to soften the abruptness of the tragedy just related, and his face lightened. "Not the entire building, mind. And, then again, nobody died," he stressed with an endearingly misplaced honesty.

"It was pretty much, sir," insisted his other half. "A setback to his ambitions, to all intents and purposes. And to ours. But we are serendipitous. We move on."

"Indeed. What was that intriguing electronic gadget called again, Cubshaw?" said Mr Quills, sniffing the air in successive discriminatory bursts.

"An Oberheim Sequencer, sir," came the rueful reply. "Rather dated these days, but, like the *Ondes,* an esoteric piece of equipment nonetheless. I believe a keyboard came off very badly and almost melted."

Such talk, at once both mesmerising and baffling, deflated Arturo, the thought suddenly occurring to him that a similar disaster here might be a better way out for everyone. And so to the bigger question. He looked collectedly from one to the other and forced a smile.

"Interesting. If I may just ask you both, getting back to the present for a moment, how do you recommend we go about this - er - job, then?"

Mr Quills sniffed again, then eyed his questioner like a quizzical bird.

"Job? Exactly what job are you referring to, my friend?"

Arturo flinched and felt momentarily lost for words.

"The - the job you've been brought here to do. Slaughtering rats. A horde of rats. In this very house," he said, punctuating his reply with a good deal of unintended alacrity.

"Ah, that. Don't really know why she thought we should throw our hats into such a ring, so to speak. Never done that sort of thing, have we, Cubshaw?" Cubshaw screwed his eyes and shook his head, as though such an activity was anathema to his sensitivities. The whole situation was becoming more bizarre by the moment.

"Then again, this is evidently a very pleasant establishment," said Mr Quills, toying with the possibilities the project might advance.

"Perhaps we may combine work with pleasure, Cubshaw. The youngsters would take to that, I'm sure. An adventure where we may relive, to some extent, former glories. If our new Ladyship wishes us to begin this - hum - task tomorrow, well, what better place to start than the library. I take it there is a library here?"

Arturo, not altogether relieved, assured him that although a library did exist, it was for some reason not a favourite haunt of the rats. Of all the rooms he'd roamed he'd never found any tell-tale activity there. Mr Quills, though, was not to be put off by this piece of private information.

"Rats are a funny business, from what I gather. Boswick and Gus have had some, admittedly limited, experience of their methods. They invariably are where they appear not to be. Isn't that the case, boys?"

A charcoal grey and a predominantly white tricolour head, refreshed from their recent sleep, miraculously looked out from the other box nearest the lamp and appeared to nod in unison, privileged to have come to the magnanimous attention of Mr Quills. Arturo gave a fresh start.

"Thus, you see, the glitter of row upon row of gold-embossed titles, the addition of a table or two of polished rosewood, a candelabra - all surely have a studious as well as splendiferous appeal to their inquisitive instincts. If such a profoundly erudite solitude doesn't catch them napping there, it will do so well enough for us."

Having dealt with the preliminary stage of the business, the pleasure presently became all-consuming.

"Do I detect a smell of warm chicken?" he said,

inhaling deeply.

"With gravy, sir," confirmed his number two approvingly.

The five other heads simultaneously rotated towards the kitchen, as the figure of Euradice loomed large on her return, balancing in her hands a stack of dented metal dishes which she presently doled out to her eager onlookers like a brash card dealer. To improve the light she dragged the lampstand nearer to the window.

"Gorge well, for tomorrow is another day," she murmured, as she rubbed her hands contentedly. "Where you're natural instincts will come into play. For - er – war, rather."

A brief and stoic 'good night' was about to form upon her lips when her ever-alert eyes caught sight of what seemed to be four strange mini torch lights hovering a short distance away beyond the darkened window. Oh! What in heaven's name was going on here? Cat's eyes! Sitting on her blasted bonnet, too, if she was seeing right! She was. Eyes that did not implore. Demanding, unwavering eyes that only stared menacingly, challengingly. Compelling her to bring them in from the onset of a wet and drenching night. Supper was quickly interrupted by an inquisitive silence when, a few moments later, the glinting addition of the four cold eyes slowly entered - bringing their very own brand of insidious darkness with them.

Cold tails were snapping repeatedly on a colder stone floor as a group of rats sat in a small circle beneath an alcove at one end of the Arena. In their midst a single sliver of unwavering candlelight superimposed itself against the surrounding darkness, a source more than adequate for them to concentrate on the task at hand. Which was to distribute broken chunks from a generous mince pie as intimately and as cheerily as the conditions would allow. It was almost dawn, not that anyone present was too bothered about the coming and goings of natural daylight, down here underground, where a feast could be a midnight one just as well as any other, and a festive pie came as a delightful exception to the norm.

Such gatherings were weekly affairs, exclusively arranged between some of the younger team members and trainees and conducted in true boot room style in which the prime concern was considered to be mutual bonding, with all the conviviality that went with it. And a right boisterous time they were having of it, as warm blood began to flow through their hands and feet once again. Each fellow smacked his lips as morsels of sugar-dusted pastry shavings laced with spiced sultanas were savoured in a succulence of temporal silence. It didn't take too long before that spell was broken, though, as the irrepressible Nobs, leaning back, looked across to one of the newcomers at the scene, who sat almost opposite, head down, busily nibbling at his portion of the pie.

"What's this we're hearing about you wanting to be a goalkeeper, then, Jed?"

Nobs winked mischievously for the benefit of the others as he sought to maintain the merriment of the prevailing mood. Little Jed kept his head down, not knowing quite how to respond to such a teasing piece of interrogation. One or two of the trainees sniggered, but waited for someone better qualified to pick up on this hilarious notion. Jed chewed ever more slowly, refusing to enlarge on the rumours of his personal ambition lest he should appear more foolish than he already felt inside. The awkward silence was ended by a tuneful, yet sympathetic, voice which came directly to his rescue with the accompaniment of a flashing smile.

"Ah! Jedd. You wanna be ze goalie? Yes? Theez a-playerrs, they come in a-many sizes, you must know. Ees-a no problem eef 'e can spreeng and a-dive. I weel a-show you how, eh? Being leetle reely ees-a no problem here."

The face beamed again in sympathy to Jed's cause.

"That's all very well for you to say, Georgio. But it's a known fact that all goalies are mad, otherwise they wouldn't choose to go in goal," said Hobs, getting in what he believed to be a valid point on the subject. "That's not to say you're a bad keeper, yourself. But you might just be mad, all the same."

A bout of convulsive laughter followed, as heads

rocked and warmed tails flapped up and down in their appreciation for such stylish banter. Georgio waved a dismissive hand, having grown used to all the jibes and frivolity of his team mates ever since his unforeseen arrival in a carpet van one wet afternoon a long, long while ago. The land of his youth still figured in his conversations. How fate had, against all ze odds, led him to a new family. Where ze beautiful game was also reverred and even played with ze panache of street fighterrs by hees own-a kind. *Mama mia!* Ah! Where grasshopperrs cleeped ze heels of stick insects to save a cerrtain goal. *Miracoloso!* Ah! Nobs patted him on the shoulder and agreed that his coming had been a marvellous turn of their fortunes.

"But for you, we'd never have had any half-decent shot-stoppers to test our predatory skills against. It's what we were hoping for, having taught you the rudiments of it. More like a modern game should be. None of those wearying 9-7 and 7-6 scores we used to plough and skittle our way through. I think all here would agree that the standard we have lately attained to surpasses anything we used to produce in those former days of our rat hole scuffles, eh lads."

This statement went down extremely well, receiving due affirmation, before Hobs got up and produced from a hidden corner a miniature liqueur bottle sealed with a loosened screw top. It was swiftly opened and handed round to celebrate this coming of age, each member allowing himself one swig only from the unidentified concoction before it left him with a hot throat and a heady swirl.

"Courtesy of Cook's brother. Left on the dresser. Goes perfect with the pie, lads," cried Nobs, relieving himself with an indecent belch of warm breath.

Georgio swilled his mouthful thoughtfully before letting it slip gently down his throat.

"Ah, I dreenk to Sorrento, land of-a my birrth! To theenk I a-climbed a rope and fell asleep on a boat. Then eet was a-float."

His listeners laughed at this unintended rhyme from their soliloquising goalie.

"Yet I never forget ze futbol. An' I a-bring my skeells to thees a-strange, darrk place of flames."

"Yes, we know what you bring. Arms, legs and elbows - to hack the ball away," implied another voice.

Hobs shook an ex-trainee named Cedric playfully by the hand for his quickness off the mark. Georgio went on undeterred:

"Eet ees neverr just catching and saving. Narrowing ze angles, blocking wiz ze arms an' legs ees-a so important. Ee-talian goalies are worrld-a-famous. My grand-father, 'e talk to me 'bout ze great Dino. He was a capitan who wonna ze Worrld Copa for 'iz countree. I a-dreenk - to Dino Zoff!"

With that he grabbed the slim bottle which, to his dismay, he now found empty save for a few drops.

"So, ok, I a-dreenk to leetle Jedd, instead. Eef 'e 'as ze courage to keep a-goal, 'e can be as victorious as Dino wuz."

The drops were promptly drained. Jed brightened at this and, emboldened by the generous measure he'd previously gulped from the bottle, finally declared that if Italian rats could wear the number one with distinction, then so could an English rat. And, who knows, all that stretching might in time make him bigger. Nobs quickly extended him the privilege of accompanying both himself and Hobs to the tower when the next match was showing and where he could closely observe some of the attributes needed to be a goalie. The offer was gratefully accepted to a background of good-natured cheering. Tails thwacked in applause against the sides of the crate on which the candle was positioned, making it flare up from the resulting vibrations. Georgio was not quite finished highlighting the fundamental differences in the arcane art of continental defending and its counterpart here.

"We goalies are 'appier doing a-not so much. For thees I rememberr my cousins and friends for ze trick of the *catenaccio*."

"We don't need reminding of cats on this occasion, Georgio," said Nobs abruptly, smoothing a dribble of runny wax around the base of the candle as it cooled.

"As for Black Art, whether he has any tricks left is pretty doubtful."

Everyone jeered at this sober enough assessment.

"If he ever had any to begin with," grinned Hobs, not to be outdone.

Georgio was having none of it.

"Eet ees not a cat or cats. Eet ees about tough defence. Zey shut ze bolt across, so no playerr can shoot to score. Life then become easierr for uz in ze goal."

"No room to swing a cat, there, either," declared Nobs, as he stuck rigidly to his own peculiar interpretation, "because if my own understanding is correct, we could be needing a bolt like that. One too tight for any cat to break down."

Hobs, his face obscured by low shadows, chided him in an equally low voice: "You're talking in riddles, Nobs. The drink has probably gone to your head. Let's not close this assembly on a downer."

"You're right, my friend," said Nobs airily with an immediate change of heart. "No news is good news, and the news from Lief and the other scouts is most likely to be grossly exaggerated."

He looked at Jed and the trainees with the barest trace of guilty apprehension. The waxy pool from the heart of the candle had begun to drip excessively as the stem withered perilously close to its sticking base. The group sat silent in their uncertainty, the darkness in front of them appearing more impenetrable than ever. Then, out of its stillness came a voice, not one of their own.

"The news, if you must know, is no exaggeration."

Without a specific pinpoint, it sounded as scratchily distant as a recorded message relaying some awful declaration of impending doom. All held their breath, the fur on their necks bristling.

"It is, I'm afraid, quite correct."

Drawing nearer, the tone of the voice gradually became more breathily recognisable as Olly's.

"There are plenty of cats up there - since last night," he said hollowly. without taking his eyes off them.

There was an added tremor to it now. He shuffled forward, his disquieting face, as though breaking the ether, materialising fearfully at the edge of the candle's weakening radiance. He tried to make his next words sound more calm and collected, in order to stem his own extreme anxiety for their sakes.

"To use the terms you younger players seem to understand: you're going - we're all going - to have to close down the space and defend our own half. Captain has just had the news confirmed and, to repeat one of Lief's nautical expressions, has ordered a very tight ship."

The cluster of close-knit ears were vaguely rust-red, bent low in the dying squiggle of the burning candle.

"All unspecified trips are banned as from now. You ignore this at your peril."

As an admirer of their singular views and their infectious bravado, Olly bitterly regretted having to announce such a devastating report. It was all closing in on them, with no real indication where relief would come from. As if in answer, the remains of the candle disintegrated in a wafting twist of smoke and the Arena once more returned to a deadness of futile dark. Just like their hopes. Pitch black.

*   *   *

Elsewhere dawn rose like a fresh wind of danger, scraping the sky with wispy streaks of a gunmetal grey to replace the slow dissolution of night. Danger might change its shape, yet its signal panged like a graze from a bullet, with no less an impact than if it had been a direct hit. Arturo sat sleeplessly in its imaginary line of fire, staring through one of the tall windows, thinking how conveniently easy it would be for a half-decent sniper in the old hayloft to take him out before the day had properly taken off. No need for him to puff out an unprotected chest, it felt vulnerably exposed enough as it was. But so was his back.

"You ain't bin sleepin' too good, it seems."

The words bit through the stale air as grittily as shovelled gravel and made Arturo turn with a start. He was greeted by a face perhaps less feline than his own, one far more pinched and weathered, and belonging more to the inextricable shadows behind.

"Name's Scrounger. Don't you mind me. Call me Scrounge, if it comes easier. It does for most. It's wot I do, generally speakin'."

Both of Scrounger's ears were split and torn from momentous past encounters, and he displayed them as proudly as any war wound, a twitchy swagger which Arturo found strangely attractive. He presently averted his eyes and peered towards the empty dishes below. A groan wriggled its way around his stomach as he remembered having eaten hardly a bite the night before. He looked up at the ruffian cat and, almost apologetically, found his voice at last.

"I never saw either of you take anything."

"Ah, well, we'd dined earlier," came the throwaway reply. Scrounger yawned, then chuckled noiselessly.

Arturo narrowed his pointy eyes.

"Birds, that is."

The casualness of the explanation seemed slightly shocking by design, and Arturo's face paled as far as his dark fur would seem to allow, his pupils momentarily widening. Scrounger followed this up by licking the coarseness of his dry lips, as though an aftertaste still lingered.

"See, that's the trouble with you domesticated cats. Too much in the lap of luxury - and so you lose wot comes nat'ral."

In the background, a collective sound of snickering could be heard coming from a shadowy heap encamped beside the boxes.

"Them's only young uns," said Scrounge with an eerie smile, yet without turning around. He then aimed his tattered head towards Mr Quills curled up in repose near by.

"Gregarious charmer now, ain't he? Me and 'im" (pointing opposite with a club of a paw to a shadowy coil wound up along the rear wall), "we did wot may be regarded as a stakeout, see. Pressed our noses to the winder, figuratively speakin', an' hung about till the missus came in with all that commotion. When we saw 'im" (now pointing back to Mr Quills) "struttin' his stuff, well, we thought it'd be nice to come along for the ride, as it were."

The audacity of these two latecomers had not been lost on Arturo, and he showed no little indignation at this leering admission so freely given. To think that, after all the indecision and change of plans he had endured, and which had eventually only brought about the selection of imposters, his mistress should, in two minutes, create a double-edged sword for herself. It hadn't taken him long to realise that the introduction of Quills and his jolly entourage to her aggressive scheme was going to be a disaster waiting to happen. And, as far as it was of his concern, uninvited guests just muddied up the waters even further. Indeed, in Scrounger, he noted something more than a vulgar raffishness. He had already seen the amber eye of his formidable partner and had at once suspected them to be a combination of quite unpredictable   dangerousness. They   were   both unseemly chancers on an altogether different level. Scrounger, noting Arturo's change of expression, sought to adopt a more subtle approach of his own.

"Now, I can guess wot you may be thinkin' - fly-by-nighters."

His shifty voice made an effort to sound frank and easy, but to Arturo he might as well have been a fat cat trader selling mangy fish-heads disguised as the real deal.

"If there's any sport to be had, we like to think our contributions will be appreciated. An' no one'll be any worse off for us takin' a slice of the action, b'lieve you me."

Arturo frowned at this statement of intent.

"What makes you think there's any action on offer?" he said, trying to match the demeanour of the other. Scrounger bared a formidable row of stained teeth and gave a ruptured smile as raw as any sneer.

"Wot? All that comin' an' goin', late at night? A crew

of cats all gettin' on nicely together? Do us a favour."

Here, it occurred to Arturo that a touch of frankness of his own might not go amiss, if he was to get out of his present dilemma. He had long known that he lacked the basic killer instinct which belonged to cats. He felt that he did possess, though, other, more insightful skills which only required support from the right source to turn things round and make him more complete. To this end the ornamental cat from upstairs had been a massive let-down.

"Alright. You've made your point. There's no big secret. We've got a problem - with rats."

Notwithstanding this bluntness on his part, with the need to enlarge on this statement he became at once almost clandestine again.

"That's to say, me and my mistress have. A pathetic, bothersome horde of rats. We want them eliminated. Anyhow. Just gotten rid of. And," without wishing to state the obvious, "this bunch of sleepy heads, in case you hadn't noticed, are not, definitely not, going to deliver."

At this appropriate moment Mr Quills made a decorous yawn as he adjusted his sedately entrenched position on one of the choicest blankets below, quite oblivious to the judgements being passed over his predatory skills (or lack of them). Arturo eyed his sleeping successor with a thought-provoking intensity, unusual even for him. What was it about appearances which made them so deceptive? His was the face of glittering honour, of unjustifiable rewards. The image and acceptable face of splendour to match an elegant stylishness his mistress believed was rightfully hers. A tycoon's tom to be stroked in a - what was it? A lap of luxury. Exactly. A trophy cat. Kitsch with kittens. A purring purveyor of empty hopes where image was seen to be all. And his own face, then? What did that represent? Was his the unacceptable face of reality? The reality of an unalluring failure from which she desperately wanted to hide? From which she now wanted to escape? Probably. He shrank from such a pitiable conclusion. Anyway, life in the seaside flat was infinitely better than the uncertainties that were being thrown up here. Maybe, sooner or later, she would cut her losses (or count her gains) and go back. To where they once belonged. His mind, having revolved in turn on these matters, was jolted back the present as Scrounger sidled up to the window beside him and studied the blurry formation of a band of cloud which had formed in the meantime. He wanted to whisper in his ear, but Arturo's body language told him to keep his distance - which remained about three feet away - to which he readily complied

"So wot's in it for you lot if and when the rats get done for? No deep secrets 'ere, are there?"

The one thing Arturo could not imagine resigning himself to was being stuck in this rambling pile tied to a host of other cats for the rest of his life. Surely they were a means to an end? She didn't have to stay here to run a health farm, did she? Far better to dismiss right away all these unanswered questions or else he'd only end up getting into a perfect panic. Time enough later to work out eventualities. He gave his inquisitor a vacant look and shrugged.

"You know. Food, drink and freedom. What do you expect?"

"Well, freedom to roam is a grand privilege, without a doubt. Just eatin' an' sleepin' ain't a fair assessment of us cats, though we do it better than most. Me an' 'im 'ave an intuition 'bout when our time is up, an' so we knows when the next move's due. But for now, if it's any consolation, you won't need to be takin' all the flak when things don't run to plan. You could even be sharin' the plaudits. There could be a deal of those, I'm certain."

"For hunting down and killing rats, you mean?" came the insistent response.

Scrounger shifted the balance of his legs in a soft shuffle and swiped through the air with a measured stroke from the club of his right paw.

"To kill a bird is to kill rat. No matter which. It's instinctive timing. Coupled with a spot of cunnin' manoeuvrin', of course."

This brief demonstration, with the unquestionable expertise thrown in, not only confirmed Arturo's view regarding this ruthless duo, but also gave him some slight encouragement for what lay ahead.

"So how about if you two take a grip on things here and start showing the rest of us how its done. I'm sure Quills and Co would be only too pleased to learn from specialists like yourselves. And then we can get the job done without so much fuss - and bother."

Arturo felt more exhilarated by the possibilities and was eager to establish this promising pact.

Scrounger bided his time before giving it his positive approval.

"Of course, we need to get the go-ahead from my partner over there. Seal it in blood, as it were. Now, don't let that worry you. Only a manner of speakin'. 'E's a sharp metal, that one. Sharper. Leaves me to negotiate an' all that, then goes for it, wotever it may be. Never turn your back on 'im when you're wanted, though, or 'e'll swish you - like this."

Once again he sliced viciously through the air, putting extra malice into the downward thrust of the swing. Arturo winced, leaned back adeptly, and tried to maintain a brave face.

"Can you not settle it between you now, so we may inform the others in good time," he said, quickly recovering his equilibrium.

"Right you are, then. We'll put the case nicely, and see wot 'e want's doin' arterwoods."

With that, the amenable Scrounger, displaying a good deal of bonhomie towards Arturo, slipped down and quietly took up a close position next to the darkly forbidding coil. The matter was imparted in a low voice before Scrounger turned back to Arturo in order to add his own hasty assurances on the deal.

"Let 'im get 'is 'ead round everythin', then we're well away."

Waiting was a tense business for Arturo, as he sat at a respectful distance from the quiet discussion in which Scrounger seemed to do all the talking in an oddly formal and deferential way. A charm offensive might have worked in any other situation, but not this one. The light had begun to forge oblique inroads to the dank recesses of the outhouse, making its cluttered drabness all the more partially apparent. Discarded and broken picture frames of various designs and sizes were stacked against the wall between two towers of rickety shelves adorned with wide-mouthed pots and several fusty fruit baskets. Apple-weighing scales, hanging by a thread of spindly old chain that threatened to bring it crashing to the floor if any sprightly cat chose to hop aboard, completed the scene of ramshackle obsolescence and neglect. In front of the frames stood a bulbous *fauteuil* which, although perforated by eruptions of stuffing and other unexplained lumps, nevertheless provided a spacious vantage point along with some reasonable comfort. It was from this majestic spot that the embodied coil slowly unwound, muscle by steel-sprung muscle disentwining from each other with bone-stretching elasticity until its eventual malevolent shape had risen like a relic of a panther god resurrected from some newly-uncovered Egyptian burial chamber. Tail and loins were captured and suffused by two shafts of pale light, whereas the merest glint of slanting amber remained the sole detectable feature in an unexposed ebony head. It turned, in due course, and fixed a hypnotic stare upon Arturo, who quelled any tendency to tremble by keeping his own hopeful eye on a relaxed Scrounger sitting beside the throne-like chair.

"I understand you wish me to take the reins from our friend Mr Quills."

The words fell out of the secret mouth as a sound of water dousing hot ashes. Unable to vocalise any words of his own, Arturo could only affirm as much by means of a succession of rapid blinks.

"It's good to hit the ground running, my friend, yet we understand Mr Quills intends to do just that. Now, it is easy for you to criticise good intentions. His methods may or may not be revolutionary, but I feel we should be giving him as much encouragement and support as possible. I consider this only fair. You agree?"

This recommendation was, by dint of a cunning eye, extended to Scrounger, who in turn ratified this viewpoint with a grave nod and a corresponding: "Oh, absolutely."

Arturo's mouth dropped aghast.

"But – but look - I thought - "

The big cat lowered his terrible frame and, adjourning the hearing with a challenging stare, endeavoured to rewind into his former position. As luck would have it, before ever Arturo could collect his senses, his nemesis broke the stunned silence by greeting him with a light slap on the shoulder. Mr Quills, as jovially fresh and sparkling as the night before, seemed eager to engage in further dialogue.

"Good morning, Archie. Cubshaw and I have just decided to post three of our more adventurous boys at judicious points outside the house. The brisk country air should keep their spirits from flagging, don't you think. Begin them with a sense of adventure, I say. Once we've all had the stimulation of breakfast, of course."

Arturo's own spirit had already begun to sag as he watched Cubshaw in the background in the process of delegating the rôles to the fortunate threesome. He could only have repeated what he believed to be the case: that there was a next-to-nothing chance of finding any rats straying beyond the boundaries of the house, especially when he recalled that frustratingly lost opportunity with the rat rolling around on the grass. It had been wrong place and - much worse - wrong cat. It still rankled, and he simply couldn't see how the present set-up would fare any better.

"Now, we don't want no disunity here, do we?" grinned Scrounger, observing Arturo's distraught countenance. "It ain't a time to be squabblin' like ferrets in a cramped place. This is, after all, a handy hole to be in, I should say."

Mr Quills concurred vigorously.

"I constantly marvel that we are so judiciously located beside a kitchen which, as every cat worthy of his digestion knows, is an exceptional choice bar none."

He sniffed towards that region and wondered if there was to be a useful bowl of something to be knocked up a bit later. Scrounger laughed boldly and, after another subtle wink to the slumbering giant to his rear, suggested that they all press on regardless.

"'E's 'avin' 'is lie-in till later on. Perhaps Mr Arturo will direct us to the library, in due course. Yes, there's sure to be somethin' to keep us all occupied for day one, in this grand ol' place."

"Hum. Indeed. The - er - cat with no name is - hum - welcome to join us when he chooses," said Mr Quills in a less than rousing tone, slightly vexed by the unnerving motionlessness of the sleeping giant.

With hunger being the least of his immediate concerns, Arturo had, in the mean time, moved to the kitchen door to check if anyone was up and about. After the night's excesses he doubted whether his mistress would be paying any visit before lunchtime (she never ate breakfast there now) to see how events were moving. But sooner or later she'd realise that outwitting the enemy was going to be a slower business than she'd imagined. For his part, reality told him he had no choice now but to dip his feet where the water flowed. And that meant a fool's choice of either swimming alongside two utter devils - or end up floundering with the rest in a very deep blue sea.

★   ★   ★

"Grandfather, I know you're listening. Grandfather?"

There are faces you will remember all your life. And from the first meeting to the last those memories will never vary, never dim. Snapshots of now and forever, indelible impressions which somehow get to be stored somewhere deeper than the recesses of a forgetful mind, and all the better for being nowhere deeper than in a shared reverberation of the soul. It is the resonance of a constant: twoheartbeatstogether.

An old man, peering over his glasses, and above the top edge of a newspaper, answered the insistent demand of the other with a sheepish, if not boyish, wink of an eye. Amusement met bemusement, but, since the insistence was certainly not on trouble, the younger face asked the question for a second time. Perhaps it was an unexpectedly tricky one, for the glasses slipped further down the old man's nose and his ragged eyebrows went in the opposite direction. There followed another interval as the paper gradually worked its way back to its former height with a rustling of full-spread resistance. But the waiting game was soon brought to a sudden end by an impatient snap of an index finger against the front page headlines. The grand-daughter's tresses hung as naturally as a cascade of weeping willow, as she leant forward to poke the same finger doggedly into the middle of the centre folds. She giggled, almost inaudibly, with an unaffected and winning charm.

"Sorry, grandfather. But I do so want your opinion. I want to know why it is that most girls simply can't kick a ball properly? You tell me. It's not a such a silly question, is it?"

Mr Brimble continued to look bemused as he tried turning his attention from the Boxing Day match reports to wrestle for a suitable answer. The paper came down half-way, allowing his kindly face to come into full view.

"If you value my opinion so greatly, and, it is only an opinion, mind you, then I put it down to regular practice - or the lack of it, I should rather say. Really, you may as well ask me why away goals count double. By the way, have you seen all these end-of-the-year fixtures? Some crucial matches coming up, you know. Often goes that way. The timing. Now I recall a season not so long ago when - "

Harriet snapped at the centrefold again and scowled defiantly for a number of seconds. Moments enough for that breath-held reverberation of twin hearts. She sat back with a trace of a smile suppressed beneath her lips. He was more than a tough game. But she wasn't about to let him off that easily, though. The second alternating heartbeat, understanding the new tempo perfectly, finally brought the paper to rest on his lap.

"Really, my dear, I'm in no position to say for certain, since I've only worked with boys, the juniors, you know, and the village teams."

Harriet sat forward to avenge herself before another word was said.

"Yes, and not forgetting me with the tennis balls. I practice as much if not more than most of 'em', so I'm quite sure *I* don't kick it all wrong."

Mr Brimble, undeterred by her vexation, and discerning something deeper being wrestled with, sought a gentler line of communication..

"Well then, why should it worry you? Besides, ladies' football seems to thrive quite well without any interference from their opposites. In fact, you would be amazed to know that the most unlikeliest of teams can do more than adequate justice to the game. And, while you're nearly out of the chair, my dear, would you be good enough to give the fire a gentle poke. There's a fair old wind out there this afternoon, and we need to keep this room nice and snug. Some heavy snow is forecast round about, which may play havoc with some of tomorrow's matches. There'll be oranges or lemons, and not just at half-time, if you want to see where the ball is."

The old man chuckled, then looked on thoughtfully as the child of his delight gave a meek sigh and carried out the request. A bright flame leapt up and caught the World Cup lamp with as graceful a gleam as any displayed by the original when it was first raised aloft one sun-swept afternoon in July many years ago. She returned to the chair to squat neatly on a large batik cushion placed beside it.

"Oh, it doesn't worry me as such, grandfather. Only it's Rory. He keeps on about how great he was when he used to play and how stupid it is to expect any girl to be anywhere near as good. He likes to show off his dribbling in our back garden. Especially when he's had a few drinks."

She pulled a face and rolled her grey saucer eyes.

Mr Brimble stroked his chin, trying to recall the name from his memory.

"Rory? Now that's a - "

"Yes. he's Scottish, grandfather. He's mum's latest boyfriend and he comes from Scotland."

The stern summation seemed almost shameful to admit and that to add anything more to his description would be quite unnecessary. But the touchpaper had smouldered down too far and, this issue being no damp squib, an incendiary crackle or two was now inevitable.

"And it just makes me despair to think that mum's

sometimes so stupid in her choices!"

Harriet knitted her fists, clenching them hard till the protruding knuckles whitened.

"That's not to say I don't like him. He can be very funny at times. He tells jokes, but even when I can't understand him he just goes on and on so. I can't get a moment's peace with him and mum larking around. You can't tell her anything, for she never listens. She's as much of a child as he appears to be, and I really don't think she'll ever marry him. Like all the others. O, I wish she would come here with me, then perhaps she might just listen to you and have a change of heart. Do you know, I really do think she's afraid to come."

She leaned back, brushing the long curls away from her cheeks in a fit of frustration, and picked at a loose thread on the cushion's edge. She wondered whether she had said too much and reacted by biting on her lip. Yet other thoughts were piling up one by one into a log-jam that clearly needed to be disposed of.

"She always says she will come back one day. One day. Huh! One day might be never. She says she doesn't want to be a hypocrite. She's cut down on the cigarettes, but I think she drinks far too much. They both drank too much yesterday. Oh, grandfather, I could argue and wail, but then she would call me a child who doesn't understand, so I really don't talk about it any more. Once I remember thinking I'd feel dreadful after talking to her the way I do - I must have gone on so - but all I could feel was a sort of numbness, as if it didn't matter any more. Now I'm just sad if I keep thinking about what will happen."

The corner clock, unmoved by these disclosures, ticked on through the ensuing silence with all the dispassionate tempo of its own rigid heartbeat. Her grandfather had changed his position to a less than relaxed one. Having listened with the sensitivities of a father, his face seemed all at once to be inexplicably withdrawn, lost in some internal grief that racked him with its own private pain. If his solitude was an enforced rite of passage, then Harriet had gradually become a pleasanter means by which a measure of forgiveness might yet be attained. Theirs was a symbiotic relationship, an essential ingredient for the private and settled world of Brokehill, if it was to remain unscathed by change and its strange and undisclosed realities valued and preserved. The old man, soothed by these inward feelings, folded the newspaper away carefully and regained his former composure.

"So what exactly does Rory do for work?" he asked finally.

"Vegetables. He sells at the market each week, I think. There are always plenty of cabbages or turnips to kick. Instead."

His granddaughter broke into a small elfin smile and bending forward, straightened her denimed knee with an aim in order to show how it should best be done.

"He'll never make a fortune, but mum doesn't mind. He gets her to help on the stall, and all that. She likes it, though. He wants to take us in that battered old van of his up to his family in Scotland.

To see in the New Year."

She looked around the tower wildly, unable and unwilling to focus on anything for too long.

"Yes, celebrating the new year is a grand affair in Scotland," resumed the old man placidly before being waylaid again.

"Rory goes on about Hogmanay and something called 'first-footing'. More excuses - for drinking - I reckon. I wasn't going to tell you, but I haven't felt like celebrating anything this week. They went to some late-night party and mum was dressed up in something awful! I wish I could've been here and out of their way."

A startlingly auburn sheen of curls revealed themselves in the firelight as they hid a flush of frustration. She leaned forward again with a renewed and improvised demonstration of her kicking prowess.

"But I really don't *want* to go. Now I've got back, I'd rather stay - *here* with you. With Prince and Cooper!"

She flopped back sulkily into a mask of annoyance and fire-flung shadow.

"Talking of which reminds me of something else I must to tell you, grandfather. When I came up earlier there was a cat, an ugly brownish thing, at the bottom of the stairs." She pulled another face of mock horror on recalling it. "I thought for a moment it was that miserable Arturo who follows great-aunt everywhere. I wanted to clap my hands and shoo the silly, skinny thing away, right out of my sight. But, you know, as I stooped down I noticed it had a much more wicked little face with ripped ears. It looked like something which had fallen from a dustcart. Then it hissed and ran off down the passage."

Mr Brimble didn't seem particularly surprised by her discovery.

"In fact, that's not all. Mr Pale says he's spotted three others this morning, shivering things, moping around outside. Two in the garden and another by the stables. In this weather! So, why are we overrun with cats all of a sudden? Prince won't take too kindly to them popping their heads up everywhere!"

Her grandfather pooh-poohed the likelihood of that happening with a forceful wave of his hand.

"Don't think it for a minute, my dear. He has an indomitable spirit - ahem! A stalwart. Rugged, for all his endearing appearance. A most resourceful and adaptable fellow, if ever there was one! He's been down there with Cooper since this morning, keeping a steady watch on those mischief-makers. There's been quite a bit of activity, so Cook tells me, both in the library and in the kitchen. She counted quite a crew of 'em - all queuing up for dinner! And my sister not to be seen anywhere. I don't think her festivities made any provision for yowling, carol-singing cats! However, they are all here under her care and keeping!"

The old man appeared jovially unperturbed by this unexpected invasion. Indeed, the presence of so many cats seemed to have put a magical twinkle back into his eye.

"You see, she's kept her promise - now we must ensure that we keep ours."

Harriet could offer him no more than a bewildered shrug of the shoulders to the last part of this incomprehensible statement. Her grandfather sprang energetically to his feet and grabbed a long woollen scarf (a labour of his grand-daughter's love) from the hat-stand behind the chair. He wrapped it in haste, leaving one end trailing so near to the floor it seemed more than liable to trip him at any moment. The wind, by this time, had shifted its capricious course high along the hillside behind the house, where it was now rising and flying, unfettered, unrestrained with the screams of a banshee. By nightfall a number of the more exposed trees would be pummelled and beaten down by its wintry blasts before being left to crack and rot beneath the veiled mists and iron-earth gloom of late December. Only the fittest survived a tribulation, as Edward Brimble well knew.

Happy to leave the crow's nest in the hands of his young protégé, he was, nevertheless, not too quick to throw all caution to the wind, however far off it may appeared to have flown. He issued Harriet a couple of concise instructions.

"I'll be back as soon as I see how things stand downstairs. Give the fire another poke, but make sure this door is shut if and when you go out. And look about you as you do. No need to encourage any more of the snoopers to try their luck up here."

He swung the loose end of scarf round his neck once more and headed off down the spiral stairs at a steady pace, whistling a gentle warning to anything that might be lurking below. If anyone was going to trip up it wasn't going to be him. If his sister's act meant war, then it would be a war on his own terms - as a dog of war.

$$\star \qquad \star \qquad \star$$

The warning words of Captain Greybands were ringing loudly in his ears as he darted up the next few steps with another short burst of calculated speed. So far so good. But he'd never felt this nervous for ages. Not since that day he'd come back from the river and had that amazing escape. He believed he was the seventh son of a seventh son, statistically by no means so improbable when it came to rats. Yet the idea that this distinction came with some special protective power was not something he wished to test to the limit. Once really ought to have been enough. But on a night like tonight he felt he was pushing close to the limit again, getting closer to it with every forward step. Captain had taken him to one side and whispered the bad news. Jed, of all people, had gone missing. Certainly, if anyone had taken the curfew badly, it was little Jed. Defiantly sullen during the day, Jed had been noticeably absent from a five-a-side match which had been arranged after tea-time at short notice to keep everyone on their mettle.

"The tower. He's got to be up there. The tower's the only place Jed would head for. Maybe he thought he was small enough to get in there without being spotted," he had speculated to the Captain.

The Twins had been severely reprimanded for putting wrong ideas into the little fellow's head with their foolish invitations; although they claimed they hadn't planned on any trip to the tower. At least not till the weekend. They were going see how things stood by then. Whether Jed had understood this tentative approach was another matter entirely. Not their fault. Oh, no.

"He's desperate to pick up some tips to prove his ability as a goalie, you see," said Olly, taking the brunt from the Twins. Greybands didn't, but agreed about the tower.

"Cats meat," was all Billy Battle had to say to describe the likely outcome. "No good for morale, but he'll be a goner. Well and truly," he added for emphasis. And if anyone was daft enough to think otherwise, then they were welcome to step up to the menu. His warning came with a swift cut-throat movement of brutal clarity. The Captain, nonetheless, took a more rational view, that something had to be done and that a rescue might be effected by a responsible volunteer. One who knew better than most how to look after himself.

"That person is you, Oliver," he had already decided.

With bad news the blow was often softened by some good news that came along with it. Scouts had accounted for all the cats that had been seen mooching around in the library, as well as those pitiful wastrels stuck out all day in the cold. But that wasn't to inspire absolute confidence. By the time he'd set off on this high-risk mission the enemy were reported to have congregated once more in the kitchen, no doubt hoping to devour another kind of flesh after all their fruitless exertions. As he passed by to the staircase he had heard the complaining voice of Cook and what seemed to be the more placatory voice of the master himself in a hurried exchange of words. He still wondered, though, whether pointy-face would still on the prowl somewhere, since his mistress evidently gave him a hard time of it. Kept his pointy nose to the grindstone. But up here everything was quiet. Too quiet. At least there was no sight or sound of *her* stalking about, like a virulent, modern-day strain of the 'black plague' (another colourful and memorable story line of Lief's). And, by the time he'd got himself beyond those enormous glaring portraits and covered nearly a dozen of the spiral stairs, he felt his former stealthiness gradually returning; every move being clinically executed in the sureness of a carpet-deadened silence. He wondered why it always had to be trials or adversity that got you fired up in this way? Yet there was no denying the difference between selfish fears and what the Captain would call a wholesome fear. The change was one of discovery for him. One had drained his spirit, whereas the other was driving him on. There was the fear of hating what you have and another fear of losing what you ought to love. Yet this was no contradiction. It came down in the end to core values. Captain had once told him these trusted beliefs would eventually lead him to where his heart lay. If he felt brainwashed, well, maybe his brain needed a good washing. Clear his head. To save another was to save yourself. As Billy had reminded him as he was leaving: giantkillers *did* confound the experts from time to time and had been known to go all the way. "So don't let the importance of th' occasion go to your 'ead afore your match gets under way, or you'll lose it afore ye know about it," had been his final words on the matter. There was always a football analogy to be found somewhere, since the game was, unsurprisingly for them, virtually a game of life.

With his breathing calmed to a steadier rhythm, he crouched in a position where he found he could get a good view of the doorway above. A thin chink of light showed it was slightly ajar. He picked up the sound of a very faint scraping that seemed to be coming from further inside the room. Getting to the landing was easy enough. Getting inside would be the hard part. What or whom he expected to see he was not at all sure. The main thing was not on any account to be seen himself. With the exception of the Master, the other occupants were an unknown quantity with whom he was still undecided. He closed his eyes and, in an odd moment of wishful thinking, he imagined he saw Jed munching on a piece of biscuit, waving to him in a friendly welcome. It was a desperate, yet comforting illusion, useful perhaps for fighting off another kind of fear - a fear of failure. However, on peering cautiously into the low-lit room, he was to discover the sight of something quite unexpected.

A figure of a girl was stooping down before an

open log fire, or what was left of it, listlessly raking away the burnt-through chips and flakes, drawing patterns in the resulting ashes with a poker. He at once recognised her as the master's grand-daughter whom he had seen before on several occasions about the house (though he was sure she hadn't seen *him*), but, of course, never in this room. There were wall lights on either side of the fireplace which reminded him a little of the sconces in the Arena. The girl stopped, stood up to yawn, brushed and straightened the faded knees of her denims, then moved towards the door. She halted as a quick change of mind made her step back. On a large oval table, beside a neat stack of books and other writing materials, was a small silver frame with a photographic portrait inside; and it was this that now attracted her attention. She studied it, winding a finger abstractedly through a ringlet of hair before wagging the same finger at the picture in a kind of chastising rebuke. Olly, as on a similar occasion, took his chance to slip inside unseen behind an armchair, where the high walls winked and gleamed at him more persuasive than any flame in the Arena. He waited. Suddenly there was a clunk. Disoriented by a forest of chair and table legs ranged in front of him, the sound of the door had come too quickly for him to react, and he found himself trapped inside with no apparent way out. He crept between a set of fat, bandy legs, looking about him here, there and everywhere, in case Jed should be cowering somewhere like a lost soul. He scrambled up onto a chair seat, then onto the oval table to get a better view of his cluttered surroundings. Seeing everything and nothing, he hissed Jed's name twice but without bringing himself to do it too loudly. The fire had all but disintegrated to a barely glowing ash heap, and the clock seemed only to be holding its breath. The thick folds of a closed curtain hung over the window end of the oval table to add a deadening and motionless effect to its place of concealment. Outside, the bitter air hovered and pressed against the glass like some poverty-stricken vagabond lured to and entranced by the rich warmth of an inner light. But as Olly raised his eyes from within he only felt cold. The curtain quivered. Then it was that he saw it. Across the table it appeared. Out of nowhere. A shape, immobile, intrusive. A dark, black bulk with an amber eye:

'The Witchfinder General stood, put on his cloak and shoon. Archly poised in a sinister mood, he was his Lord's true son.'

Without a warning sign it sprang forth, laser-tipped eyes blazing, skidding over flying sheets of paper and scattered books. Where opposites meet. And worlds collide. An unexploded warhead slamming into its objective with a force that hurtled it high, head over heels and backwards to the floor below. To writhe in shock, stomach-punched, fixed and seared by those merciless, searching eyes. Heat-seeking, blood-seeking. To spill. To kill. The falling of a lampstand between a maw of fangs. The heaviness of the gilded, unfurled wings that belonged only to an angel of death. Falling with a thudding crash, deflecting a razorswipe of claw with a twisted loop of flex. The feeling of pain filling up. A slashwound to the heart. A heart stab stinging. A spray of warm drops oozing, then flowing, to a trickle. A rush of numbness freezing the limbs like morphine. A swing of a door. Then a growling thrust of a mighty foot as a blinding dark mass passes overhead with a shrieking snarl .An enmeshed ball of yin and yang spinning away in a blur of blind fury. The long, tall shadow of man blotting out all that remains of a dying vision. Jed? Jed? Is it Jed? Shaking uncontrollably beside me? To die for. To die for. The lights are going out. Fading ... fading … fading fast ... dead. Dead.

Or not dead?

Mixed with the dried-out fruits of autumn's Indian summer, compacted earth, dark and uncut, lay smothered in an icing of decorative whiteness, preserved for the coming of another year. For those lying buried deep below, sun-baked or snowbound, another slice of surface life prepared to pass them by, the temptations of its fresh ingredients to remain forever out of reach, untouched and, therefore, untasted. After two days of intense snowfall the upland slopes and lanes had succumbed to undulating drifts as featureless as any to be found on the frigid wastes of Pluto, and where no crystalline footprint, whether animal or human, had since dared to cast its mark. No footsteps could be heard or felt inside the old house either, whose billowing swathes of cotton dust sheets, thrown over the furnishings in the great rooms of Brokehill, made more than a passing chill resemblance to the windswept desolation beyond its walls. The high tower, in contrast to all this, basked in a cosier ambience of quite another kind. Suffused by the wintry morning light, its fire-reflecting ochres danced about with a celestial glow upon the wainscoting to provide an unexpected, though not unwelcome, sight for a recovering patient lodged favourably at the window. The invalid's eyes, though, were presently turned away and aimed weakly through a low square of mullioned glass. A new scene - of fields, fringed with faraway trees, glaring their whiteness beneath an iron sky. The intensity of the scene gradually grew more painful and made him turn away for a few seconds. Snow-seared outlines scorched the blindness of the optic nerve with transmogrifying concentric rings of many colours before slowly resolving into another image. One of much closer proximity, and startlingly familiar. It was a daunting face – but one without those unforgettable, burning amber eyes. Eyes, though, also unforgettable.

"Hello agin, straynger. Yew've bin in a right awld skermish, and naw mistayke."

An unmoveable icon: the cream cat, snow-lit and softly clad, and peering down at him in the same manner as he had once done before. Sitting at the far end of the window, he seemed relieved to have his own attention drawn away from the monotony of endless fields of snow. Though the reflective balm of his eyes might almost seem capable of turning everything to a wavy green. They lightened, as Olly's own eyes showed a hint of recognition.

"Yew should be feelin' plaised t' be up here raither then rawlin' arownd down theyre as yew were awhile agow. You've got merster and mistriss t' thank this toime fer keepin' yore hed jest abave th' water-loine. Me and DH thought yew was a gonna."

Olly had no choice but to return the look and await the possible consequences any change in his demeanour might bring. But there was no mistaking it. Those eyes didn't burn, and that they were unlikely to seemed a fair conclusion to reach. He tried to

108

adjust his position only to discover that something else certainly was burning - inside him. From the left shoulder to the groin he was wrapped in a neat bandage which gave off a yucky, syrupy smell as he moved. He had received a wound which had, fortuitously, not ended up as a death blow. Without seeing, or wanting to see, he fingered the sticky scar of dried blood down its length with a tender touch, as if to measure, not just its size, but its soreness, too. He relieved his discomfort by allowing his eyes to wander over various striking points of the cluttered room. Frames, figurines, glass cabinets, a brass telescope all shone with an individuality beyond their collective presence, with the blaze from a vast log-fire adding to these nuances its own aura of gold-spun gentility. Even the cream cat with his curly coat looked almost seraphic. Prince, by his own admission no angel, had decided a few words of comfort were, nevertheless, in order.

"We reckon yore a hero, fair dinkum," he said, with the grin now converted to a smile of genuine admiration. "Seems you was up here after the bowny little fella, thow he couldn't saiy too much. Yew moight be plaised to knaw merster got 'im off home smartish. The big feller, well, he was noicely booted into touch loike the beast from Brisbane, en' we ain't seen 'im arownd here since. En' Oi can say that gledly, even thow he was one of me ohwn koind!"

From the vicinity of the fireside there came a heavy snort followed by a sharp flap of floppy ears.

"That's not to say they won't keep trying. Nice to

see our friend's alive, but it'd be better for us if they thought he was dead."

The gruff voice with its harsh, weighty words made Olly sit up despite the inconvenience of the bandage. Their meaning pained him more than the injury itself, and his eyes met the cream cat's with a plucky, burning defiance. Prince hurriedly tried to pass these comments off as a misunderstanding by giving him an unconvincing wink of assurance.

"Down't yew listen to 'im. He down't mean it. Just a tad disgruntled, he is. Yore safe, recuperaitin' here."

There followed another snort as DH lolloped across to the table with the deceptive speed of a cantankerous elephant before heaving himself onto a chair under the window's ledge and bringing his gargantuan head right down to the tip of Olly's nose. Shoved aside, it looked to Prince as though they were going to slug it out.

"Listen, titch. There are no misundertandings here. Nothing personal, neither. I'm not for or against you rats, as things go. It's a question of strategy, see."

The small rat's defiance kept him from trembling. Greybands had beaten on about strategy before now, but he'd never heard it applied in this sense. The bloodhound moved back an inch or so from his nose.

"You see, your little friend told us enough. He knew there was a whole coachload of danger roamin' about here, there and lord knows where. So, then, why take such a risk, up here in the tower, of all places?"

Olly edged his nose away very slowly, as he

pondered on how to answer. It was obvious that Jed hadn't told them his reason for being there or how his rescuer knew where to find him. DH, however, didn't wait for an answer of any kind.

"We like to be one or two steps ahead of the game. It's how we would like to operate in the present circumstances. If they think you're dead, then they'll believe things are looking up, and the next one will be easier and so on. That's when the opposition let their guard down and make mistakes. Only thing is, your attacker seemed to be a headstrong sort of villain who won't have taken too kindly to being bowled out of here in a hurry. We need to be vigilant so none of 'em comes up here again. Not him, nor any of the others. In other words, one of us has to stay up to ensure you don't get back under their radar. So if we're a bit on the defensive for a while, then at least we don't gift 'em any more goals. That way, once we get to know the lady's game, we'll get onto a winning streak and score a neat one ourselves."

The footballing phraseology was not lost on Olly and he perked up at the thought of how he might gain more sympathy for his plight. Prince sat upright, stretched and began to yawn loudly, shaking out each foot in turn, as his immediate thoughts began to dwell on more pressing requirements.

"It's a pretty toime fer yew to be cummin' rownd," he said chummily to Olly. "If you fancy some brekkie, mistriss will be bringin' us a boite soon. Ever since she saw sum reg-beg apologee fer a cat sniffin' on the stairs she provoides us with a personal service. A chip o' baycon moight do f' yew ok. It's jest wot th' doctor wud've ordered, Oi moight edd,"

"All the more need to keep on the watch, then," argued DH, as he returned quietly to his former spot by the fire. Consumed by the heat once again, he made a quick résumé of how things stood. Governor had been under a cloud at first, but seemed oddly to have snapped out of it as the weather changed for the worse. He'd considered the idea of keeping Olly tucked in beside the log pile, where he had slept the last four days, a good one. A tough piece of gristle, as rats go, he was. And not much more than gristle he would have been, come to think of it, but for his own last-ditch intervention. At this very moment, as if his mind had been read, he overheard Prince describing to the wide-eyed rat exactly how that life of his had been spared and of the tremendous kick that had been executed to achieve it. It had been a fair old scoop to lift the big cat's massive underbelly clean over the spilled table.

"I seem to remember you playing your part as he landed," DH briefly reminded him out loud, knowing how his compatriot liked to eulogise such run-of-the-mill deeds at great length.

"Aw, yes, we was oiye to oiye, an' bowlin' along jes' loike one hewge daisycutter, until the merster decoided to split us with a few prods from a stick kipt by the door. Big fella went tumblin' downstairs like he niver knew they was there. Still, it was the kick what did it. A blinder."

"I have to admit it was a good un, as they say," DH

112

finally agreed, "probably down to all them dead balls I like to lob back into play from the touchline."

"A sizzler," added Prince with a nod to Olly.

Appreciating the fact that his salvation had come from a snap shot of apparently pure playing skill, Olly decided to make the overdue confession to his saviours as simply as possible:

"We all play football, too, you know."

His small voice was thin, but unfaltering. "We have our own pitch. Below. Honestly. That's why Jed came up here. In fact, some of us have come up to watch the real game many a time in the past."

A short silence was followed by another snort, this time one of incredulity.

"Did I hear right? You don't mean on that over there? Courtesy of the governor? Whorr!!"

DH stabbed a lazy paw towards the wide-screen television sitting incongruously between two antiquated display cabinets littered with the contents from a similar age. He smiled wilfully to himself, amazed at how infectious the governor's own enthusiasm seemed to have become. Audacious little devils! Perhaps these footballing rats had their own way of staying alive, if they did indeed have a love for the game. Maybe that famous quote of it being more important than life and death was, in their case, quite possibly true. He shook his head, but said no more.

Olly, in the mean time, eased himself flat, turned over and stared out through the glass again, as the cream cat, waiting patiently for breakfast to arrive, gave him another wink. The magnified illusion of a miniature seasonal paperweight, unshaken and undisturbed - a mirror image of his own protective bubble - soon soothed his smiling eyes and gradually lulled him dreamily to sleep.

*   *   *

'July 1642:

Pevenston Marsh was a thriving village made up of around twenty cottages (possibly twenty-one, if the stonemason's unlisted rubble of a residence was to be included) that straddled the river Dadge, a dribbling offshoot from one of the main tributaries further north beyond the valley plain. Though the marshes were not extensive at the time these events took place, the land was as evidently fertile as it had ever been during early Saxon times when, according to local legend, a settlement was established; even if potsherds from an earlier Celtic period seem to provide a more accurate and conclusive testimony on that score. Some isolated poor farmed the margins beside the Manor, while others, living in rough-hewn stone huts along the southern edges of a straggly wood, plied their trade as best they could as fullers and weavers. The remainder consisted of a small community of farm labourers who had worked under Sir Richard Pevenston and his family for generations. Poor harvests had bedevilled them on and off in recent years, but natural misfortunes alone, according to Sir Richard, posed no serious threat to their general prosperity and good will. Accustomed as they were to allow for such occurrences, it was only the exceptional, cumulative effect of other ructions that seemed likely to stretch the fabric of this peaceful existence. If some things were predictable, almost inevitable, a war of opposing ideologies was not one of them; and its unknowable outcome gave Sir Richard a mounting sense of anxiety. A headstrong parliament was testing the King's stubborn resolve, it seemed to many. To others like Phillip Pevenston, his father's only son, it was the other way round. Although Sir Richard's wish was to remain neutral in any displays of fiery debate, Phillip showed no such qualms in expressing his own forthright convictions. With his petty restrictions and intransigences the King was resisting the will of the people. Could his father not take to heart the self-fulfilling counsel of Proverbs twenty-nine and verse two? His father could not, preferring to remain in the ways that did not drink from a cup of confusion, ways as familiar as the tracks and paths that crossed the Marsh and wound away to the farthest end of the valley. As they always had and always would. Phillip duly returned to London espoused to a calling that seemed to be gathering with an obdurate, restless momentum, and for which an imminent declaration of war, not just of the mind, but of the body and its spirit, could not come quickly enough for him.'

Harriet stopped short at this second mention of war and ran her finger thoughtfully over the coarse texture of the manuscript. The hand-writing itself was not crabbed or spidery, but well-defined, the ink greyish against faded, yellowy sheets which were held together with an old-fashioned string fastener. She dug her toes deeper beneath the duvet in an effort to wring the last drops of dampness from their joints. Trudging along through an orchard knee-deep in depressions of unending snow may have given her an enormous appetite, but some tiredness was now unavoidably catching up, and her concentration began wavering, as she skimmed over the page and gave up counting the number of lines it contained. Why had he given her this - what was it again? An archive - of meticulously recorded history, he'd called it. Facts and information gleaned from diaries, letters, word of mouth and so forth. What was so special about this Civil War thing? The labels 'Roundheads' and 'Cavaliers' were the only history lesson snippets that came to mind. See what you can make of it anyway, he'd said, dropping the slim file on her lap soon after lunch. She could ask anything she wanted to at tea-time. His permission to remain here and not to be subjected to the trials and tribulations of a Scottish New Year was all she wanted. But she feared she wasn't going to get it. All because of the mayhem with that evil-looking cat. Caused - she felt sure of it - by her own sheer carelessness. It had been a struggle to keep the little creature alive, but there was some hope that he would pull through. She twirled the frayed and grubby string attached to the sheet round and round her index finger, before a random word from the next entry caught her eye and refocused her flagging attention. Forgiveness.

'November 1642:

The escalation of the conflict had now reached the dreaded stage of outright war. Yet an inconclusive confrontation on a recent, late afternoon in Worcester served only to strengthen parliament's designs. From his son Phillip Sir Richard had heard nothing, except for a short (an all too short) and adulatory account about his meetings with members of the Trained Bands. Of his position with Swaynes, the Fulham silversmith, there was also no word. Thus it was with great relief that he opened a hastily written letter on a rainy morning during the last week of the month cited above: "Father, I am sitting amongst men jocose and jaunty from the sharing round of wine, the effects of which they suppose will allay the fear of dying in a road or being otherwise flung grievously wounded into a ditch. The battle lines look staunch and are firm with intent, though the waiting is interminable. Perhaps, as it is a Sabbath, it is better to do nothing. Rumour says the King will not chance his arm today. I believe I shall return to sleep tonight still in one piece, as God's time may not be yet. If so, I am oddly glad, and my hands do strangely tremble, despite no drop of drink having passed my lips. I beg forgiveness for these unforeseen frailties. I beseech, not only the Father of my spiritual life, but, unable as I am to hold back this confession, you also, as the father of my fleshly soul. This discipline lies uneasy with me, as I fear the correction of this weakness may be harder than expected. Forgive me if any seed of uncertainty

117

has planted itself in the soil of an otherwise steady heart. I must try to follow where God leads. Your devoted son, as ever, Phillip. Turnham G. 13th Nov.'

Her eyes fluttered back and forth, trying to coax some meaning from the emotion that falteringly revealed itself in the letter. One or two unfamiliar words didn't prevent her from sensing the young man's fears. By comparison, anything she had ever had to fear would probably be regarded as minor. But how she wished she could express her own troubled heart in a similar way. If the mother she loved, so wanted to love more, would only listen. She remembered facing her own enemy: the twilight that all too quickly ushered in a longer night with its encroaching loneliness. So many times, as a child at the window, waiting, watching the darkening walls of the room. Where the orange street-lights projected a shadow play of low, groping branches as they wavered in the wind. Those weirdly disconnected, umbral arteries: deathlessly yo-yoing - bloodless and withered in the wind. She had been too afraid, too panicky, to move. Yearning, through tear-brimmed eyed, for the taxi lights that never came, before drifting off into sleep. And then, it was too late. Always too late. But with grandfather she had lately found herself feeling much less of a child - that vulnerable child - yet without ever feeling desirous of running roughshod over *his* authority. All that was heartfelt could be unburdened. As though he had gradually become the caring father she'd never had. The father of the mother she had always wanted. She would read on.

'March 1643:

Talk of the plundering and terrorising of neighbouring villages was the sole topic on every sober tongue in the Marsh. Royalist garrisons were seeking, not only quarters, but retribution. Spring had unleashed bitter clashes as both sides sought to make inroads in an attempt to gain an upper hand. Neither the Marsh nor nearby Brokehill or Stanmore Harden could consider themselves immune from the upheaval, as swift-moving forces of cavalry tried to cut a swathe through the eastern end of the valley. Sir Richard had friends at Oxford who, 'for sums of monies, would seek to avert further calamities befalling specific regions, using such influence as they possessed'. Yet, being averse to such unwarranted bribes, he feared it was only a matter of time before he was exposed to similar threats. And in this he was inevitably proved correct.

On a cold, misty Saturday in mid-March, like a forbidding masque of the apocalyptic vision, four horses trotted slowly, one by one, down the sloping path that led to his courtyard, their mud-spattered riders cloaked and anonymous against the opaqueness of the horizon. The soldiers dismounted, leaving the horses to nose each other in a circle where the steam of their exertion rose in a thin smog above their buttocks. The men were ushered inside to a long room with an equally long table where, after brief introductions, Colonel Wennard and his fellow officers seated themselves at Sir Richard's request.

Had they eaten? The colonel suggested his men might devour his Lordship's pantry out of venison or good beef, given the chance. But no, they must decline. While wine was served, the colonel, eschewing the usual pleasantries, hastened to give his reason for paying him this opportune visit. The men, forming a group round one end of the table, looked on, sullen and constrained, as Wennard endeavoured to be brief and to the point. They possessed an insufficient number of troops to defend the town, much less the triumvirate of villages that guarded the valley at each end. Powder and munitions were currently low, with only a small chance of keeping supply lines open. If a compact unit could be established here, near the main road, to maintain the viability of the bridge, there might be some hope of holding to an obstinate defence till the end of Spring when reinforcements would be mustered. Sir Richard's girth seemed to fill the whole width at the opposite end of the table as he listened to this passionless plea. There was no fire lit in the inglenook, which lent the low room an air of austerity and impotence. The men shifted uncomfortably, feeling uninvited and out of place. Wennard waited for a response with a look of resentful graciousness.

"Gentlemen, you must do what you must do. You are richly engaged in an atrocious affair, one which, I fear, will strangle the nation till they know not, neither care, who or what they fight for."

"You are no fighting man, Sir?" Wennard made it sound more of a statement than a question.

"I am a landowner of no especial grandness. I farm the ground whereon I stand and feed those on my land."

"I fought abroad against papists, for the preservation of our religion and our people."

"Now you are pitting yourselves against men who feel the same."

"The King must exact his rule, else we have only an excessively pious sentiment which will, sooner rather than later, water down that rightful power which is his royal prerogative."

"The King is thus to prove his own divinity? If he has God's approval, then he is welcome to his rule."

Wennard straightened to stand with a slight sneer on his lips.

"I am informed your son flies with the rebel forces. You are not obliged to answer, sir, but your position is highly insecure."

He got up, scraping the chair heavily. Sir Richard remained unmoved, with his eyes on the others.

"For my part, colonel, I pledge myself to my king and country. I, likewise, cannot and do not dismiss lightly so many centuries of monarchal authority. However, though I be no pilgrim, neither am I my son's conscience. There is still time, I hope, to curtail this madness. Misunderstandings require a measure of humility from both sides, before matters escalate beyond all manageable control."

"Humility is in short supply where parliament is concerned," said the colonel abruptly.

"There is surely yet room for both to exercise it."

Sir Richard bowed. None had touched their wine, whose dark, inverted triangles remained in full measure above dim, fluted stems.

"You have not said, but we shall advise you when the men are ready to occupy your land this side of the bridge. We may requisition a barn or two as needs be. Good-day, Sir."

As Sir Richard watched them go, as uneasily as when he had seen them first arrive, he had a foreboding that the outcome of this initiative would inevitably lead to a perilous dismantling of their freedom. Freedoms long cherished. He spent as much as an hour writing entries in his diary later that day, and, on clearing his mind, wrote a letter of encouragement to his son. Though he knew not how or where to send it.'

Harriet yawned involuntarily and wondered what sort of letter the father would have written to his wayward son. What dangers were to be expected? She felt she could side with someone like Sir Richard. He came over as reasonable, much like grandfather. She had heard him trying to come to sensible terms with great-aunt over the cats roaming about where they ought not. She had treated him very high-handedly in return. Like the house was already hers to do as she wished. As if the so-called trouble wasn't worth discussing. Worth putting up with for the riddance of the rats, was her unchangeable opinion. *They* were the trouble! Some people only enjoyed wars. Great-aunt would've got on well with that colonel.

'April 1643:

To Sir Richard, dispatches meant simply life or death.
 Seemingly by providence a letter arrived in the Easter week of the new month. Delivered in secrecy by a stable lad coming over a back road from Brokehill, its inscription was a welcome relief to Sir Richard. The tension, as well as the immediacy of its contents, however, was unmistakable. Philip was assigned to a force under the command of Sir John Gell and had been part of a detachment sorely pressed by a fierce blast of Royalist artillery near Stafford. The clash of the armies was viewed from a novitiate's perspective.
 "Being in a rearguard position on the flank, our purpose was to pick off the cavalry as it charged in full cry. Our resistance suffered unexpectedly from unerring shots of musketry and salvoes of cannon that accompanied no little confusion. I cannot be sure if any of my bullets hit their mark as intended, before some wild fetlock glanced my side and threw me down dazed. I landed sandwiched betwixt a stricken rider and his dead horse, and whilst taking cover under that poor beast, I saw their charge cut great furrows through the centre, where men fell like so many skittles. It reminded me of the comedies, for I fully expected them to spring to their feet right after for a repeat performance. Though my untrained eye observes little method to the pounding madness of hooves and cannon, still never did my brain feel in better temper than it was during those bizarre moments. The grass is mingled with blood and with

broken swords and pikes, and the smoke of musket hangs in the air. Yet I am without a graze, and, though we have retreated to our camps, I feel ennobled. Another day shall again, I trust, meet me more than halfway in God's own cause. May you remain ever in my thoughts. Phillip."

Some soldiers now guarded the bridge from the Marsh side and took quarters in a grain storage barn less than seventy yards from the farm with its sprawl of stable and outhouses. On some days the Spring sunshine blazed and turned the road into a rod of white gold as it dipped its elm-lined course between the rolling meadows beyond the bridge. The setting was more suited to a hunt meet than the surreptitious mobilisation for a planned regimental attack. To Wennard a lull always preceded a storm and was but another tactic designed to wrong-foot a sleeping fox. The fox may gnaw on a staple of bread and mutton if he must, but never at table where only the victor feasted in his victorious celebration. Sir Richard, meanwhile, wrote in his diaries and prayed for peace: a cessation to contention and the emergence of wisdom and good sense. Wherein faith in majesty and parliament might be rebuilt. Could he but only have seen the barrels lodged beneath each end of the arch of the wide-spanned bridge, fused and ready to be ignited at a moment's notice, such fragile hopes would have been the first to have been shattered.'

Some things are best left unread before you go to bed, others scarcely less so on a late afternoon in mid-winter. But that one word - Brokehill - now gave a sense of place and purpose to this unfolding drama. The link was perhaps three and a half centuries old, but maybe there was a story still to be told. Though a happy ending before nightfall might be quite another matter, she thought.

'May 1643:

Desertion would be a strong word to describe the action taken by of all but two of his working men, and Sir Richard was not inclined put it quite that way. That he did feel let down was certainly a disheartening acknowledgement of the demands being made by this pernicious war, those which made captives of men - whether through patriotic feeling or pressurising fear - and steadily, inexorably, eroded the day-to-day order of things. According to his only remaining servant, most had been marched off to the town to help strengthen defences there. "They be digging their own graves 'ere the battle begins," was the old retainer's view. Even the weaver women were dragged off to slave at a work more pitiful than they deserved. It was, however, Sir Richard's hope that if parliament's morale continued to be shaken his workers would be returned before the harvest-time - and, thus, both would be saved. The final week in May proved him to be never more wrong.

On the morning of the first day, a rebel army force began to arrive, manoeuvring their position on high ground to the north-west. By mid-day, without warning, a siege attack on the town had begun. The

125

crack of musketry and the thrum of an advancing cavalry reached the edge of the valley like a sound of distant thunder, as Wennard's men maintained their own position and waited. The noise of fighting rose and fell during the afternoon while Sir Richard waited for any useful news of its progress. The soldiers dotted around the bridge and dug in below the avenue of elms remained impassive, but on the alert. By seven o' clock the noise had subsided and, as he could no longer bear the uncertainty, Sir Richard returned to the requisitioned barn which had been vacated for most of the day. The sky, stippled with the pastel remnants of a westering cloud, was luminously serene, the departing sun concealing itself behind a copse of old oaks spread out along the far bank of the river. A soldier had dismounted and was apparently tending the wounds of another he had carried down from the road. Propped against the half-open door, a dull red gash was visible under the silk lining ripped away from the victim's tunic.

"They are hiding in a circle, almost upon us. At the bottom of a damned field, less than a pistol shot away. Midnight will come too late for him," muttered the soldier with some feeling, on seeing Sir Richard's own pained expression. The man gave a slight shrug, then pressed a small flask into the other's trembling free hand.

There had been a brief exchange of gunfire about an hour earlier and this had been the unlucky result of the sniping. Smaller sounds were carried further through the stillness of the evening: a clink of metal, the scrape of a boot, pebbles clucking beneath the shallower levels of water that gurgled beneath the bridge. From beside it, with the twilight lingering more pronounced upon its stonework, the drab figure of Wennard was seen to emerge. His horse stumbled on the slope before cantering up a well-worn track toward the two men.

"You exact free quarter and give me no adequate protection, at least no assurances of such," Sir Richard said angrily, as the colonel drew up.

"In heaven's name I would prove to you, though my sword be not two-edged, how swiftly the division of joint and marrow may be accomplished," replied Wennard as cold as the steel he was wearing.

"What, then, is to be the outcome?"

"The outcome is that we take our leave tonight," said the colonel with a peremptory wave of a gloved hand. "Better than to sit trapped like cats in a sack. We head east to the farthest side. A longer detour to reach our destination, admittedly, but one an enemy of base tapsters and plough boys cannot follow so easily. While they sup and persist with their prayers for a sound recovery from the shocks of battle, we shall regroup and return to fight another day."

Sir Richard ought to have been warned by this plan, but any reaction on his part seemed muted. Wennard nodded grimly to his man, who hastened inside the barn and brought out two prepared torches. On being lit the order was given, and the burning orbs were hastily flung back into the barn. The colonel, satisfied by the ascending crackle of the hay bales greedily engulfing the upper beams of the roof, wheeled his horse round and turned once more to Sir Richard.

"Our parting gift, sir. Consider yourself lucky, since your lot lies tenuously with the king. This is of necessity - as well as a slight reprimand for the weak conscience of your son."

"I will not forget a single word or ungenerous action, of that you may be sure," cried Sir Richard, as the riders shunted past his stationary figure.

They sped off back into the semi-darkness of the bridge, their shapes sharply lit by the all-consuming conflagration beginning to rage in their wake. Without having time to think, Sir Richard swung round and, crouching low to the ground, jerked the wounded soldier over onto his back, then dragged him, in one frenetic movement, from the certainty of an earlier death. The right sleeve of the coat was almost torn clear; his knuckles, clenched and streaming with the blood from the well-saturated shirt, reflecting the gilded lick of the flames in its runny flow. The air's hotness made him gasp for breath as he heaved himself into a nearby declivity and looked away, unable to witness the spectacle of blazing rafters now collapsing, one by one, into charry destruction. As though in obedience to some malign signal, another fire ignited the distant sky like a ghastly beacon in a coastal chain. A barn and several stables next to the farmhouse looked to be well and truly alight and, without manpower, certainly without hope of being extinguished. The man at his feet groaned, yet remained inert. Wennard and his devils were gone - but not before twisting the knife with one final revolution to exact the most pain. There was a blinding flash, quickly followed by another, succeeded by the muffled roar of exploding masonry, as jets of dust and smoke fanned out into the night sky. True to his word, Wennard had left no stone unturned. The bridge was destroyed.'

Two and a half miles from Brokehill there was a garden centre with an iron bridge nearby and a tea-room which she remembered was called the Marshes. And that was it. Mr Pale once mentioned a Pevenston Wood, that you could cycle past it on a rough track from behind the house. But, if it existed, it wasn't on any local map.

'July 1643:

"They have plundered most of my corn and as much other provender as they could find, most of my coinage in extortionate tax, virtually all of my labour force, and - "

"Yes, your barns. It is, indeed, a pitifully insane business."

The person sipping his wine in commiseration with Sir Richard was John Brimble [aka Brimbell] his closest neighbour from Brokehill manor.

"And, to be sure, this is likely to be the last of the wine, man. I had to hide a little amount beneath my bed to guarantee myself a drop on their departure, untimely as it was."

John Brimble laughed heartily, though unsurprised

by the drastic steps taken by his friend.

"At least, despite those singed eyebrows, you have your life. You are yet tolerable. Parliament's officers may be priggish and some of them more distastefully pious than others, but they have yet to exceed the bounds of barbarity shown by the king's troops."

"Really, John, I feel as if I have *nothing* left to lose." He flexed his large hands on the table resignedly.

"They show little will to patrol this part of the valley, their concerns lying with the strengthening and keeping of their precious control of the town. The broken bridge also serves their interests inasmuch as it does hinder any approach along the road from the north, and a single guard on the south side of the ruins remains their sole requirement. Wennard's disadvantaging me has not disadvantaged them."

He laughed bitterly at this analysis of his reduced situation.

"For my part, I may sink or swim," he continued, "and the cottages lie empty while the harvest remains an unfulfilled blight on the land. Perhaps you are luckier not having to worry about servants or work force."

"My abode is not so extensive ever to have needed 'em," replied John. "Hugh, of course, thinks it a madness, this lowish life I lead. But I tend to my bit of lawn and dine contentedly at Stanmore as the occasion demands. 'Tis enough for me."

He stopped there, having perceived of another intractable problem regarding the labour shortage.
"In your own case, even should a minority be allowed

130

or be persuaded to return - "

"God forbid the impossibility of that happening," interposed Sir Richard bluntly.

" - by a generous calculation, with, say, a fraction of your labour, you would get to reap two or three fields. However, to be sure, they must need to keep a still tongue in their heads for fear of mindless intervention or reprisal."

"Precisely. In whatever form that might take. For then we would be doing it for ought. Besides, we are overlooking other factors. Threshing and storage. My barns are no more and, besides, my position, like that of the cottages, is far too inconveniently exposed, therefore risky. Forcing entry would, in their case, like forced prayers, be an unconscionable presumption."

"Aye. And, of course, to cap all, the miller fights for his own daily bread - with a pikestaff."

John Brimble, nevertheless, seemed hardly perturbed despite adding to a list of negatives. Both he, the erstwhile Oxford scholar, and the widower farmer, companions of more youthful days, shared a bond which went much further than merely singing from the same sheet of ideals and beliefs. Sir Richard was shrewd enough to allow his younger friend some leeway.

"This is so much talk, John. I feel you are leading me somewhere. Perhaps some inimitable, madcap plan or adventure sits between and behind those nonchalant eyes of yours. Ready to take on and, no doubt, outwit the dullness of the opposition."

Sometimes events shaped circumstances, and

the chance to make them work in one's favour was a challenge too good to miss. John paused in his reply, making it sound like some vague prologue to what was coming.

"Allow me to explain," he said quietly as he prepared to put his case. "Forgive me, as I am rather inclined, indeed, compelled here, to spin out a grossly overblown tale."

His brother-in-law, Hugh, had of late come to the conclusion that his retiring and homespun disposition required the compliment of a good wife.

"My sister Lucy agrees, by the way, but pretends indifference. Your manners and wit are of the highest order, Hugh ensures me, but since London's vigorous attractions are so far besmirched with intrigue and animus (his words), the discretion of its gallants questionable, and the general conduct of its fashionable spots more befitting the lewd bustle of a Turkish harem (his words again), then we must look nearer home. He loves the unfashionable, bucolic air of Brokehill, does Hugh. None too far to stir a roving Cornishman's passions, he hastens to add. A middling fair manor with much potential, he declares. So it comes about that three years ago, as you will recall, I had the lumber room and two unwarranted servants' quarters enlarged under his direction - to facilitate feasting and entertainment. Into a goodish enough ballroom, to be precise in his description. A cellar was excavated but, due to a lack of funding and enthusiasm on my part, there it has remained, propping up, well, precisely nothing. However, Hugh refuses to be outdone. All such banqueting must be accommodated with a corresponding wine cellar, he assures me. Banqueting! I'd sooner have a presbyterian supper! Perhaps you are somewhat aware, Richard, of his business interests in Cornwall. He has affairs in a tin mine near Polreath. He is ably assisted by capable engineers who work their skills in preserving the shafts, the adits and much else besides. Some have fought already for the king in Devon, so the mine has come to a halt this past Spring. Last month he sent half a dozen good men with his foreman, Trannion, to Brokehill with the sole aim of finishing my cellar. We share in paying them a wage for their labours. I have to tell you, if yours is a cupboard, mine was, you must admit, an upright coffin without a lid. Almost burying me alive, if I dared to enter for a pauper's bottle. But from two weeks ago it is changed! - positively a gentlemen's taproom in its spaciousness! Below stairs, it has become a cellar the generosity of which my good contractors are convinced not even the king and all the most foolish of his advisers could gainsay on inspection. With its own appropriately earthy coldness, too. Ahem! Thank you."

Sir Richard rolled what was left in his own glass before pouring a generous amount into both from this, his last bottle. He added another faggot to the impoverished fire.

"Do go on. While I am going into decline, you look to be bursting at the natural seams with these modern expansions of yours."

"Well, let me just say that I am truly grateful for Hugh's largesse. Through it I have become acquainted with men whose calling belies their practical intelligence. Mr Trannion and I take supper upstairs where he ensures we always sit away from the curtained window. You see, we are off the beaten track, but it is his valued opinion that in lonely darkness a lonelier light can be an unwanted attraction. There are raiding parties from both sides, always on the prowl of late, he explains, looking to plunder what they can under cover of night. So convinced is he in this that he has consistently kept his men on site in the cellar, where both he and his bedfellows sleep warmed by a brazier with a few candles for their repasts and conviviality, and kept alight for vigilance's sake. They are well used to the gloom of the pit and the mineshaft, and prefer it, is his opinion. The night your barns were destroyed our fire upstairs was low as usual and I was asleep beside it when Trannion woke me with his concerns. He'd seen an evidence of fire and heard the rumble soon after. His conjecture was correct on both accounts."

John of Brokehill sat back, rubbing his palms like a storyteller exercising another judicial pause to heighten his listener's interest.

"Which was?" Sir Richard finished the wine to its dregs without taking his eyes off the other.

"If not your farm, then a barn or other nearby buildings. He suspected, with great perspicacity, that the blowing of the bridge was what followed thereafter. He even heard the horses cantering their circuitous route by the lower end of the lane a short while later. The valley is a great relayer of sounds which may travel far enough in the stillness of the night. As it was too dangerous for him and his men to depart, it was agreed they would stay as long as they wished until conditions became more settled, whenever that should be."

Now the crux of the story was reached. Since ascertaining the way things stood, another plan had been contrived. The plaster had but hardly dried on the end wall before an altogether new tunnel had been marked out. To be dug deeper still. A pause led to a longer silence. Sir Richard seemed to have quite misheard what was stated, much less its implication.

"A tunnel? What do you mean by tunnel? Below the cellar? Wherefore the need of a tunnel? Come, John, I am not one for riddles."

John Brimble leaned back further still and stretched out his legs to the renewed warmth of the inglenook. His eyes twinkled in affirmation.

"Why, my dear friend, so you may have a tolerable harvest - and the war be damned!" '

Harriet, in contrast to her pragmatic ancestor, drew her knees higher and reread the vital line over again to ensure she had not misread the word herself, as it spilled from the page in the declining light. Like successive clues in a treasure hunt, without which any journey could not be completed, the mention of a tunnel seemed about to undermine even the most profoundest depths of her own unbridled imagination.

'August 1643:

Eight men, concealed by clouds drifting wraith-like across a full moon, stood at the river's edge in whispered consultation. The six, carrying coils of rope and utensils colloquially referred to as 'rimmers', were men of few words. Using these slender, hook-curved crowbars, they would be able to loosen and extract the required stones as economically and as skilfully as possible. Not just the flagstone slabs imploded into a precarious pile below the ruin of the yawning bridge, but also stones from the bridge itself, which had been flung out into the river through the power of the blasts. They had decided to work in pairs, beginning with the amputated stumps of the bridge where the water slopped along at will, frothing and flowing into bifurcated channels between the debris. The sentry had long departed (his ill-discipline matched by the emptiness of his stomach, said John), as the men waded in knee-deep from the slope of the nearside bank with the ropes tied about them. Each of the seconds carried thin reedy torches offering a barely sufficient light for the other to work in, and these were discreetly wedged into convenient spaces between the rubble when the chosen items were ready to be handed from one to the other. John and Sir Richard stood and kept guard at the bank, peering down as they waited beside the horses, four of which were secured two abreast to a couple of sturdy wagons brought from the farm. To work a rock face above ground was an evidently welcome change, as the leading men, with sureness of balance, probed at the gaps and fissures, before freeing up the slabs of paving deemed the most suitable. One by one, these were finally lifted back to the bank and laid out on the grass to glint like unmarked gravestones in the fleeting moonlight. How Sir Richard wished he could hire quadruple the number of these multi-faceted miners this very night. He'd have the bridge rebuilt in all its splendour by morning, before anyone was awake to begin their false prayers for divine assistance! His neighbour found himself reminding him for a second time, albeit light-heartedly, that such constructions were better served elsewhere. That the lord doth catch them in their own cunning was a very worthy reminder and, scripturally, quite apt, but, meantime, they must proceed with theirs, was John's expressed opinion. Trannion clambered up beside them, having heard the end of these murmured exchanges.

"Liberty is different things to different people, sir. But it is a relative thing in this restless world of ours. I leave behind the sea birds' cries, the rush of the sea waves in their hurry and all other things I know and love. But the ground here may be walked on also as God so gave us breath to do. Not all the men have always worked the mines. Mr Silverwood, here, and Mr Tunstall were carpenters by trade for one of the big houses near Truro. Some were fishermen formerly. Like the apostles of old."

Hearing his name mentioned, Mr Silverwood's eyes darkened and winked mischievously as he sat at the rear of one of the wagons, tipping water out from his boots.

"Some of us here have experience of shipwreck. Smugglers stowin' the - I will not say ill-gotten gains - in secretive hideaways. Howsoever, the workman's worthy of the gift of his wage, so it be said. So may we be of ours, sir. And if we can repay thee by preserving an ounce of thy liberty, may God be for and not against us."

He chuckled, then took a deep breath in the belief that he had said too much already for one night. Trannion drew an arm round the man's broad shoulder, complimentary to his forthright, yet honest submission.

"Not contraband, sir," he reassured Sir Richard. "A little wetness on the knees has stifled him higher up in his cranium, as mebbe do the clinks of rowlocks which work and grind 'gainst the changing forces of the tide. Mr Brimble will know what I mean, and agrees with me, I'm sure."

John assented with a smile. Within an hour a sufficient number of the slabs had been rescued and, after a brief refreshment of bread, cold stewed quails and a drop of Brokehill's best brandy, the men returned to scour the river bed for the other stones. Whereas the slabs had been prised out without too much difficulty, fishing for similar trove, sunken and embedded below water, would prove more difficult. Night was coming on apace and the water was murky brown beneath the smoking haze of the rushes. The ropes were extended to their limits, as the volunteers removed their jerkins and went in up to their waists.

The hour was after ten and all six men struggled for a further hour and a half before thirty or so granite blocks of varying shape were dragged forth into the second wagon. With the task complete, the reeds were tossed into the water and allowed to float gently downstream. Finally the men carefully stacked the slabs according to size before wiping themselves as dry as possible with their wrung-out shirts.

"So gentlemen, a satisfactory conclusion to our evening, you must agree." John Brimble mounted his steed in a contagious mood of complete satisfaction.

"The Armada itself could not have given up more to us than what is needed for one night," said Mr Trannion in his clipped tone.

The men, too, were quietly content. For persons well used to the treacherous vagaries of the storm-fed sea tonight's labours would be considered only a mild diversion. If any backs were aching, they did not show it, something which astounded Sir Richard, as he was well aware they had only yesterday partitioned the tunnel at Brokehill with an area maybe half as long as the reconstructed cellar above it. The stones would be the finishing touches to an extraordinary excavation. He was not allowed to see it until its completion, not that his imagination, knowing the character of these men, could fall far short of the reality being so craftily fashioned underground. With one as driver and two to steady the loads front and back, the wagons moved away slowly, their noise minimal on a dirt track parallel with the river bank. Progress slowed still further with the ruts and bumps growing more prominent as they approached and joined the farm road. Sir Richard drew alongside, lifting his collar to its limit about his ears, to observe these toilers at close hand. Rough-hewn they were, yet not roguish. Hardened, but not harsh as from war. Silent, child-men whose humility, simple and uncalculating, was a heavenly reflection of some lost, earthly humanity. Led by principles which, as anyone could see, went beyond any loyalty to king and country, they arrived like some Greek chorus, as a theatrical laughter from the waves upon a shore; observing the players on a restless stage of briskly ever-changing, scenes, yet without claim or recourse to any greater godship or authority of their own. Reform or die was a formidable and too sudden a rock to climb for this nation. Men who insisted on moving the mountain somewhere else by the repulsive hysteria of their religiosity or by some other undue force would find their conduct perhaps to be much less acceptable than the morality exhibited by these men. Was it a war without an enemy? There were always enemies as real as life itself. 'You must be perfect as I am perfect' did surely not mean without flaw confessed or flaws basely ignored? Puritan or Pharisee? It was a tragedy with no need of a sequel. Yet, how he missed the plays. How he missed Phillip.'

Not all secrets worth telling were worth knowing, 'Arry. It depended on who was doing the telling. Rory had said that. But she'd thought he'd been drinking. Mum always claimed people who were drunk came out with the truth. Mum liked to confuse her with stupid comments like that. Whoever had written all this clearly believed it was worth the telling. See what you make of it, her own grandfather had said. She wasn't now so certain that there wouldn't be any light at the end of this tunnel. Though it was getting late.

'September 1643:

Where the hill began to sweep into a gradual north-easterly ascent lay the chosen and secluded fields of Sir Richard's solace. Dawn to midday days of toil having whetted the sharpness of the scythe to reap as much as any salty harvest plundered from a teeming ocean, they lay denuded in a stubbly frazzle of chocolate gold. The tang from the cut sheaves remained in Sir Richard's nostrils, his forehead browbeaten, flushed by sun and sweat, by the dust of stalk and haze of ear compounded in the vigorous race against time. He felt optimistic today, as did the man sitting alongside him beneath the shade of a hedge, munching on an outsize apple. John was in one of those talkative moods which had become more frequent with him as the project moved ever nearer to fruition. The farmer had the disarming and slightly disconcerting feeling that the scholar had been reading his mind. John had always possessed this confounded ability to render him completely transparent. Your checks are assiduously infectious, Richard! However he could ensure him every blade of the crop was appropriated and presently converted into more grain than there were Puritans left alive in the entire New World.

"'Indeed, 'twas certainly a blasted heath to delight any previous sower of seed. Yet I strongly suspect that your thoughts lie elsewhere today. The scripture recommends that we observe the ant. If ants contain the blood of Cornishmen, we do well in obeying that advice with all our powers of observation. These remarkable men have furnished me with embellishments finer than any other where the moth and the rust do indeed consume."

Sir Richard wiped his brow and determined to say nothing, lest his dear friend should deliberately clam up as a result of any fresh earnestness in his part. John took another large bite at the apple and chewed on, studying it pensively. His eyes eventually gave in and made a feint dart to the other man.

"I may as well tell you, Richard, Hugh had intentions on a broader scale than I imagined. If anything, the dining-room was intended to be a ballroom, and I truly believe the cellar was in reality to be a kitchen! Hence there is enough timber to roof and support this tunnel of mine. They garner shoots from the old coppice near the Stanmore road. A daub is carefully mixed for all the rendering of the tunnel's walls and slapped on. But the jewels in the crown are, of course, those chosen stones. Levelling and digging with every infernal contraption of rod, plumb line, gauge and whatnot - with tallow in their caps as a lamp to their feet! As well as to their hands, I should add. A politic construct, indeed! And to what effect? Why, my friend, you never did see such a cathedral!

Where even the king and his pompous commissioners might sit at table and dine delightfully before agreeing most profoundly to disagree in all their detestable talk! It is a cave, a dungeon! Yea, a first-rate palace! And for what purpose? Merely for the storage of grain and a horde of my choicest Honey-tops. A mere forager. But as a man of the pen, I am humbled!"

"Mr Trannion must believe that this war could escalate and drag us down further for him to have assisted in so much. To lend us the hands of four men for the fields was indeed a kindness for which I cannot thank him, or them, enough," said Sir Richard plainly as he got up to scan the garnered prospect for one final time.

"The miller's old father didn't need much persuading, as I had suspected," said John. "He don't see a case for fighting among ourselves, any more than we. The last of the grain, I understand, can be taken tonight. Though I do fear Trannion thinks something is afoot. His ears in Stanmore Harden have once again sensed change in the air, my friend."

"Well, the mill's in a pretty spot, where we must but hope our movements are not espied upon and followed, that we may reap only what we have sown. Let me hope this new creation of yours is yet more temple than charnel-house. I have been kept at bay long enough. Forgive me, John, if I appear to misappropriate that biblical designation."

Both men rose, shook hands warmly and parted, each to his own domain to await the hour.

He had been cursed with an irrepressible urge to

set down with regularity the majority of his thoughts, however momentous or trivial, during the bitterest of these days. To reorder this harum-scarum urge for uncontrolled change. For many weeks some normality of progress had seemed possible. An audacious shift of purpose had provided some hope, something in reserve for better times ahead. He was, however, no John, in this regard. It was but a log of events, a diary of personal sentiment, perhaps for the grandchildren he might never have, or, then, at least for the posterity of the Marsh. Much more than a mechanical obsession, it became a balm to the troubled spirit that never quite left him, a panacea to an anguish the root cause of which his neighbour had not fully discerned. A modicum of the harvest was in, and still this acute sense of lack which had severely oppressed him all day persisted. He raised his tired eyes and looked out toward the path by the river. The afternoon was all but gone, where a few stars spun their early paths into the bluish velvet of an eastern sky. A stretch of grey descended through the trees, fringed and tinged with the departing gold-edged embers of another dying day. The primordial majesty of yesterday and of many days long before. Something moving, as though resurrected from the deepest shadow, caught his attention and he began to follow its progress with a more than curious intent. A pale rider drooping in the slowness of his journey. But a lone soldier on reconnaissance would not stumble forward so lethargically, so exposed. Sir Richard could not take his eyes away as an inner turmoil struck at his soul. For him there was no perspective to view. The fervent request he had murmured daily in his mind now resounded its tremorous catechism more loudly against his heart as each second lapsed. From there at last to soar heavenward - to the grace and compassion of the listening God who now answered him - as an unexpected tear dribbled unchecked down his cheek. The spirit had replied to words unuttered. The light fell upon the stoop of a horse. And from a long way off he recognised his son.'

'Where'er you walk you shall have no fear. For tho' time has flown, to all its passing hours you are insensible. Come, descend no further, for a love that lies deeper doth protect you.' Alone in her bed, the unbidden words sounded gently through the centuries into her heart. The words, though unwritten, were not fearful. The tunnel was now beginning to close in on her.

'Five men dressed in dark clothing sat around an old deal table and waited. No longer was there a brazier of glowing coals to supplement the several candles that still burned in two holders spaced apart on the table. Phillip, though supported by his father's arm, shrunk from their spectral sight. But this was no base court sitting in pitiless judgement over his fate, for the swarthy faces showed no obvious malevolence. John bade him sit, before handing him a glass generously filled with a dark, purplish wine.

"Drink this, my boy. 'Tis a French vintage from a Catholic estate, evidently far too good for Communion, yet not too good for toasting the likes

145

of episcopal skulduggery, methinks."

The men smiled, as the young man did what he was told. The starkness of the cellar, though now rearranged with a number of tall, wooden cupboards and half-stocked with a few empty flagons and casks, left Phillip shivering as he took a seat. Having ridden most of the day the exertion, coupled with the stresses formerly endured, had begun to tell on him considerably; yet he declined any further assistance. The faces of durability watched him closely as another tentative swallow of the wine eased the dryness of his throat and appeared to steady his senses. He returned the men's look with wearied, sunken eyes.

"My father had a dread of us being followed, hence nothing has passed my lips since early this morning. My bones feel jarred - but that is of little consequence. I am, however, indebted to you gentlemen. My father has related your exploits in some detail on our way here. It seems that if you have laboured long in the honesty of sweat and toil, I have found my own engagements to have been rewarded only with that of blood and tears. I will not say so much of the misery it has afforded me. The treachery of traitorous men who slaughter first women and children, and thereafter skewer the dying e'er their terrifying groans do fade from their lips, and all without compunction, is sufficient for me to relate. Would that I had died the prisoner I was, but that God saw fit to release me - to bear these mental wounds forever and a day."

He drank a longer draught of the wine before becoming silent in the weakening state of his agitation. Sir Richard looked on with some distress as his eyes met those of Mr Trannion. After an interval of reflection the Cornishman was the first to respond, his voice quieter and more controlled, as he summed up the latest state of affairs.

"King's troops have been seen in Stanmore. Some have asked questions while bragging of conquests in their cups. The inn lad there is a reliable messenger and this afternoon he rode over saying that soldiers were asking about Brokehill. Were there stables? Quarters? You understand the line of enquiry. Casual intelligence gleaned from gossip which be laced with threats and fear. It could mean an unwelcome visit."

Sir Richard shook his head and stared at the wine in his glass. He remembered well their predilection for violence, and had no wish for John to experience the same backlash. Again, Mr James Trannion's was the voice of calm, sound reasoning.

"My men and I leave tonight, as agreed. Best it be to go under the cover of dark. From Stanmore we shall proceed to Bristol forthwith. I am informed that an attack is to be anticipated in a day or so, thus this region may well be a high hotbed of rage and resentment, possibly worse than any previous. Sirs, if this young man is discovered, either here or at his father's house, both you and he may fare badly together. We must act at once, and shrewdly, lest the dangers escalate and we are overtaken. Robert, call Mr Tunstall to prepare the horses."

While this was being done, he turned aside with a nod of intent to the man next to him, as though he had already considered his next move.

"What do you have in mind to do?" said Sir Richard, following the Cornishman's unblinking eyes with a quickness of his own. "Whatever it is, I feel happily confident that you possess the cunning to outwit the Devil at his most devious."

From behind Trannion's chair John Brimble lowered his head and crushed under his boot the few grain kernels that were scattered in a trail from the stairway. A fiery musket ball speeding past his ear could not have distracted him less as he drew erect, stock-still, with his face towards the shaded terminus of the wall. He then made a bow to the remainder of the men seated at the table.

"Ah, Mr Trannion, 'tis a fact that great minds do think alike. Mine's not yet so great, but I am catching up fast. Forgive me, but if you propose what I believe you shall, then we have need to repair immediately."

He ran his foot lightly over bits of exploded grain which had been scattered along the boards of the cellar floor, knowing the answer he would receive. With the click of Trannion's thumb and forefinger Mr Silverwood obliged by taking up one of the candles and stepping back towards a great, ebony cupboard which had been but recently positioned there. With the light burning low beside him, he knelt and, using a small knife, ran it along a decorative join below its midway point. His fingertips eased it to the left as something within gave way and the panel before him opened outwards with a solid smoothness usually reserved for an artfully constructed trapdoor. A space darker than the wood itself emerged to blow gently against the candleflame.

"'Tis a fitment of fine precision, well disguised, and which will be easy to break open when necessary. So a man may remain hidden from the unsuspecting eyes of the world without. If you can manage to slip through here," said Trannion, beckoning Phillip with due consideration, "we can keep you from harm's way and thus guarantee your safety for the duration required. Many more such places may be built in future times, for the safekeeping of things other than earth's fruitage. Howsoever, in your case it will most certainly be no more than for your very life."

"Only till this troublesome business dies down, then a better means of escape may be arranged in a day or two," insisted John. "These nobles have, unfortunately, already eaten me out of my house with mutton and roasted potatoes on the brazier, so we are left only with this half a loaf - minus fishes - and a cut of cheese in their stead. Oh, and some water in a flask."

Sir Richard clung to his son closely, gripping his wrists to feel the fullness of their pulse, before releasing him. Phillip turned and, as an afterthought, made a brief request of John:

"Allow me some ink and pens. Some few sheets of your choicest paper. I shall endeavour to compose my thoughts by means of a letter to Swayne in London. Perhaps my insomnia will only by such means have its work complete. Just as water, too, may cool and suppress an overheated mind."

The young man, too beaten in spirit to otherwise resist, then allowed himself to be led through what to him appeared to be an earthen pathway of unearthly narrowness. Down, till a lowish arch of stone was reached; to slither feet first through its barrel-wide partition; to rest at last, hunched low beside several stubs of candle wax fused to the newly-mortared floor of whinstone slabs. Leaning through the gap, with one large hand supporting him on the top stone, John handed the bread and cheese he had taken from the table and proceeded to console Phillip as he would a younger brother. Another lighted candle followed.

"There appears to be a sufficiency of light to keep you both warm and tolerably sane for any number of hours. There are Honey-tops in those barrels, but do resist the grain sacks, my friend, as they are sealed as tight as Gloucester's very gates. We will escort these men homeward safely, have no fear, and return with all due haste. If all goes well, and I see no reason why it should not do so, the three of us may yet enjoy a late supper above. If they may only bake us a fat rabbit or two at the inn."

Both John and Mr Trannion scrambled forward, reaching out in turn to grasp the young man's hand, as he wished them Godspeed. The writing materials were subsequently passed through the aperture which was then carefully closed. As he had arrived, so his guides slowly departed. As sleepwalkers glide to the end of their dreams, as the beating of a dying heart surely fades, the upward footsteps fell away noiselessly into the residual muffle of the tunnel. In the paucity of the light the gaunt walls closed in oppressively, the low beams above threatening like the triune arms branching from a gallows tree. It was a leaden tomb. And, with an unrelenting pain, Phillip Pevenston was left alone to endure the silence of the candles.'

The lyrics of one of her grandma's scratched old 45's raced through her mind: *I Think Of You* with its wistfully lonely tune, sung in a plaintive key. She heard him calling to her - when the night was cold. Plucked by a lute, it would almost be like: anothertwoheartstringstogether. She sighed and then turned the next page.

'At eleven 'o clock they rode homeward. The moon was no more. And the Polreath miners were no more. A unspoken sadness had since taken their place with the two men returning from Stanmore Harden.

"The boy is uncannily correct in his report, Richard. We travel a lonely road and are therefore all better for it. It is to be hoped our fine acquaintance with Mr Trannion may not be long in its renewal, whenever our countrymen can bring themselves to resolve this disgraceful squabble and put an end to these evil hostilities."

John Brimble patted his horse and reined him in closer to a dark line of hedge to his left. Something flitting from a bush. A fox on the run to his lady dear. His companion drew back, trying to scan the field, though without much success.

"I shall not be free of the terrors, John, till we pass the crossroad up ahead. The day has been a long one. Too long, I fear."

He tightened the collar of the greatcoat around his neck and wished for the flintlock he had been recommended to carry. The younger man stifled a yawn and gave out a short laugh to himself as he revolved the day's events through his mind like the recollection of a schoolboy's adventure. To have outwitted the opposition (whoever they may have been) at every turn, with every device in the *modus operandi* implemented to exactitude, was sublimely satisfying. He drew rein.

'Tis not far now. I hope *we* are worthy of our day's wage."

They followed a measured bend in the road where the overhanging hawthorn bulged considerably for some yards to deny them a clearer view of the road ahead. Sir Richard trotted almost to a halt, before running a gloved hand involuntarily down the inside of his coat to confirm the absence of a sword at his side. As a rule he was not one to carry a weapon, but tonight he felt unarmed. The turn was completed slowly until they viewed the crossroad where a familiar landmark of a clump of elms rose to the right. It was at this intersection (nominally, a lane to a few poor cottages) that a cluster of black shapes rose up - like a cast of hawks slouched upon a promontory. Hatless riders, whose restless horses were pawing the ground, snorting. Two small lanterns hovered in mid-air like demonic eyes, each with a bluish flame. One lantern moved higher still to reveal the predatory eyes of its holder, deep-set, and staring out above cadaverous cheekbones. At twenty paces the two men stopped.

"Good evening, gentlemen. A bold night for travellers. Perhaps you have forgotten there is a war on.

"God save the king, sirs. We have always something on our hands, do we not? Perhaps blood? Is it never to be overlooked? Let us pass in peace, man."

The cluster of horses remained motionless, as the light bearer drew his pistol and pointed it at Sir Richard's head.

"It is you, is it not, Colonel Wennard? If ever paths were to cross again, I was sensible of it one day being ours."

"Once in a lifetime might be considered a poor return for faces you never forget. Your son's face, as an enemy of the king, would be a worthy example of that," said Wennard, spitting the last word out in contempt. Steadying the lamp, he cocked the gun coolly and lowered his forehead. Sir Richard sat erect and braced himself in the saddle.

"I will face you and your henchmen, lest to shoot me in the arse would give you more satisfaction. But you shall never see my son. That I do tell you gladly to your face."

The courage of Sir Richard was unmistakeable. Wennard, triggered by the response, exerted the lightest of pressure to that of his wheel-lock as it grated. A crack lit the night with a puffball of smoke.

The figure of Sir Richard slumped forward and slid awkwardly from his startled horse. Three more pistols were immediately raised and aimed towards his lifelong friend. As though kick-started from the shock of a sordid dream John Brimble reacted with a desperate shout of anger.

"In God's name, what have you done! Venal dogs! You have murdered a man of the king for no good reason!"

Wennard snatched up another loaded gun and pointed it with a snarl. A volley of discharged barrels blitzed the stillness of the air with the flash and stench of powder. The Colonel's features creased, then froze in a shock of horror. For neither he nor any of his men had fired a shot. He swayed in the saddle, his gun-clenched fist pointed forward still, before falling dead - dead to this world and all its petty disputes and vain acts of vengeance. Never to see the face of the renegade son, nor, for that matter, any other, in this most mortal existence. The trees came to life as rebel soldiers with muskets moved in to finish off their work. The thicket snapped to the creak of leather boots, as a cavalryman swung out across the defenceless man's path. Helmet and sword steel burnished the darkness in front of John's unseeing eyes.

"So the papist hounds kill a man of the king, eh? Whither do you fly now, my lord?"

Courage born of anger took over as, raising his arms high to the starless night, he called out to his captors:

"God help me, gentlemen! But *I* am for the king!" '

The poignant thought occurred to Harriet that one of these men must have survived for this bit of the account to have been recorded. Else it was all just a pointless fiction. Someone having a laugh, playing with the emotions of a gullible reader. Historian or basket-case? Fact or fiction? She swallowed hard. It did have a ring of truth about it. But what did it matter? Live or die, they were all dead now. But somewhere beneath her feet lay a tunnel that would not let her fold up the book and go to sleep. Not just yet. There was one more page still to be read.

'Oct 4th, 1643: The confession of Phillip Pevenston.

He stared at the flame, an eye-level incandescence enlarged by his own morbid obsession. Where such a light could heat the brain to a madness, if all else failed. There was no sound, save the murmured undertone of his own lips counting down the dying seconds of a candle's life. Counting out time to no purpose. He began to write again.

'Yes, there is a mad coolness here which exists beyond this light, and, when the flame is soon to be extinguished, I shall be assailed by a darkness more so profound than anything snuffed out by an unseeing night. Where the visions of heavenly riders on their ghostly steeds will return to haunt me from the rafters, as they did when I fled the battle's field. O Lord Jehovah, Preserver of my soul, inform me if my poor conscience be not already ripped and torn away entirely. Do not allow a deadness of spirit to run me through - and I am then no one's no more. Were I to conceal myself in the blackness of the deepest cave, You would be certain to find me there. Make all my calculations cease, and supply to me a crowd of humming angels that these ears might better hear the funereal song prepared for my deserving remains. Thus might I justly die the more compliant.

I have slept. Today, if this be day or night by any surer estimation, I write with a steadier hand, and so Swayne may yet hear of my grand fate. It seems my God has given me a congregation of rats for my company. At least it seems there was one eye that glittered, aroused by my presence, tho' meek in its curiosity. And no unworthier example do I set between these blurred-edged hours of burning candles end to end. Both of us may hunger and thirst and listen for each other's presence, yet the very nature of another dark life terrifies me still. If there be any air of lingering hope which may descend as sweet as a faerie's breath and circulate over the freshness of these trimmed, new-laid stones, I am insensible to it. To go beyond these walls frightens any present inclination. For another angel stands invisible, turning in obedience his flaming sword. Here, at least, I may eat to satisfaction, for to bite dry bread and sip cold water is no more forbidden than to imitate the simplicity of an earthly Christ. But in this pit there is a heaviness of sins, where I dip my pen as upon a heart of ink in an outpouring of my lifeblood. I do recall the drops of blood which fell from my Lord's face when all the weight of this imperfect world was upon his shoulders. He afterwards prayed: 'Forgive them for they know not what they do'. Now I beg for such forgiveness, for I know not what I have done, and my prayers be incoherent. If one father has forsaken me, will You do otherwise or the same? Looking on in secret, repay me in my secret place. From the storms and silences of this burial-ground may you shield me. In this madness of a living death am I afraid to die? O from a rock-tomb may I arise! There is nothing left for me to say. The essence, or what remains, of my spirit is poured out into a scrawl, lighted only by the brilliance of a nimbus so pure, so refined in its shimmering. One candle left is all there is. And the light from its beginning is unchanged. From change to change there's no beginning, as I fear there is no end. Where the history of love and hate continues to be an unmade bed unfit for temporal rest, much less a place for sweetest sleep. May the power and the glory of the Kingdom belong to the true Majesty forever. Ere sleep shall blend with the permanence of a shroud of darkness, the agonies of my last words are now written:

"For the time hath no consequence and leadeth me to nowhere" ' '

A knock came at the door. There was no reply. The silvery head of Mr Brimble peeped inside to find his grand-daughter asleep with her head on her knees. He carried a tray with a mug of cocoa and a plate of Cook's home-made biscuits. As he gently placed the tray at the foot of the bed she awoke, drowsily disconnected from the dream whose closing words were formed as a charm upon her lips. Harriet blinked several times before noticing the old man sitting on the bed's edge with his eyes lively and twinkling. The last page was open where her hand had fallen. She read the epilogue line from memory without once looking down. Grandfather raised his eyebrows in appreciative surprise.

"People never talk or think like that today, do they?" she said. "I - I don't mean just the words in themselves. I think some, maybe most of 'em, are a bit difficult to understand. But it's the way he made me feel. Like somebody whose pain is so bad they can't tell you straight away how it is. Only in gasps, and - and - anyway, you can tell when it's bad and not faked. Take away the big words, and it's still there."

Mr Brimble touched the edges of the manuscript and leaned forward, as if counting the pages.

"Phillip's experiences were by no means unique for young men alive at that time," he mused. "Many a lord's true son or those of humbler station had their spiritual integrity put under test. That is to say, they tried to act in a way which they felt was both just and met the approval of God. To fight for what they felt was right. Even brother sometimes fought against brother."

Harriet stared at the tray before taking a biscuit without thinking.

"Are you saying they had to choose who to fight for? Seems to me that each side thought God was with them. There doesn't seem to have been much difference in their hatred of the other, though."

"My dear girl, people have made a love of God an excuse to kill their fellow men ever since they came to be on this earth. Though it wasn't just a religious issue to begin with. For a conflict of any kind was a chance for some to kindle old rivalries and exact revenge for disputes and hatreds best known among themselves. But there were enough good men who believed certain principles were at stake and were prepared to put what they believed in ahead of any personal gain. For the love of country. With each side confident that it alone had God's blessing. All the same, it was a terrible, confusing time. They were all moving into darker places, places where they had never dreamt of being, much less foreseen. And with no ready solutions to their arguments. Here, drink this while it's still warm. If you break the skin you can twist it onto the spoon and out of the way in one go."

The old man demonstrated the movement with the back of his hand still resting on the manuscripts. Harriet took the cup and swashed the fragrant, milky warmth of the mixture round the inside of her mouth, as though to refresh her thoughts, before allowing it to slip gently down her throat.

"Well, he's gained my approval that's for sure. Poor, poor boy. I understand something about madness when I think of the worries I endure with mum."

She stopped and held her hand to her mouth in a kind of hushed horror. She felt acutely embarrassed, for she had realised immediately the incquality of any comparison: "Oh! Grandfather! What am I saying? I know I can be mad, that is, in a frustrated sort of way. His was, I suppose, more – well - different."

"Despite disagreements with his father, a domestic battle of wills was far from his mind at the time. But you musn't feel so bad about it."

He observed the wise humility for her age as she returned his look.

"Oh! Now I'm making him sound like he was alive and well somewhere. But, of course, I don't know what actually happened to him, do I? Did he die alone, here? *Was* he a real person, even? And if - "

"Oh, yes. As real as you and I. The records were collated - hem! - gathered together by my great-grandfather and later set down as a history by his son, Arthur. What we have here is an annotated - oh dear me! - a shortened, more lucid - er - readable account made by my father just after he left school shortly after the first world war."

The present Mr Brimble was only the archivist, a keeper of the chronicle. He smiled. Harriet closed the manuscript, feeling like someone who had been avidly reviewing the film script of a book she had never actually read.

"And if - " she began again, hardly daring to give voice to the inclination of her thoughts.

"There is indeed a tunnel and with it its place of isolation," he said, reading them.

Her grandfather looked benign, his whole purpose having reached this moment of truth. She flashed back an enlightened glare.

"Where a whole orchard of Honeytops were once buried! And there's me tramping my frozen toes over all that snow looking at dead apple trees! But not so dead are they, grandfather?"

"Perceptive child," he said, patting the hand now resting on the tray, "I knew my faith in you was not misplaced. Our story begins with a journey and ends - well, I don't quite know where it ends yet."

"So, if there *is* a tunnel, surely the journey ends where *it* ends."

She wriggled free and pulled on the hastily discarded socks which were now dry. Expectation to make a heart grow fonder or perhaps beat faster had been built upon slenderer promises. She had slept off her tiredness treading the harsh terrain of an England at war with itself and in wondering about the fate of the missing persons who were a part of it. It was nearing eight o' clock and the half-drawn curtains now betrayed a heaven more imaginatively tunnel-black than when she had first begun to read about it.

"What you expect to find may not always tally with what you actually get, you know."

161

This sounded as sly a warning as any a sorcerer might offer to an apprentice about to cast his (or her) first spell. Or so it seemed to Harriet.

"What do you mean? That it's just a hole - dirty and dangerous? All the better, if it is."

She wasn't going to be put off by anything he said. Besides, this might be a way of getting him to let her stay. Mr Brimble hadn't expected this reaction and changed his approach in mid-stream.

"No - no. Not at all. Quite to the contrary, in fact." He was equally determined not to say too much.

"However, you must allow me to give you some additional history lessons as we go along. I assure you, It will make this visit more understandable by the time we arrive at the Arena - arrm! - our destination."

His grand-daughter handed him the folder with another of her challenging stares. She had not misheard.

"Arena? How big do you call an arena?"

"A mystery tour is waiting to take you away. And, like an old song I used to know, it is a magical one. However, patience is a virtue and you are going to have to exercise it for - hmm - another two hours."

"Two more hours!" She finished off the cocoa in a rush. "So what am I supposed to do for two whole hours? It will be ten o' clock by then. Why so late, grandfather?"

The quizzical met what seemed to be the quixotic with a look of endearing innocence.

"Your mother was always impatient. Impatient and, thus, impetuous, too. Ah, I know you've had so many hard words to deal with tonight. But they go well together. She was rash and over-eager when it came to decision-making. Foolishly so. I suppose my actions do appear mysterious, but I hope you will forgive me for the lateness of the hour."

Harriet turned up her nose at the mention of her mother.

"I wish you would change you mind about tomorrow. Nothing's changed there. Mum's most likely to be just as rash and over-eager in Scotland as anywhere else. And those resolution things won't make any difference, either."

Her grandfather made a mild remonstrance with his hand.

"No. You should go. To keep this family together is so important. Your mum will appreciate the fact that I have no intention of pulling you away from her when she needs you."

"*She* needs *me*? Well! I never get noticed when I *am* there! I've wanted to help, but she won't listen to me."

Harriet slumped visibly at the shoulders as she recalled the most recent rebuff of two days earlier. But her grandfather was adamant.

"An enforced estrangement would be the last thing I would wish to bring about. Don't feel you have to make your presence felt by treating her like some younger sister, lecturing her at every spare moment. Look for the good, and believe me, you will find it, and praise that. For all the rest, say not a word. She will notice you then, I am certain. I am relying on this

163

from you to help me get closer to her myself. How I envied Sir Richard at the moment his son returned to him. I live in such a hope for my own redemption. Hmm - how can I put it? My own chance to make amends." There was a humbleness in his plea which she hadn't seen before. "Now, remember, not a word." He repeated it as a mantra with a finger to his lips. "Not a word, now."

She sighed resignedly, as their eyes met in an understanding. If love believed all things, then all things were possible. She bit her lip.

"I'll try, if you think it'll work for both of us. I will try."

"It's an approach I'm adopting with my sister as well, you know."

"Mmm. It doesn't seem to be working in her case. It looks like she's waging another Civil War for some reason of her own."

Mr Brimble took a biscuit but did not take a bite.

"Ah, you see, it takes time. No, not forever. But you have to - how can I explain it? - touch the soul. Let them discover, or either reveal, where their hopes really lie, what they value most, what it is they ... treasure."

He hesitated at this point and held the biscuit up closely in front of him, although his face gave nothing away other than the explicit belief in such a subtle course of action.

"By not saying too much you may also, indirectly, lull them into a false sense of security. Many a good manager has flummoxed - er - caught the opposition out - by keeping matters close to his chest. My sister thinks she has a trick or two up her sleeve, so a squad of cats is brought in to speed things along. Ha! Her problem here is one of, let's say, impatience, only helped on by what she perceives to be a weakness on my part not to intervene."

He shook his head gravely, as if almost chiding the foolish lack of insight from someone who should have known better. Known him better.

"So you do have some tricks up your own sleeve, then, grandfather?"asked Harriet more in hope than any sure assumption. "Apart from acting cool, I mean."

"Apart from leading suspicious cats on a merry dance around the house with Cooper acting as a decoy? No. Not as such. But it will do for a while. Tires 'em out, lowers morale, and makes 'em think rather more of their own stomachs. An unfed army becomes only a distraction to itself."

Harriet laughed heartily as she saw the contrast.

"While the rats are kept going, getting theirs filled with cake bits, nuts and bacon rind!"

Here the Provider of such provender nodded with a hint of mirth.

"I wonder if that's anything to do with why we've to wait until ten o' clock?"

"Your aunt, I have noticed these past four days, has got into the foolish habit of giving her boys supper around ten. Having exerted themselves to dropping point, with no reward for their pains, they're glad to refuel and subsequently feel disinclined to wander

165

about more afterwards. Mind you, I can't say whether or it will have the same effect on all of them. There are those not part of the clan (taken in out of pity, according to Mrs Dains) - now, I've not seen them about since."

His grand-daughter pulled a face.

"Ugh! Those horrible, ugly things. Nasty, too. But I don't think they will try it on again in a hurry."

Mr Brimble nodded as he got up, and told her to wait until he and Cooper appeared, and the all-clear was given.

"He's coming along as what you might call a minder. Prince will be staying up top to keep guard. He seems to have quite taken to our recovering patient."

Harriet yawned and rubbed her knees. So the tunnel was to remain out of reach for two more long hours. But not too long for her to close her eyes again and light one more softly blur-edged candle to Phillip Pevenston.

★   ★   ★

A piece o' white lightnin', *he* wos. A blonde bomber to shake 'im a bit, if ever there wos one. Phew! Never saw 'im taken down a peg like that afore. Images to stay in the mind, they are. Still, he'll bide his time, an' the dog lump won't forget 'im in a 'urry, either. Never saw that bruiser arrivin' on the scene. An' where'd 'e turn up from, eh? Wot I'd like t' know. Too late by then. Bad job, that. Goin' in for a big one without

166

takin' a proper lie o' th' land. Too clever for 'is own good 'e is. Anyhow, knows wot we're up against now. That - wosisname? - Arty-Farty. Yeh, well, he wos right on that score. And that gang o' kissmewhiskas. Ho-ho-ho! We've got their numbers taped. Fancy followin' that wallopin' lump uphill an' down t' other, roundabout an' back agin, for half of th' day. 'Eadless chickens, if ever there wos any. Best on me own, really. The woman's a tartar, though. All gooey smiles. Then shriekin' for th' evidence. In me 'and, she sez. I wanna see a dead rat in me 'and. Full stop. Me? I'd only need t' see one on me dinner plate. Early days, tho', ain't it? Brrr. Bleedin' cold waitin' here alone. Sez 'e wants to be incognito for a bit. Hmm. Nothin' t' stop 'im doin' a night shift like this. Wot we wos meant for, as Scrounger's me name. Old lenses don't miss much. Top peeper. Nothin' flash in this business, boy. Just keep on the watch an' melt into th' dark shadders. I reckon I'll get a good butcher's of wot's wot from this spot, mind. Handy ole brolly-stand this. Tuck in behind nicely an' watch that door. An' them stairs. Funny how th' ole bloke nipped down here arter th' scuffle an' headed straight for it. Had 'im in me sights all th' way. Odd move, that. Locked th' door 'e did, too. Some fancies tick all th' right boxes, I sez. Gotta be onto somethink thick here, as 'e's bin goin' down same time each day since. Like clockwork. Talkin' of which, there goes th' ole ding-dong. She's bin gorn off t' bed ten minutes ago, so let's hang about an' see wot we get tonight, then. Bin a pretty quiet place since. Too quiet, if you ask me. But there ain't nobody askin', is there? Brrr. The rats in this 'ouse ain't normal, either. Got a kinda sixth sense about - hello, hello? Wot have we here? Dark on them stairs. Let's get a steady shufti. Creepers, if it ain't th' old un' agin - with company this time! You've hit th' jackpot tonight all right, me ole son! Blow me if it ain't Lumpalong with that stroppy kid. Wearin' a coat over all that hair like this mornin'. Impressionable she is. Worth keepin' tabs on. There they go, sneakin' inside that door. Shhh! Well, then, let sleepin' cats lie, eh? Wot's with that place down there? S'wot I'd like t' know. 'E'll love this when I tell 'im - if I tell 'im. Nah, matey. Nah. Not yet. This one's for me.

★   ★   ★

They were all squeezed inside, when Mr Brimble eventually snapped on the lamp. An oblong box was clamped tightly under the same arm.

"Sorry, children. I've never been down here before with company. Plain sailing all the way from here."

He shone the light to the keyhole and turned a knobbly-headed key in a grating, clockwise direction. A little more of a twist at the end was needed. Then the click.

"There! Now it's locked. Unlike the front door which, as you know, never is. It's very important we keep this one well and truly locked, particularly at this time, and presently you shall see why."

He pocketed the key carefully and went down a step. Harriet pressed the torch she had been given and swivelled its beam about the dark, wooden stairs below her feet. They creaked ominously, as Mr Brimble led the way with a solemn-looking bloodhound in the vanguard, ineffectually sniffing the indistinguishable scents of any lurking foes who might choose to impede their gradual progress. A strong smell of undetected turps and white spirit hung about the cool air below. Where once a meagre selection of sealed case bottles from John Brimble's coffin might have stood, could now be seen rows of pots dunked with brushes of various sizes perched above several lidless boxes of screws, nails and other hand tools. Cooper (DH) offered a jaundiced eye to these modern-day equivalents and sniffed, again to no avail, as the pool of light moved on ahead.

Seemingly belonging to a sombre line of cloistered monks at evensong, an interconnected spine of low-lit, close-knit shadows traversed steadily along the right-hand wall, obscuring fissures and cracks that breathed only the secrets of their antiquity. The old man picked his way along sure-footedly enough without so much as a suggestion of a stumble or even a need of light. Despite the lateness of the hour, cocooned as she was between the others, Harriet felt safe. Any tenseness she'd felt on starting out had changed into a controlled excitement as her dream moved towards an imminent reality. She swung the torch beam to and fro along the vague shapes which reared up out of the dark on either side before finally getting it to merge with the ring of light her grandfather's lamp made in front of her. They reached the spot where five pairs of sympathetic eyes had once long ago looked upon the plight of a disturbed young man, and it was hereabouts that Mr Brimble halted and raised his lamp higher. He cleared his throat for lesson number one.

"I can confirm that John Brimble survived his clash with the parliamentarian ambushers. He was taken prisoner, where he apparently proceeded to win over the jailer and his wife, not to mention a few of the other officers, with some wonderful recitals of impressively tall stories told with such down-to-earth wit and good nature that it seems not only to have contributed to the easing of an acute sadness, but also to the lessening of his time in captivity. He was allowed to return here about three months after - to find the house empty."

It didn't tell Harriet the one thing she wanted so much to know. But this was soon put to one side as her torch flashed upon on two considerably less benevolent figures before they reached the end of the cellar. The air here tasted of bitter earth and sour, old onions. Two untidy sheaves of fence posts and bamboo rods were each stacked and tied at the waist by several feet of plastic washing line and surmounted by any amount of caked mop heads, rakes, and bristles of broom heads that straddled the tops in a deliberately life-like manner. Exposed all at once by a combination of torch lights, Olly's formidable giants had more of the look of sparse, tightly-bound guys waiting to be consumed on a massive bonfire. Surveying their grotesqueness, more in curiosity than in fear, Harriet nimbly side-stepped the long hoes and staves lethally cocked like Olly's spearheads and javelins. Cooper (DH) indicated his own misgivings by offering another symbolic sniff of disapproval and padded past with eyes figuratively in the back of his half-turned head - just in case he got a parting prod in the rear from one of these dubious figures of fun. Woodentops. Grinning as the lights passed 'em by. Guard on. Mr Brimble's invasive eyes knitted momentarily within a pool of collective light.

"Ah, yes. A little, or shall we say, larger-than-life joke which Mr Pale helped to construct a while back. Scarecrow sentinels - to frighten off any unwanted - er - visitors. Effective, don't you think?"

It was getting to be more of a guided tour than she'd expected. Harriet edged beside him and made to say a word, but was stopped before she could whisper anything about the purpose of scarecrows. She flicked some hair over her collar and patted the bloodhound on the neck, as he sidled up behind her and waited. The old man turned and ran an apologetic back of the hand down a much older exhibit. It was the last barrier that stood between them and the final part of the revelatory journey he was taking them on.

"Dear, dear. So much dust. As it is with the dust of time. Unfitting, you may think, to have a curtain for the grand entrance to a tunnel. Yet wholly suitable, I would say. My grandfather might once have had a door of some sort fitted. There have been a few renovations completed here over the years. Necessary for its maintenance, really."

He held the lamp up higher.

"Tunnel floor. The walls. Tarring of the supports. That sort of thing. Preservation, you see."

He waited for a response but, as in most history lessons where the dates rarely sank in, neither did these details or their implications. He loosened the lid from the box he was carrying without opening it. His grand-daughter had been wondering about its contents ever since they had started out and what the connection might be with the tunnel.

"Of course, you're waiting to find out what's in here, and I won't keep you in suspense any longer."

But he kept the lid closed and, resting the lamp on top of it, seemed to make some silent calculation before stepping inside. Whatever it was changed his mind.

"N-no, not yet," he faltered. "We shall go in with the lighting we have. For now."

Harriet's torch formed a perfect ring over one of the generous, grey folds before being squashed into a kidney shape lower down. Her grandfather's face softened as he groped for the aperture in the fold.

"Many people wonder whether life exists on the other planets of the Solar System. Even beyond. All I can say about what lies below Brokehill will not necessarily prove or convince you of the former. Yet strange and beautiful miracles do occur every day right here on earth. Beneath the earth, we might say. And they *are* truly something to wonder at."

With that, he pulled the curtain at its nearest end and held it open for both girl and dog to follow him

172

inside this other world on earth.

Although the stones of the walls and floor had a smooth and cold feel to them, a distinctly earthy pungency filled the low headroom as the three figures slowly descended. It was claustrophobically dark and the guiding lights were indispensably aimed straight ahead. As the level of descent petered out they found themselves at a gradual turn where the tunnel widened a fraction. Cooper (DH) liked the narrow confines not one bit and kept rubbing his sides against the inward slant of the walls as he tried to focus on the light flaring about ahead. Beneath his feet, beneath a layer of flat stones, rat tracks of three hundred odd years may have lain hidden, but, somewhere down the line, something not too forensic seemed to tell him their owners, past and present, were somehow involved in this peculiar caper. And what a line it was turning out to be and all! His governor paused to test the air by inhaling slowly.

"Mr Trannion was quite an engineer. At some stage, probably when they began to excavate down, he added a flue pipe of improvised air-conditioning for his men. A piece of thin lead piping was driven up to the surface from just inside the entrance where the depth is obviously not so great as it gets further on down." He exhaled a puff of mist and shone the lamp to the cross-supports above his head. "My grandfather added another wider vent for his own purposes, and both of them come up a few feet beyond the library window. Each have a fine wire grille over them to keep leaves from blocking and allowing the air fairly free access. Mind you, since there is no door any more, we breathe the cellar air more easily still, I suppose."

Harriet inflated her cheeks and blew warm air slowly through them as she came to the ripe conclusion that to be confined here alone would be more than just a nerve-racking experience, and that maybe to die of suffocation might be a less dreadful option than to remain alive for some length of time in a deadness of isolation. Could loneliness, that feeling you had even when people were all around you, be compared to an aloneness that came with some inexplicable fear of being watched. Alone, though never alone? Close your eyes. Something unseen touching you. Inhuman voices. Let them come. Let them come inside. Inside your head. You cannot destroy me, for I am secure in my loneliness. Can't you see into this darkness? I can. It's incomplete, intangible. But I like it just the way it is ... A movement of air. The tunnel of life was whispering more insubstantial tokens of someone else's despair. She wrinkled her nose and looked down at Cooper sitting awkwardly and snuffling at a greasy, concave patch along the curve of the wall.

"Sorry, grandfather. What did you say? I was somewhere else. Why did they not keep it straight?"

Mr Brimble lowered the lamp and shone it against the curve.

"They encountered rock and root stocks, so my father said, which would have slowed them down considerably. So they did a sixty-degree turn and hoped for the best. They keep on a level at this point and stay with the clay. After a few more feet the vault itself was dug out without any further trouble. For apples to lie just beneath the orchard of trees that bore them. For a living son to be buried beneath the earth, even as his own father lay dead elsewhere upon its surface." The old man grew uneasy as he pointed forward. "If you aim your torch this way you will see a small wall of stones. The Arena lies beyond."

For the first time since leaving the tower high above the oblong box of secrets was released from its master's grasp. His bowed head scraped against the roof of the tunnel's end as he hunched his shoulders and wrapped his hand around a rust-scarred ring set into the wall at waist height. An aged, expert safe-cracker doing one last job, breaking a code he knew only too well. His grand-daughter's torch flashed closely, as he pulled away at the iron, catching him literally red-handed. He halted and looked up.

"Treachery and destruction sometimes knew no bounds, my dear, and this was indeed sadly the case even with Parliament's forces ... as with many a stained-glass window, so, too, with the Marsh and its surroundings. John Brimble rebuilt this wall in homage to Sir Richard. But more of that later".

The old man might have known them personally, such was the affection with which he said their names.

"To seal it forever. But it was my grandfather who opened it up again. So he could play his knockabout games without interference - on the most perfect of new-found courts."

Games? Court? What game was he be talking about? Harriet kept her eyes on the ring, as he tugged once or twice, giving the block to which it was attached a bit of a lift at the same time. Then, with a scraping sound, it came away.

"I'm quite old enough for this. Too old, I fear." He heaved the section to one side leaving a rectangular hole about four feet high with just over half as much in width. "A proper door was out of the question. It was sacrosanct to him. Hmm - a place set apart from any other, let's say. But he drilled air vents in each of the top stones of this arch – up here. Still, like Egypt's boy king, it is forever Phillip's rock tomb."

He picked up the box and, lowering the lamp, crept through the gap as surprisingly lithely as any enthusiastic archaeologist. Harriet stooped to a squat and threw an arm round the bloodhound in the hope that he would be the next to follow. But Cooper (DH) was having none of it. This was new territory for him, too, and though he had no compunction about going in smartish, he'd be blowed if he'd let the governor's mistress slip in last. He sat down, sniffed resolutely and ushered her forward with a nudge from his otherwise insensitive snitch. She could see the light from grandfather's lamp shedding its rays weakly from within, and decided she really had nothing to fear. Tilting the torch towards Cooper's great paws, she took a deep breath, reminding herself that the real thing was never as impressive as the picture-book image you created from the words on a page. Just wish-fulfilment, really. Though her heart still skipped a beat. Anyway, here goes. She flicked some stray locks from her ears, ducked, and slipped inside the Arena.

A glimmer of the stones: grey-gold in the pulse of their subterraneous albedo. It was ever thus so. Twenty-five feet by nearly thirteen - a truly diabolic dimension for a field of dreams. Yet no dream could ever contain it. Never those hollow, snapshot dreams of déjà vu pressed and pummelled into the tired depression of her pillow, where stray strands of auburn hair lay lank with wetness. Yet never was a chamber more truly suited to the charms of a mistress designate. Its appearance *was* dream-like. Illusory. Candlelights burning their simultaneous phantasms of sun and moon, where sometimes it was day and sometimes night. Where evening and morning merged: chimerical stones forever skimming water. *Atlantis in excelsis.* The Arena was more impossibly beautiful than any words could express, so she made herself comfortable on the top step and said nothing. It was so quiet she could hear herself breathe. She saw the ticking. Undeterred time ticking away from the one thing of beauty that she wore: an unusual 'Black Sheep' swatch watch which her mother had given her and whose starry face spoke only in words, in a universal language of peace. It was presently *Sogni d' Oro* past *Süsse Träume* - with more sweet dreams to come. Almost twenty-five past ten? Well, she didn't feel tired. Besides, black sheep always got to count their blessings in no time at all. There were narrow ledges below flaming sconces along both lengths of wall, and on them she noticed dark ornamental objects positioned in their relative places opposite one another. These strangely-shaped, shadowy fixtures, hunched like goblins, made her wonder if they, too, were a product of someone's inflamed imagination. Such was their attraction, she hardly noticed the rump of warm, slobbery bristles brushing against her cheek, as the faithful bloodhound crept in from behind to take his place beside her in the silence.

"A penny, or perhaps a pound, for your thoughts, my dear."

The sound of a voice was as incongruous as a busker tuning up within the sanctity of a mausoleum. Her eyes reverted to the bottom step where her grandfather sat with his hands wrapped tightly around his knees, staring up at the roofing, whether in absent-mindedness or in reverence, she couldn't tell. He seemed to be very small and cowering. Like a prisoner from long ago. So, it had that effect upon him also.

"It's so – so - oh, I think even a pound would be far too cheap for my thoughts at this moment, grandfather," she stumbled, before finding her own voice at last.

"Priceless? Your thoughts? Yes. The Arena is just so. It is just so ... "

She waited for words that never came.

He tailed off in deference to, and overpowered by, the silence once again. He had wanted to continue the lesson, to unfold further pages of the history, but it now seemed muted and somehow irrelevant. Buried beneath the stones of destruction which could not be made to speak. Hidden away from the world their formation and reformation, he knew all too well, shouted out loudly enough. So what further reason was there to teach? What more needed to be said? Harriet fiddled with her watch strap and tried to count the number of star-riddled sheep along it, but one of the candles had fizzled to a low point and the added gloom made them hard to pick out.

"If I dare to describe it, well, it's a - um - a grotto fit for gremlins. That's not saying much, visually, I know. But if I think again, why, then, it's the equal to the highest room in the house. For quite different reasons, mind you. Then again, I think what you've done to make it look so - "

"Ah, wait there. You don't know what you are saying. There are plenty who clap their own applause here," interposed the old man, contracting his bushy eyebrows into a wrinkly display of seriousness. He had noted something moving on the ledge facing him. Harriet picked up the torch which the bloodhound had handily pushed inside with the sort of touch usually reserved for poking a log fire into life.

"I think the batteries look to be going on this." She stopped. "Still, it would've been more of a thrill to explore with just a lamp - or our own candles - to guide our way. As you said - like breaking into a tomb."

"Not scary? Phillip Pevenston found its solitude overpowering."

"Nope. Lighting a candle in the dark would be so

much more - oh, I don't know the word I want? But, after all, It's what that poor boy had to do."

Mr Brimble admired the generousness and braveness of her spirit.

"Perhaps 'authentic' is the word you're after."

Another noiseless movement was observed from the ledge nearest to him.

"Still, you have to admit you've been cheating, grandfather. To make it look more presentable, I imagine."

"I see. What makes you think these candles were lit by me?"

"I bet that's why I had to wait two whole hours before starting. You probably gave it a little sweep through as well, by the look of it. But you needn't have. Aren't dust and cobwebs - um - authentic, too?"

Her grandfather shook his head slowly, his spirit of adventure seeming to have been a little dampened by the accusations. The light was reduced and fading fast.

"I can assure you I did not come down any earlier to - to tidy things up, as you make out."

Her smile was one which took nothing at face value. She appealed to the dog beside her.

"How does it seem to you, Cooper old fellow? Gleaming grey, eh?"

A weakened ring of torchlight clinically targeted the smoothly-scrubbed flagstones below. Cooper (DH) offered a cursory sniff before guiding his eyes in the direction to which those of his governor's were clearly aimed. The old man prodded the box he had placed at his feet and steadied the lamp that was balanced upon it. He turned to face Harriet's chastising stare.

"Remember what I said about people looking out into empty space? When there are plenty of mysteries to be discovered closer to home - right here on earth. No need, really, for us to create a kind of parallel world of make-believe. Many questions have answers which may make us feel uncomfortable, and there are some which seem to have no answer at all. We should be meek enough - that is, teachable - to be able to take our place in this grand scheme of things and learn to live with them. The world will keep turning, knowable or otherwise. There, I've probably overdone it on the lecture front. I'm sorry if I sound complicated tonight, my child. Instead, perhaps to keep it simple, you must use your eyes to grasp what I mean."

His voice dropped almost to a whisper as he pointed to the almost quaint transformation taking place on the ledge opposite.

"But then if you - "

The new mistress tried to speak, as her not-so-simple eye became overwhelmingly spellbound and the inner light of her mind still more confused.

"I - I - must be hallucinating. This light is playing tricks. Just like it happened to that poor boy!"

"Yes, but he suffered from what might best be described as a spiritual torture. You may sometimes feel alone in your thoughts, but you are not quite so alone as all that. Tell me what *you* see."

"I think – I think I've just seen a face. A baby face."

"You see them. The candle lighters. They are just waking up. I suspect they fall asleep from the warmth emitted by the candles when they are fresh and bright. We must have just missed the latest game."

As in acknowledgement to their presence, Mr Brimble took out a handkerchief and wiped his eyes and forehead. There could no longer be any holding back of the final history lesson. It needed to be told. He turned on the lamp and shone it down to the end wall where a compact outline of a chalked goal was revealed. The other end was the same. Penalty areas were clearly marked out. All on a vastly smaller scale, of course. A mini centre circle was where the light was strongest. He reached out an arm, allowing Cooper to sidle down to the level of the floor.

"You know where we are, don't you, old fellow?" he said, as the dog scanned first the ledges then the vault itself with his analytical mind working overtime.

The old bloodhound had seen a few surprises in his time, but this one took the dog biscuit, fair and square. So this was the place that little beggar was goin' on about. The nose mightn't be up to anything, but he could see all he wanted with the aid of the governor's lamp. Very nice playing surface, even though it wasn't grass. As good as any *astroturf* or the latest cleverer stuff they used up at the school. Wasn't a slopin' pitch, neither. Ball would run true and even, then. Wonder what ball they used? No bigger than a golf ball, he'd wager. Had to be. As all the talking had been done in low tones he reckoned the sleepyheads hadn't yet cottoned on to the fact that they had company. But there were others. He peered up and down unhurriedly, the realisation of where he was now having relegated most of his initial uneasiness into those darker corners from where he suspected those very others would likely be watching.

Harriet shook herself out of her trance, her grandfather's last words echoing loosely in her head.

"Um - did you say game? What game have we missed? You're saying these rats are - ?"

"Sporting rats, my dear. The Arena is their venue. Look carefully at the chalk markings. Our game."

Her grandfather made the statement seem as though it was the most natural explanation in the world.

"What I can tell you won't take so long. They say all that glitters is not gold, but the eyes set upon us are jewels beyond compare. Perhaps our young man saw the first rat to make this place its home, perhaps not. Where you create openings and store foodstuffs, then their arrival is virtually guaranteed. At any rate, after some unspecified period, they made the Arena their abode, and generations of them have resided here ever since. John Brimble held it in such high esteem that it appears likely he recalled some of its original builders to help restore it some years after the war. Nothing is certain, but more work seems to have been done to strengthen this roof." Mr Brimble ushered some light towards the array of cracked and ancient beams above. "Then we get to the mystery that's so dear to your heart - Phillip's outcome. I say mystery, because nothing was found save the record he compiled while in hiding, part of which you have already read. However, no knowledge of his whereabouts was ever uncovered. According to John, some of Parliament's soldiers did quarter at Brokehill for a short time prior to his return, but the fact that the grain was untouched, and the papers were found inside a barrel by John himself, suggests that soldiers did not find the tunnel, and that Phillip Pevenston, at some stage, had got away safely."

Harriet heard herself sighing deeply once again. She remembered the ambush.

"So his father did indeed die, then?"

"Oh yes. Sadly, there is a very sure record of that. Sir Richard was buried at Stanmore, and it is recorded that John later reconstructed the entrance wall behind us using several stones from the great Marsh House and from the ruins of the cottages, in memory to the total devastation they suffered during the latter stages of that bitter, see-sawing war. Very few stones are left to declare the demise - er - destruction of Pevenston Marsh. Neither is there a mill. However, there is one final chapter to this part of the story left to tell. Twenty or so years later, long after the war, a stranger visited Brokehill and asked about the existence of the tunnel. John, who was absent at the time, learned of the stranger's insistence on seeing the cellar and was amazed to discover what can only be described as a parting gift left outside the tunnel's rebuilt wall behind us. Whether this person came inside is not known for he kept his identity secret and he never returned. The gift, however, is in our keeping to this day - but I will say no more of it for now. Do you feel the cold in here at all? We're directly below a dry layer of rock, and where the roots of the apple trees take up most of the moisture. So little dampness gets down here. Perceptive of Mr Trannion, I would say."

His listener hadn't really noticed, what with her preoccupation with the Arena and its bizarre attendants. One question still puzzled her and needed answering directly. He had mentioned something about games being played. What exactly were these games?

"An excellent question to ask. I was expecting it. Its answer will, I trust, link the present with the past and show you why I wanted you to see this place with new eyes of understanding. As the rightful inheritor of Brokehill."

Her grandfather's hands trembled slightly as he lifted the lid of the box to shed the required light over its contents. Piles of candles. Matches. Tapers. Some chalk. And two small candle holders.

"Twice yearly I become the keeper of the fire. And of the secret it holds. So freedom may run its timeless course, you see." He checked himself. "No, you don't see. Oh, what am I saying? Now I know I'm talking in riddles, and you've taken quite a lot on board for one night, as it is. But I've no intention of keeping you from your bed a moment longer than necessary. As you know, my grandfather was always a keen sportsman from his youth and revelled in those games of public school tradition. It's where the seeds of both rugby and football were first developed into something more substantial, that is, shaped into what they are today, having a code of laws and conditions, etcetera. One game in which Arthur Brimble did excel was the more exclusive game of fives. Rugby fives to be exact. It's enough to say that fives is rather like squash without a racquet. You just use your hand, gloved or otherwise. Well, Arthur had a close friend, a cousin whose elder brother had previously played football for the famous Royal Engineers. So, as you may imagine, whenever these two weren't smacking a ball against a fives court together, they could be found kicking one into a goal somewhere. There was only one suitable stretch of wall behind the house for fives, but playing there was frowned upon by his mother due to the problem of some very prominent windows. The ones beneath the ballroom. They were encouraged to think again."

Harriet shook her head vigorously in mock-frustration as she rolled her eyes at the problem this must have presented.

"Tell me about it. Discouraged, I'd say. Mum never likes to see me wearing a club shirt."

"I understand. But Arthur was not one to give up, and was typically astute in hijacking part of the cellar, using old oil lamps to light up a makeshift court. Needless to say, it wasn't long before he rediscovered the entrance to the tunnel and, in doing so, he found the place he called his idyll - the Arena - which proved to be the most perfect venue for rainy afternoons during the holidays. With his father's forbearance he gradually came to restore it, as I have said, and later added these ledges. How old the sconces are is anyone's guess, but eventually more candles were stuck along the ledges for many a wild kick-about when they got tired of playing fives. The candles, fives balls and marker chalks were always kept at the back at that end."

The wary bloodhound threw a cursory glance to the alleged region and let out a derisory half bark, half grunt. He noticed the little chaps underneath the sconces drifting back off to sleep. Too tired to eavesdrop on things that didn't merit their interest. Not half as interested as he was right this moment in getting down before a cosy fire, one which was waiting for him goodness knows how many feet above this nippy cell. His mistress, on the other hand, was giving the governor more than the usual attention to his stock of information.

The storyteller bent closer to the lamplight, which was acting as a kind of intimate campfire between them. As keeper of the fire he then freed a long candle from beneath the exposed pile. His voice kept low.

"Now what happened during this early period is quite strange to relate. They had always possessed an intensity, a competitive edge to their play, but no sooner had they installed themselves in here than they began to experience an overwhelming sense of - of - shall we say - er - a strange dislocation. Another of those words! Of not knowing where they were. But that time seemed to matter - well - not one jot. Not in the normal, exuberant sense, I mean. But that time itself somehow stood still. Perhaps an hour or so of playing went by in, literally, no time at all. My grandfather wrote something about the feeling of being first juggled in a kind of capsule, then of being tipped out without any warning. He said it was like seeing himself from behind , without having so much awareness of his opponents movements - a sensation both compelling and scary at the same time. What your mother might have called an 'out-of-your-head experience'. A trip. Hmm. Simply put, it felt nice at first, but wasn't at all, really. Like being lifted up by your legs on one of those gravity-defying funfair rides. I don't expect I've got it across very well, have I? But, then, I have never played here myself. To make matters worse, their watches always stopped. If anyone brought along a time-piece, its mechanism would stop working - in a blink of an eye. They left the Arena alone for a while, although my grandfather was loathe to give in entirely to these odd forces. That's when he decided to research his father's records, including most of the papers compiled which recorded the tunnel's beginning."

"This house has been kept and swept up by a host of grandfathers, it seems," mused Harriet as she began to lose track of who was who.

"And wept over, too, to complete the rhyme. We were not always so. Grandfathers, I mean. The three men before me all died before they could be called such to their face. In wars not of their making."

He gave a sigh as he brandished the candle as though it was a short sword. Harriet thought how sad it was that each of them had barely lived long enough trying to preserve something which had not been not of their making, either. Yet still worth having.

"Three wars on foreign soil. Great-grandfather George died in the Boer war, Arthur at a place called Vimy Ridge, Arras, in 1917, and my father flew on one bombing mission too many in the Spring of 1944. Never to return."

The old man became silent and watched the last flame sinking in its sconce. The shadowy figures below it jumped down with surprising speed now that their job was done and the temperature had noticeably dropped. He rose and, after managing to light the candle by means of it, moved across to a darker recess of wall which some of the scurrying rats presently adorned. Warm-blooded in their cold concealment. Like fruit bats. Lyke-wake bats. The watcher of their souls then returned to his previous train of thought.

"Arthur finally came up with an idea which was to have lasting consequences for this place - in a way completely unexpected. It was a simple premise, really. He took the gift kept by his father and brought it back to where it had first been deposited. It is a timepiece in its own way, you see. Shrewd boy, was Arthur. Then, in quicker time than it takes to kick-off or take a penalty, the candles no longer burned down ever so quickly, and you could tell the time again. Extraordinary, really, don't you think?"

Looking at her own watch, which was now *Sueños Dorados* – a quarter to eleven, Harriet had begun to follow her grandfather's footsteps with a sleepier eye than before. Cooper (DH) sniffed at the dry air as though some usage to his nasal passages had returned.

"Not only that. The presence of this timepiece extended its influence further," the old man continued, with his emotions rising. "In the years that followed candles were often discovered burning on their own and several fives balls would be found dotted about the floor as if they had recently been played with. Someone was playing a game of their own, it appeared. One day, not long before the outbreak of the Great War, the big mystery was revealed. He saw them. Groups of rats chasing a ball over the markings of the scaled-down pitch. Even a penalty area had been roughly sketched out. As they are now. He thought they might have copied it from an old programme he'd left behind, but my father was never able to say for sure. Nevertheless, he felt somehow indebted to the influence that the gift had brought to the Arena and to the rats in its care. And that is how he became the keeper of the fire. After the war my father did likewise in his memory. And to his grandfather's also. Twice a year he carried a box of candles, matches, tapers and a set of fives balls - like these - for their convenience. So I have done likewise for many years past. I was just six years old when my own father led me here for the first time. Wars have come and gone, but this game of life the rats keep playing remains ever burning."

He balanced the candle in a flat holder before allowing the newness of its slender flame to leap up beside an upright wooden box, a box which had been there for more than a century. He then knelt and lifted out the enigmatic gift inside its plush lining. It was a half-hour glass, as wonderfully designed and constructed as the Arena in its own way, exquisitely caged in rings and connecting rods of solid silver with delicately carved knobs of gold at one end. Its glass was divinely proportioned and resembled angels linked by their fingertips where the lifeblood of the silvery sand was imparted from one to the other. The bluish whorls of the bases were each studded, above and below, with twelve deep and dark, almost black, prismatic gems that seemed to change colour, as the keeper of the fire turned them gently in the light. The silver was tarnished, but that it was an object of enticing and stunning beauty could not be denied even in the poorest of light.

"My father discovered the stones are tourmalines. Or black schorl. They are dichroic - ahem! - that is to say, their colours can vary in the light. And they provide a force of attraction when any heat is absorbed. Perhaps the rats feel its pull sometimes. I like to think they are imbued with the spirit of the missing man and this gift is a remembrance of his time here. As a relic of his own salvation. Its energies are released with each inversion of the sand of time. Genius cannot be taught," he theorised, "but, once bestowed, perhaps it may be mysteriously passed on."

He tilted the sand into a sparkling flow. Cooper, having followed his governor, now leaned over to gaze in earnest upon the talisman.

191

"You recognise this, too, eh, old boy? Ah, yes, yes, I think you do," said his master in a very subdued voice.

"So it's a kind symbol - of freedom, then."

Harriet was awe-struck that such a treasure could be at the very heart of the vault's strange powers.

"And of all things - footballing rats! Who could imagine it!"

Her grandfather couldn't agree more.

"To think of their dark lives being bound up with a game as unpredictable as football, is itself as unpredictable as anything could be."

"It's also the most romantic. Which most people probably wouldn't consider a rat to be."

She looked around her guiltily, but the sentries had fled into the niche when Cooper's curiosity had first got the better of him. She held the lamp closer to her grandfather's face. He winked back.

"Well, it is the beautiful game, and you don't have to be a Brazilian to appreciate that. Or even human," he added with a touch of his own finesse. While in thought, he returned the still-flowing half-hour glass to its protective place. The mistress of Brokehilll was gradually feeling the lateness of the hour and discerned from her grandfather's face that it was time to go back. Back to where a world slept not so deeply.

When dreams are sweet, remember the rings of studded stones: from change to change unchanging, bestowing gloom with glory. As in heaven, also in earth. Also in earth. She shivered and felt cold. Her grandfather took up the box of celestial lights and pushed it into the recess. Wedging another lighted candle into the second holder, he handed it to her and led the way up the steps.

"Like life," he reflected, "football is a game of incidents - some elegant, some brutal, some foolish - to win or to lose. And here am I bringing scraps of light into their darkness, while I remain in a darkness of my own, with no one to brighten my path. Until a day of victory dawns, whenever that day should arrive, when there will be no need of a light. Yet have I done the right thing? That's what I constantly ask myself. I hope you will not think me a little mad tonight, my child."

The candles glowed in the blackness like stars from an unknown constellation. A flicker of anguish was caught in the girl's tired eyes as well as in her soul. An echo-location, sounding forth by heartbeats only.

"Oh, grandfather! I'd love you even if - if you were – certified!"

The three figures ascended, with the grim, grey winding wall blowing, blowing at the flames. Blow it out! Blow it out! One by one. Before the new day shall catch them listening to the sighing and repeated prayer that whispers, whispers through all the ages long:

'O save me, O save me! From every stoop and bow.
Fire my hymns by candlelight,
and Christ receive my soul!'

"If you ask me, I think the whole thing's become an obsession."

"Nobody is asking you, so you may as well go back to sleep."

"Who's sleeping?" The replier yawned as if in answer to his own question and contented himself with freeing the last bit of breakfast from the bowl with a lazy scrape of a protracted claw.

"You, baby-face. Sleep-walking or sleep-talking. Much the same thing. Some of us round here are trying to pull our weight. You, as well as that polecat over there, are just showing us up."

The said cat was doing his best to live up to this description by bounding between two precarious stacks of upturned baskets, all but oblivious to the scatter-gun arguments being sprayed about like bad blood below. The squabble, which looked to have subsided a few minutes earlier, was building up a fresh head of steam and seemed all set to fly off into one of greater vehemence.

"I'f gog as muff righ' chu fpeak my mund alsh alnywun."

A last chomp of jellied chunks was sluiced down with a good gulp of the gone-off milk.

"Grief. How can you put that muck down you, like that? Don't you go kidding yourself you've got any valid input here, Squealy. Too many cooks an' all that.

Leave it to those who have real ideas of strategy. One thing's for sure, the usual methods are no good here. We've got to explore new ways of approaching this."

Boswick wiped a paw several times over his eyes, something he always did when he felt stressed.

Gus looked up sharply and gave him an incredulous glare, along with a jaw-dropping fang or two.

"Don't start that again! Is there an insect tapping somewhere inside your noddle? Cooks? Aw, come off it, Boswick. Where? We don't have any. Anyway, you were all for the daft idea of keeping tabs on that dog when he was really -"

"Shut it. Just shut it," came with a dismissive hiss before any more of the painful escapade could be dredged up again. "You can't say you weren't toddling along nicely like the rest of us, Gus, so long as things seemed to be looking up."

"No. I won't shut it. You were one of its chief proponents, as I recall, and just look where it got us. Perhaps Squealy's right, we are too obsessed by what *they* do. Or don't do, come to that. Why can't *you* come up with something more original, then?" With that Gus jabbed a challenging fist of pink toes towards his defensive neighbour.

"All this stuff about new tricks makes me laugh," remarked a high voice in their midst. "Anyone seen a dog in here? Let them worry more about our movements, I say."

A basket behind was tipped over. Another, disturbed by its fall, turned towards the scene of commotion with a familiar expression of resigned weariness. Though Arturo didn't expect his own reasonable views to carry much weight any more, he felt he had to say something.

"Can't we just stop all this nonsense before it gets out of hand? We should be seriously discussing workable options in unison, instead of flinging accusations here, there and everywhere."

He had suspected it would all be going off into a stink soon enough, and, sure as bad eggs, it had. He wasn't addressing anyone in particular as he spoke, but the reactions were not slow in coming. There was a hoot of derision followed by catcalls.

"Yah! Hangdog! You've always got an option. Back up to mummy, if things get too hot," said Gus with a blatant sneer of contempt.

Boswick had to snigger behind a paw at this.

"Finish it, Gus," said Sabre, one of the youngest three, who was more determined than ever to be heard. "Seems to me he's right. It's not Arty's fault he was here before us. And so I say again, let's leave all the guesswork to *them* and make them start worrying about *us*."

Gus spat some saliva and went back to glaring at Boswick, before shooting an irritated glance over his shoulder at the so-called polecat struggling to disengage himself from the fallen basket.

"And you, Diggsy, are a drop dead plaything. Are you on any accessible wavelength?"

"Ain't done nothin'!" squeaked the athletic Diggles who, without pausing for breath, took another daring leap.

"Exactly!" came the quick-fire reply. Gus again spat bitterly in disgust. "Like everyone else in this madhouse!"

Yells of objection rose into a dissonant free-for-all. The noise only died down when the kitchen door opened and a slightly distraught Mr Quills flounced inside followed by an equally dismayed Cubshaw.

"My, my, boys. Why are we getting into such a tizz this morning? We can hear the clamour from the other end of the kitchen. If it's food rations that are the problem again, you only have to say."

For some of the others he was clearly not on their wavelength, either. Cubshaw, somewhat aloof to all the noise being generated, cast a magisterial look towards the basket-flier.

"Get down from there. Or do I have to raise my voice as well? Get down at once."

"Hey! hey! Oi! Can't you lot keep the cackle down a bit?"

From the corner shadows yet another disgruntled figure emerged, steering a bleary-eyed course over to the group with a rasping cough.

"Me an' 'im are trying to get some kip, y' know," muttered Scrounger to the nearest agitator.

"Yeah. You're half the trouble and all, you are." Boswick could see where the fault-lines lay, but wasn't content with that by a long chalk. "Bin on a bit of over-time, have we? Neither of you two seem to be working for the general good. Think we haven't noticed? If there was ever an advertisement for going it alone, you'd be the star. You're up to something, but

I don't expect we're about to be let in on it. Anyway, I, for one, don't want to know. But I'm warning you, if anything goes wrong it'll just make things tougher for the rest of us. And as for his Lordship back there, when he's finally formed his master plan, will he be so good as to tell us about it?"

The interlude had allowed Mr Quills to push his way in between the arguers, but he was no longer the centre of attention. Boswick spluttered and wiped his eyes as though they had been offending him. Scrounger looked around his audience in general acknowledgement and produced the street-wise grin which was his wont in these situations.

"Come, come, gentlemen. No need for any of us to put a spin on things. All's to an advantage. You've at least got to know the extent of this ol' 'ouse by now. An' as I sez before, 'e'll bide 'is time till the right moment. Then the smell of blood'll soon be in our nostrils. Meanwhiles, we need to 'ave patience, me lads. Guerilla warfare, see? Arter all, Rome wasn't built in a day, as the adage goes."

Mr Quills, typically impressed, cleared his throat and added a measured: "Here! Here!" before quickly grabbing his opportunity to carry on in case any further interruptions started up again.

"There's an important item of news we've just learned from the ramblings of our dear hostess - hum - the cook."

"She's havin' to stop leaving certain people turkey skins and hunks from off the choicest cheeses, is that it?" jeered Gus, furthering the line of his own brand of cynical sarcasm. There was a titter.

"Fraternising with the enemy is definitely one way of improving your diet," agreed Boswick drily.

Cubshaw was having none of this and threatened to raise his voice again. There followed some overdue silence as their rallying chief composed himself once more.

"We are given to understand that the young mistress, going by the name of - hum - Harriet, is leaving us this afternoon for an unspecified length of time. Some of you have found her less than accommodating, and therefore one less distraction can only be to our benefit as we go about our routines, in which we shall inevitably begin to make headway in our fight against the - hum - enemy within as their – hum - resistance weakens."

The chest heaved as he rattled off his speech in a more than usual punctilious manner. No one seemed to be lifted by it. If Scrounger felt a jolt on hearing this piece of information, his features betrayed no corresponding emotion whatsoever, schooled and skilled as he was in the black arts of bluff and deception. Boswick and Arturo both eyed him carefully, nonetheless. Twenty-twenty vision wasn't required for his brand of chicanery. He scratched a rip in his ear and gave it a wiggle, preferring to survey the yard outside where a noticeable thaw was slowly converting ruts of icy mud into rivulets the colour of cold tea.

"Well, me old chums, it's a mish-mash of a new day out there. I'll take some breakfast, then see how the land lies. Another day and another year will soon be gone. As logic dictates, as logic dictates."

He smiled relaxedly. A fake smile which was so very nearly convincing.

★   ★   ★

She felt terrible. After closing the tower door her conscience had pricked her just enough for her to wonder if it was a risk worth taking. It felt awful stealing him and slipping away like that while Prince dozed by the fire. With every guilty step taken the weight of an injured rat in her coat pocket began to feel more like the weight of the world. On the stairs, she tucked the flap down tight, fearing his head might bob up at any moment to look for a way of escape. Any unnecessary exposure would only make her feel more stressed, not to say more guilty, than she already was. Let him go now, and all hell would be let loose. A cat or two were sure to be about. She had already seen what mayhem they were capable of. She didn't dare trust them an inch. Reaching the bottom stair unnoticed, she waited and listened once more. A clatter of crockery followed by voices could be heard coming from the kitchen. Grandfather? Had he come back in? He always was an early bird, even when it was late, and someone who might just catch an unexpected worm, if she wasn't careful. The clock signed off for twelve-thirty with a single, accusative bong - and made her start. Lunchtime. It was too late in the day to wish she'd got up any earlier. Probably the only good thing about the timing was the tendency of the cats not to ignore lunch But she had to be careful. Though there was no going back now. Don't even think about it. Deep down, it still felt right. It was the right thing to do. After the night before, how could she ever have let things be. Something grandfather had said about the constant energy of the hourglass had connected with her. If it was a force for good, and she had no reason to doubt it, she wanted to make her contribution count before leaving. If her going home was to be for the good of her family, so then, getting this creature back to his would renew and strengthen their resilience. The power of the Arena would surely do the rest. To keep the fight going, the flame burning. There was no room for doubt, just one way. Forward. Having fanned her own flames with this line of justification, she turned and made a bee-line for the forbidden door. Get there. Just get there and get inside.

She patted the bulge in her pocket while groping for the key in the other one. It was stuck under the torch handle. She breathed in hard and yanked it out. Just had to keep calm and not make any noise. The key wobbled stubbornly and refused to turn at first. Her face flushed uncontrollably. Oh, please, please. Then, with a small crick it turned, and she stumbled inside. As she closed the old door a cold reek of darkness enveloped her: to bring back the memories of another kind of darkness. Even warm fur and wriggling feet punching about for space against her sweaty palm could not dispel it, as she eased the pressure on the pocket. That darkness of punishment, of being shoved beneath the stair cupboard, when her razzled mother had gone beyond drinking herself to a maudlin excess. Being mortified by its cramped isolation, knowing all her screams were ignored or possibly never heard. Alone, and always alone. She fumbled with the torch. It flickered unsteadily to life and brought her back from the trauma of those childish fears. To this present moment. Where a measure of control was hers. To lock others out - where they could shriek and gnash their frustrated teeth in a darkness of their own. Having pulled the key free, she began to repeat the manoeuvre from the inside. Again it refused to make things easy for her. She juggled it back and forth, desperately wanting it to turn. There was a final unsuccessful wrench, before the torch, blinking its own disbelief, promptly gave up the ghost. The batteries! She had forgotten them. Dead. So maddeningly thoughtless! She remembered seeing an old lightbulb, grubby and dust-filmed, hanging by a plaited twist of wire at the foot of the stairs. But where was the switch? Might as well be miles away. Alone again.

The steps groaned, as she leaned against the wall to guide her way down. Three awkward steps, before a door hinge wheezed and a greyish light slit the top step behind her for about the same number of seconds. There was a fidget, then the head inside her pocket poked out and peered back. Sensing the smell of danger, tensing to each creak of the dark. The dark. A fourth step. Then a fifth. Where she turned and instinctively pressed the torch. Only for its futile, tremulous beam to flitter upward and die upon a masked grin of red-roofed yellow teeth. Before the image vanished. A long limb struck out and seemed to make a succession of swipes through the gradations of black oblivion between them like the rapid jabs of a prizefighter. In the shock of the second it had taken to recognise the intruder's coarse outline, she let out a short scream of angry loathing, fell forward against the invisible step and banged her knee. The torch flew from her grasp to greet the oncoming attacker full on the nose with the crunch of a headbutt. There was a yelp as the feline form drooped and went out like the light that never was - before bumping down the stairs with all the unseen acrobatic grace of a disjointed rag doll. The door above kindly creaked a fraction wider to allow in enough light for her to gathered her senses. The torch had luckily bounced onto the top step, and she climbed up hastily to grab it back. What to do now with the cat at the bottom? It couldn't be left in here to its own devices. She peered down and put her finger to the torch button once again. It still didn't work. But the predator was clearly made of tougher material than she had imagined. Dazed and grazed, it came staggering up out of the darkness with a scuffle and barged its contorted face through the gap in the door before she could do anything to stop it.

She looked down at the key still in the lock and, as though waiting for an answer, began to turn it with an extra inward push. An eventual click told her all she was dreading. She then recalled her grandfather's explanatory words, but too late. What now, if more cats came lurking outside? And if great-aunt should swoop down at any moment? The consequences would be too awful to contemplate. She had to hurry. Having no light to guide her down, she had little choice but to release her passenger onto the stairs. He'd find his way into the tunnel somehow. Her hand moved intuitively to her pocket - but the bulge was not there. Gone! She clutched at both pockets in helpless agitation. Nothing there! She scanned the dark depth of the cellar for any sign of movement. Nothing! Nothing to disturb its lifeless gloom. She struggled to free the key before cautiously stepping out to relock it with the same trembling hand. Hardly knowing what she did, and with self-condemning thoughts raging within her, she stamped heedlessly back up the stairs, no longer caring who might be watching.

It was just as well that there was nobody about as the incriminating key was tucked under the rug in its secret place beneath the leather chair. There was no Prince in sight. Perhaps he had gone off looking for cats who were looking for rats looking out for cats. It was all getting to be a complicated game of cat and mouse, except that it wasn't of mice. Part of her wanted to just go off as well, or hide away somewhere till it was time to leave. Yet another part of her seemed to realise that a confession being inevitable, it would be better made as soon as possible in order for her to leave with her grandfather's affection undimmed. She ought to have been punching the air in relief, but instead found herself thumping the arms of her chair in a frustration of failure. Tears welled in her eyes and fell one by one. Too late for tears - as mother would say. She could picture her with the expression that usually followed. Yes, go on, say it: "You're too headstrong for your own good." *She* could talk! But she had mimicked her mother's usual stock reaction rather too loud for it to go completely ignored.

"More strong-willed, *I'd* say. There's really no need to admonish her, though. Her intentions are good."

If one resident grandfather seemed to tick loudly in remonstrance, the other had timed his entrance on a more upbeat note. She sat up and looked round on hearing his words. But they made no difference.

"Sorry. I didn't hear you come in. Anyway it's no use. I'm already mad with myself and, as you well know, what I intend is not generally what I do. The same as *her*."

Her grandfather presented himself with his tie askew, strangled beneath a curled-up collar, and his hair dishevelled. But his words were more reasonable and assured.

"Like mother like daughter, if you insist. But I maintain it is an unfair comparison."

There was no misunderstanding his mood, despite him having just endured a prolonged harangue from his sister. There had been a cat with the bloodiest of noses careering round the kitchen like a demented demon. And he sincerely hoped Cooper and Prince had been enjoying an easier time with the rest of the opposition. Harriet sank back into the deep chair. He hadn't yet mentioned the disappearance of the rat, but he wasn't one to miss much. Did he already know it was missing? And if he did, whether the injured cat had had anything to do with it. She had carried out this half-witted plan without consulting him, based purely on gut emotions, and now that it had gone tragically wrong, she felt too ashamed to confess it. Instead she found herself looking for forgiveness from a higher authority. That this error was not the start of some inevitable downward spiral. That the power of the Arena was going to continue as a protective one. And that she could still have the approval of its keeper of the fire.

"If - if angels are messengers, do you think someone will have heard any cry of mine?"

She grew somewhat downbeat and felt unworthy of any response, knowing that her grandfather probably understood the implications of what was meant. He was sure to have take in every nook of the tower with a searching sweep of his eye.

"Ah, if you're referring to our little friend, well, we were going to get him home anyway," he said complacently and without making it at all obvious that he might have been disappointed. "The cellar is their highway. It's where I left the smaller one, remember? If we have the key, then we're no worse off in maintaining our objective - to be unbowed by any fears of what I will call 'raticide', while resisting any latent -ahem - lingering ideas of - er - 'caticide'. A balance worth keeping to, don't you think."

The rhyming joke, although said in a quiet tone, was intentional, and made him sound a little more generous of heart into the bargain.

"The key is back where it belongs. So you know why I'm so mad with myself," she said quietly, no longer able to contain her feelings. "There was an accident, and I lost him, grandfather."

"Hmm. If an injured cat was anything to go by, then I'd say our friend will have survived in one piece. I'm sure he's learned *his* lesson about going it alone. The cat, I mean. There's a lesson for all of us there. He didn't look too pleased with himself, I can assure you."

"Neither am I. Headstrong, remember?"

"Whose intentions are good. Mistakes can be forgiven, you know. As far as prayers go, and they surely cover vast enough distances, I'm convinced you will find a listening ear there, too. Have you eaten anything, by the way?"

Her day so far had been one of complete nothings. She hadn't slept. She hadn't eaten. She wasn't hungry.

"Cook doesn't want anyone to think we don't look after you, so she's packed you something for when you go. She likes to believe your mother's the one who can't be trusted!"

"I really do think you're amazing sometimes. No, that's wrong. All of the time."

She stood up at last and straightened his tie. He stretched out his arms as if in submission to a hug.

"Hem. Not so amazing as a certain group of others will prove to be when they are called upon. Then we would really see something never to be forgotten."

He gave his mistress designate the awaited long, conciliatory hug as the mutual heartbeats began to settle into something like their regular pattern.

As she stepped outside, the church resounded its dual note for two o' clock. The count of time kept marching on, even if she felt she was being given the long kiss goodbye. Soon there would be a new year where changes beckoned. Never-changing time that changed everything and everyone else. Perhaps your resolve, even. No, not that. Not when love never changed. She raised her reddened eyes skyward. Stony, unmoveable cloud revealing only streaks and striations of blue. A love of the blue that warmed to a thaw. Teams came and went, but the colours and the badge remained. The path to the gate was soft and slushy and the ha-has were liberally emblazoned with tiaras of trickling icicles. She tore off her gloves. Her palms were moist and cloying, but her heart felt dry. People only got excited about superficial things these days: lottery numbers that became the one-way ticket to everything - everything except freedom. Phillip chose freedom and left behind something to evaluate the never-changing time it stood for. She closed the gate and trudged beyond the high elms, her bag sagging and scuffing along the wet road. The battered maroon van was waiting at the bottom of the lane where she'd hoped it wouldn't be and her heart sank even lower. Drops of rain began to fall. Turning round, she raised her face to the formidable dark stones, whether in prayer or in pleading she knew not, whether in the name of Phillip, or to the supremely higher power he himself had turned to, she did not know. As the rain plashed and mingled with her falling tears, all the anguish, unchanged and ever unchanging, of three hundred and sixty-five years - a year for a day, a day for a year - cried out from her lips : 'Don't forget me! Don't forget me!"

★   ★   ★

There was a curfew. Where pockets of restive heads, some counting their blessings, others their wounds, seemed glad of the long siesta extended for the rest of the day. Still others, though, were only too glad to spend it cursing their luck. Two figures, softly delineated against the fading light of the window, were perched like young ocelots on a low bough. Sitting side-by-side, they were not shivering, nor did they suffer so much from the distractions of tiredness or hunger. Any detectable movement of their bent heads was evidenced solely in the shared lowness of their voices. The taller charcoal grey took up the agenda again on a new tack: "Look, has it occurred to you that - ?"

"That we're struggling?" interposed the stockier tricolour with more than an air of deadpan finality. "Tell me something I don't know, Bos."

He straightened his back and leaned forward - an act in which his rear markings revealed themselves to any knowledgeable observer to be a fairly accurate

209

representation of the Antipodes, in which the southernmost polar region was entirely reduced to a narrowness of speckled tail. This movement was followed by a resentful sigh, one that no simmer of even the faintest aggravation could possibly restrain.

"Yeah. We've been here nearly a week and, as if I haven't noticed, it's been practically uphill to hell all the way. Anyone could tell me that!"

A charcoal paw was wiped obsessively into the corner of a right eye several times, as a forerunner to the composure of his thoughts .

"Yes, yes. I couldn't agree more. A funny business. But look at it another way. These go-it-aloners - they disappear and come back, right? But with the spoils of success? Hardly. Just a splitting headache and a bloodied nose, respectively. I mean, it's obvious that if we carry on at this rate we're doomed. If they can't cut it, Quills and Co have next to no chance. As for the heir apparent, well, that's why we we're here in the first place, isn't it? We'll be lucky to even catch sight of a rat what with all the opposition and the deceptive goings on from upstairs. You have to say she painted a pretty enough picture for us at old Vasey's."

"A pack of lies! Like being sold a pup," affirmed tricolour with a caustic sneer and a southerly antipodean shift of the rump. "And that's all we are in the end - dogsbodies. To be kept in this antiquated, clapped-out - kennel!"

Charcoal blinked rapidly at the repeated usage of canine analogy, although being forced to agree with their sentiments. Tricolour hadn't yet warmed to his theme as he spat something indigestible out from the corner of his mouth onto the floor.

"Food fit for a doghouse, as well," he added, without wishing to alter his turn of phrase regarding the traditional mortal foe.

"Well, *he* was never going to miss it in his condition," observed Charcoal with a nod to his rear. "So you did well to snaffle the dish before anyone else noticed. Better to make the most of it, since these extras won't be coming *our* way too often."

"Yeah, but that's partly my point, too, you jerk! It wasn't meant for either of us! We're the ones being stuffed - with nothing."

The brown patch of Australia bridled and began moving momentarily northwards again.

"Quills and Co do very well, as do those other three jokers in the pack *We* get overlooked. Odd ones out. And why? I'll tell you why. Old Vasey lumped us into the deal 'cos he couldn't stand the thought of being lumbered with us any longer. Didn't want to clean up any more of our piss. We were thrown in as a clear-out. The left-overs. Geddit? And here we are, ending up performing like midges on a swing."

"Yes, yes, I see what you're saying. Still look, getting back to these rats for the moment, I do think we're - "

"Yeah, thwarted at every turn. So you keep telling me. The Indian sign, and all that."

"Shut up, will you! Listen, if we do get mainly mush, then we're better off not having to pull any more weight than we do at present. And I tell you this: whenever the crunch comes - and you know it will, as well as I do - it'll be every cat for himself. Me, at any rate. We can tag along for now, but when the game's up - you'd better work out your options carefully."

With these prescient remarks finally out of the way, followed by a further brief stint of eye-wiping, Charcoal slipped back down, curled up into a ball, and returned to the depths of his shadowy nonentity. Shortly after Tricolour made the same move, leaving Australia to dominate a world in which Antarctica and practically everywhere else had simply ceased to exist.

★   ★   ★

Nowhere. If it was somewhere, it was nowhere. Somewhere where anywhere was nowhere, if it didn't lead to somewhere. Where the Word Whisperer, the Knower of All Things, returneth and causeth its hearer to press in through the narrow door. Except that it wasn't a door. But a black crack in the wood that led to … well, nowhere. A downward slide, and though not yet dead - where you would discover that everything was simply nothing - downwards anyway, till you realised you were only going … nowhere. Anywhere but nowhere was almost as good as somewhere. But a downward slide? Always inevitably led to … a late tackle … a red card … relegation … degradation … isolation … this. A funnel. Of a tunnel. Where the trick was to stay alive. Not kicking, no. The goal was just to stay alive, unless death kicked you first and you paid the penalty. Which might be

212

never … or might not. Foot-tapping over the gum-chewed grits of bone that got in the way. The scraps and remains of the toothless suckers who made this. Tip-tap. A professional foul by the last man standing. Old habits died hard. And so would you. When time was turned on its head, so would you be. Where the man in black waved a white flag, and you had to surrender. Whistle or no whistle, hack him down if you were being closely marked. For you were going to go anyway. Down. Where there was no safety net, and the ball bounced off the heads of the poor paying public if they dared to get in the way. No ball to lash here. Just earth. Walls and floor of suffocating earth. Kicking rock. Where I behold in the visions of the night: eeny, meeny … mene, mene … o, u, t spells: OUT. The writing's on this wall and you're found wanting - if you're to be found at all. If no one wonders where you are, let alone comes looking, well then, at least you know who your friends are. No one and nowhere. Like the lost star that fell to earth to lose his shine in a premature grave. You could catch a smoker's cough from standing in the pouring rain, stamping out the cold on a muddy pitch in Sunderland where, as teacher's pet, you got to do all the work, and the ball did nothing. Saturday's memories of fag packet, ticket docket, hands in your pocket, please put a sock in it, and don't you never, ever knock it, son. It was only a b-game, but with the usual b-words flying around. With nobody to tell you what this offside was all about. Pick it up as you go along. It's where 'e is the moment the ball's played forward, not where 'e is when it gets to 'im, if you get what I'm sayin'. Two-player, now. See th' linesman flaggin'. Stupid b-----d. Always gets it wrong. Well, nearly always. Early days? Eh? Pull the other one! Overrule 'im, ref! Music-hall joke, you are an' all. Who's yer father, then? Ain't got one? *Le moment où.* No one but everyone joined in at Stanmore, where a badly-shaped ball was a riot. Wassailing laggards lumped into the gutters by a festive and lawless mass. Mob rule for a day. Till they came down hard on 'em and banned it. To stream back onto the playing fields of old England, where a game fit for gentlemen could once again be played by thugs - and followed by mugs and morons. That's what he should have warned us about. Oh, where were you, pa, when we finally won the Cup? Never there when it really, really mattered. Dad's diddly watching from the other side of the pond. He may have got so near to Billy he could've got a hoof in the chest for his pains, but he'd never have believed it seeing the ball burst twice, as uncle Jack claimed it did. Twice on the big day. And the flayed cow wasn't a white un or a light un, neither, as it 'appened. Nor were England on a better day. Bloomin' disgrace really, Jack said. Winnin's the best that can 'appen in football, but that wasn't one of 'em. Thought it was all over? And it was. Over and over again. Good day sunshine? Strike a light. You lucky, lucky boy, you! Your mother married a builder from Campden Town, who kept her on the straight and narrow and put you in his barrow. Baron of Brokehill. Dying in her arms without leaving a ha'penny to his name. He never knew your secret, although he loved the game. Under an umbrella, a-weeping for the great big feller. Tooma-looma-looma-looma-lay! It's in the back of the net! Hooray! Where the strawberry jam tasted rich on earthy cuts of rye grain pumpernickel wrapped in silver paper, as we watched the zeppelin floating over the wasteland. Those bomb-shelled street corners were pa's pieces of a foreign field. *Fussball noch auf Schinkelstrasse? Ja.* The kids were all the same. Weltmeisters. Tripped up the Magyars, hadn't they? Someone knew the exact spot where the plane had fallen and showed us. There was no plaque or anything like that. Nor for the ball that had almost, but not quite, crossed the line. You can be magnanimous even in a dubious victory. When she died all the treasured past was bound up in biscuit tins. Lousy letters of love's betrayal. Glib lies casually written with a pencil from behind an ear, but where you could still read between the lines. Dog-eared, decal-edged sepias of sombre faces in studio portraits. Uncles and aunts in high-hedged back gardens. Box camera photos of the races, of Jack the lad and a dad with women you couldn't put a name to. The RAF reunion dinners. The wide lapels. Faces having fun. Knitted jumpers and deckchairs on the beach. Good ones of the school team. Those awful handed-down brown boots with the hard toes. Dated in those days. Heavy and squelching in the wet. Three junior championships with them. Phddunk. Ooff! Stuck. Now what? Their idea of a catacomb isn't funny. Captain called them that. More ratacomb, surely?

The dead-march excavations of the past, he said. Meandering and straddling the foundations like a system of overgrown and forgotten canals. *He'd* never been inside one, he'd bet on it. Deadened air, too? Be damned! Whiff of a winding whip-snapper. But level, at least. The shoulder ached again. The airborne cat had clipped him near the groin. The near-miss clout of a nano-second. A clip: where only that nauseating foulness of cat hair lingered longer. But it was the shoulder that played up. No point in shouting, just push on till the pain ended up throbbing between the eyeballs. Pushing on was never looking back to where a morbid claw gashed and gouged to reshape the beauty of the earthworks, playing catch-up while smelling his own blood in a mole of a hole of his own making. Going forward was never having to turn and face the option of death. Where the ghosts of old navigators travelled on only in whispers - to keep you in the past, keep you living in the visions of the past. A vision. A vision so entirely perfect that I couldn't take my eyes off her if I tried. Stooping, as she did, to peer timidly through a telescope pointed heavenward above the hill. The overhanging cherry tree reflecting dark arabesques of its foliage upon the moonlit pool below, as she looks down. O, so far away and so exquisitely clear, she laughs. But i' faith, she simply cannot see this star that she is supposed to. A sheen of hair strands brushed away from her brow appear more interesting to me than the quirks of astronomy tonight. We have no need of the candle, which my father holds out of normal courtesy, and whose presence I find slightly irritating. Any attempt to refocus on what has been missed fails, as she touches my arm, and the blood rushes up as a blot upon my powers of observation. Though science blinds her, she by every means blinds me.

"I do believe you should be on entirely safer ground with a comet, my love. Yet no such grace and favour comes our way this night," I say at length. "However, Mr Halley, the esteemed Astronomer Royal, ensures my grandfather that the very display we seek shall, if we but wait, attend us in another twenty years - exactly."

The captivating eyes widen, limpid in amazement.

"Like yourself, she is a coy lady, but punctual by habit. If our friendship endures that long, you may consider it time well spent to improve your knowledge of such pastimes."

I think the joke was on me. The naked eye that seeth all - before that all be quickly spent. Within a year, she was dead. And across my dazzling universe I drew a morbid screen of sackcloth. To marry Aurora, sweet, intelligent Aurora, who, as the perihelion of the rest of my existence, lived to see the return of the comet. And I, in its expectation, never to forget the one that got away. Away from here. Have to get away and be in the dressing-room by two-thirty latest. Someone keeps playing the same flipping single on the jukebox. Buddy Holly. A new hit. But I'd give a sixpence for something else. If she sees me here, I'm sunk. Think I'm with another girl. Her annoying paranoia. Too much mascara with her nails all mottled and flaky pink. Riding a man's bike with the saddle lowered and where her pleats get caught in the rusty chain. Hope it tips down. Let her come back later, when my sister and her brand new banker boyfriend will be tempting her with a woodbine or plying her with gin and tonics till she feels sick or passes out. Woozy floozie they call her. Never eats anything. Only squares of fruit and nut and nescafe. I reckon this trial might take me up a level. Athenian league, they are. To carry on with my final year, and who knows? To play for love or for money? Ha. Always the love. Put on a bit more muscle, and we'll see. Like our defenders toughened up. Coaching's going to change. People with clever ideas getting noticed. Don't like us shipping so many goals. Tougher at the back. Potential's one thing, ambition's another. Plus a spot of luck when the scouts are on their game. And they turn up. A light touch as perfumed breath wafts against my neck. The cherry brandy lips. Do you still love me, then? That'll be the day. Lonesome, moansome. I'm a rat. I smell of rat, so the answer's pretty obvious, if it was me being asked. I never am. To play for love. The same as you, sir. Every moist blade of grass crushed beneath my feet. As you have, too, by the sound of it. But the next level is leading me to the middle of nowhere. The way it always does. Then downwards again. Down. Where a crossroad lies full of rubbish left and right. So on down it is. A shaft. A gulf. Where fortune's flying in a wind! Way hey! And here we go, here we go down! Down, down, down!!! Down where the

218

battercomb, buttercomb bees of Brokehill are buzzing. Better brake the bounce before I break a bit of bone. From Bach on to Beethoven to Brahms who belts the ball to the madcap black cap rovers beached on a marsh with a dead man's skull on their blackshirt chests who boot it to Buchan to Bastin on to Blanchflower to Ball to Best to the best of Brazil to Bonds to Brooking to Beardsley to Bruce to Beckham to Billy Battle - to bang it beautifully into the net! Breathtaking! Major Marindin and his merry men motion to me as I make my move to where the saturdazesun-to-the-sundazemoon of the hour-glass gleams allure. Can I but hold it? I shout and curse. Had you not better just win it first? Give us one more cross to beat the last defender as he chases for the ball. 'Over 'ere. On me 'ead, son, on me 'ead, on me 'ead, on me 'ead!' Gotta get a grip 'cos this guy knows where the goal is. Back-pedalling, out of puff and out of gear. He's gone! Off and away like a comet, where the posts get larger and the ball gets smaller. Kick it! Kick it! Just - Rattus Norvegicus Anglicanus shoots to the roar of the Arena! It's a dipper and a spinner of a shot! Oh, no! Don't let them lower the crossbar! Don't let me go and miss the -

gggooooooooooooooaaaaaaaaaaaalll!

Wuummp! Ker-rip! His nose popped out and one eye peeped down at a centre circle marked over a glimmer of smooth, grey stones. A small figure standing almost on the halfway line looked up to the rafters where the noise seemed to have come from. Their eyes met.

"Is that you, Oliver? Something told me you would be coming home tonight."

It was the unmistakable voice of the Captain that broke the silence of the candles.

"You always did have your head in the clouds, young man. Have you anything to say for yourself?"

Olly pressed his head further through the torn tarpaulin fabric and, gulping in more air, leaned heavily against the wood of an ancient beam. He looked down in grateful thought.

"Have you considered the idea of one day playing a match on grass? I really think it would be the making of us, sir."

The Light Of Darkness   Chapter 8

It was enough to make you weep. But she wasn't one to shed a tear. No, not her. An ill wind, most generally said to blow no good, had shunted Euradice and her New Model Army from the old year into the new with a blast that showed no sign of any letup. The trail had blown cold and the grand plan continued to look more than modest in its accomplishments. She shuffled into the kitchen where, to her surprise, there was no unwelcome stare to greet her. It was empty. Like herself. Not only was she getting tired of flogging a dead horse, but her chariot's wheels seem to have fallen off, one by one, as well. Like the floundering Pharaoh bent on keeping what didn't belong to him, her progress was impeded at every turn. Not that she allowed herself to dwell on such a chastising scenario. For she wasn't that religious. Was Edward keeping her at arm's length in order to show her *his* power? Nothing had much changed, and she'd ploughed a lonely enough furrow before now. Yet, if the only rat to be smelt was of the suspicious variety, just to think how her reliance on these cats had practically come to be a complete one irritated her intensely. Pah! She shuffled a bit further to where two or three well-scrubbed plastic dishes sat in a row underneath a deep stone sink and eyed them with consternation. Other words sprang to mind. Advice which her long-departed husband had often stated by way of a reminder when it came to business. You had to invest for a while, perhaps a fair while, before you saw a return and eventually got to reap the profits. Business. Lorelei! She'd never had a head for business. Except for the business of spending it, mind. For nearly two months she'd fed her workers with little sign - correction - no sign of any return. Starting them off on packs of cat food had been astronomical for ten on 'em. So she'd soon put a stop to that. Scraps and leftovers were, however, never enough - they looked highly indignant if they didn't get double portions each sitting. Rationing just made them more yowly and rowdy than they already were. Add that to the mortifying, ridiculously sky-high cost of buying them in the first place - with all the running around that had involved! Well! There you had it. Week in week out, throwing good money after bad ever since. And both the good and the bad would presently be turning into something very ugly if she didn't get the results she wanted soon. She never did have the patience of Job, and any similar relief from a divine source didn't look likely to be coming her way in a hurry. It seemed the antiquities man was taking his time, too. Research, it was. Specialist consultants, and everything. The unusual took longer, she supposed. Still, the photograph was genuine enough and a good one for black and white. She was sure that little man had put a cambric hanky or something over the flashbulb, so far as she could remember. Fussy little man in a green, polka-dot bow-tie with a pocket watch-chain showing. She remembered that, as well.

She had wanted so much to touch the golden twists, the etched glass, the black cut stones - but father wouldn't allow it. Oh, no! Had to sneak a furtive finger along its silver rim to feel the smoothness. She snivelled. A cursory glance across into the outhouse revealed the usual random selection of sleeping heads tightly wedged into groins well hidden behind draught excluder tails. She noted the chair further down where the two nasties had made their private and exclusive abode. Burke and Hare she'd nick-named them. They were the only ones who had dared to add their charmless presence to that of the west wing drawing-room. Seeing them clinging on to the dust sheets, lean as vultures waiting for carrion, was enough to spook anyone. Except the rats. More than enough of *them* to stiffen their resolve. The devilish things continued to outwit every useless cat in this ramshackle of a house. One or two may have been foolish, but the rest were no longer so fatalistic. No doubt they had a good deal of help from the menagerie. A *trois*? Or was it *quatre*? She sniffled. Partly out of self-pity and partly from the lingering effects of the bout of damned flu which had laid her low for such a while. If this was Edward's idea of a war, a war of - what was that word he used? Like malnutrition. Trition. Ah, yes: at-trition. To wear your nerve ends away to a frazzle. With nothing to keep you going, it certainly *was* more like malnutrition.

Her blue-powdered eyelids drooped and closed dreadfully like the metallic doors of an alien spacepod. She shivered, then reopened them ever so slightly in case something had been missed. No. Only a life! Borrowed and blue! She put the kettle on and sat by the table, wrapping a woollen scarf more closely around her as she waited for the water to boil. It had gone on too long. Life out in the countryside in the middle of winter was miserable and boring. These confounded draughts everywhere had lowered, not just her morale, but her resistance, too. There was something morbidly pestilential about the air. Again, down to those rats! Any thought of trying to convert this fetid foothill into some semblance of a holistic health retreat seemed just a pipe-dream, way beyond reach as things stood. But she knew what she wanted. Damn the rats! A plague on them! They could all go and hang - rats, cats and everyone else! Rot in hell! Wherever that was, if it wasn't here. She looked up. The kettle began to whistle before any more murderous thoughts could suffocate her. She made the coffee and inspected her face in a small, round retro mirror sitting on the dresser. Drawn and weak. Weakness was vulnerability. She smoothed the lines around her mouth vigorously and followed it up with a hasty rearrangement of some unruly swathes of hair before absently sipping at coffee as black and bubbling as the seething steam of her mind. Nothing could change that. But a rush of air from an unexpected swing of the door (one, though, made with much less force than on a previous torrid occasion) brought about a change that clearly took her by surprise.

It was Cook. She marched in, yet couldn't resist pulling a face on seeing the figure hunched at the table. She was the first to speak.

"Oh, it's you," she said, brushing past her to the dresser in a huff. "Well, you'll 'ave as much business to be here as anyone from now on. As I won't be puttin' up with it no longer."

Euradice knotted her brow into a puzzled frown. What was the foolish woman on about now? She'd dwelt enough on business, sordid as it was, for one day. Cook picked up a folded sheet of paper lying under a large mug and checked its contents again slowly. She popped it into a handbag with more than the usual deliberation and began doing up the lower buttons on the coat she had on. Euradice took another sip, trying hard not to look too inquisitive.

"What I was sayin' was - that I'm a-goin'. Them half-starved cats are gettin' me down. An' I aren't puttin' up with it any more. So you c'n 'ave free run of my kitchen from now on, missus, to do as you please. As you gen'rally do with 'em."

Cook held the bag in front of her with an iron grip. Euradice was now all ears, although rather wishing instead to know what the note had to say. She sat back and gave a weak smile. No need to throw any verbal hand grenades today.

"Surely not. As bad as all that?" she replied with the most amenable voice she could muster.

"Ah now, them little uns, bless 'em, aren't too bad, but they're an unruly lot, gen'rally speakin'. When I thinks that they're all here contrairy to mister Edward's desires. Not that he wishes them bad in any way, mind. Well, not most of 'em, 'cept for them

225

mean-lookin' ones - which you declared you never brought here in the first place."

Cook carefully eyed her master's sister as that deceptive woman gave an insipid yawn. Euradice resumed, and then maintained, her weakly placid expression.

"I didn't. As I've told you several times before. You must excuse me, Mrs Dains, as I am not yet fully over this - this bug."

The confession was concluded with a short groan, in the hope that a little pity might go a long way. Cook humphed and did up the top button of her outsize raincoat, which made her look slightly more slovenly than she ever did normally. Be that as it may, what she now had in mind to state would be better shaped and of a much tighter fit.

"Ah, but you let 'em in, anyways. An' a deal of trouble they 'ave caused. An' there you go worryin' yourself about a few rats. Rats or no rats, them cats of yours need to occupy their selves with less aggressive expectashuns. Get 'em out an' about in the open as the days gets better an' lighter. Not moochin' an' mopin' under everyone's feet. As for those of us wishin' for better 'ealth, well, feelin 'appy is a good way to start. We can't add not a cubit to our life span by bein' worriers. So I ain't goin' to let these cats get *me* down. Out of sight is out of mind. An' I've decided to leave you to it till mebbe you sees a bit of sense. Besides, the 'airs on our heads are all numbered, so to speak. An' so's my time, missus, talkin' to you."

With that she plonked the bag on the table and

made up an efficient headscarf.

"An' I aren't the only one agitated this mornin', missus," she went on, in flat contradiction of her previous intent. "While you've been a-lyin' a-bed, Mr Pale's been an' gone off 'ome, too."

Euradice brightened ever so slightly on hearing this.

"Why? I can't think that the cats ever troubled him since the day they arrived," she said with just a hint of her revived inquisitiveness. "Is it the flu as well, then?"

Cook shook her head vigorously.

"Oh no, no. None o' that. Not Mr Pale. Robust 'e is. It's Mrs Pale it is who's in a state. You see, today's her golden weddin' anniversary. An' Mr Pale agreed with Mrs Pale they would be havin' somethin' special like put on. A barn dance was what she wanted with all their friends. His sister it was who says she wants to hire the village hall an' arrange for' th' food. Anyhow, this sister goes an' gets a bout of the flu, like yourself, an' there's us thinkin' she'd booked th' hall for Saturday - which is today. Which it turns out the stupid collop of a woman han't done no such thing. Forgets ev'rythin'. So yesterday I says to Mr Pale just you leave it to me. I 'ave an idea to save the occasion 'as the 'all was already since bin taken for a bric-a-brac fair or some such. I'll get Mr Edward to let us use the old ballroom upstairs. Which 'e is 'appy to agree to. Just needs a spot of polishin' up on the floor and table an' then things will go on a treat, 'e says. So I says I can do a bit of food, an' Mr Pale can polish up the room in the mornin'."

Cook gathered her breath at this point and took up her bag again.

"Very astute of you, Mrs Dains," said Euradice, wondering how this fitted in with her not staying on.

"Yes, I'm sure it was, till las' night." Here Cook picked up her bag and carefully wiped a few crumbs from the table. "Till that daft Mavis Marcomb, realisin' what she's done, or rather not done, comes snivellin' her apologies to Mrs Pale who weren't s'posed t' know anythin' 'ad gone wrong. There she gets in a state as if nothin' could console her. Mr Pale don't want her to know about them all a-comin' 'ere as a sort of surprise, see. Then he comes to me an' says he'll 'ave to keep his eye on her tomorrer in case she takes to drinkin' th' sherry an' then she'll be in no fit state for dancin' later. Give me the keys an' you stay 'ome, I says. What will the master say he asks? No point nor need to be botherin' yourself about that, I says, as I shows 'im th' note as I 'ave just put in 'ere. Mr Edward insists you takes th' day off with Mrs Pale as it's your big day and leave the rest to me, it says. As for Mr Edward, e's gone off early this mornin' with Miss Harriet to watch some important football match it seems, an' won't be back till latish. 'E apologises for not sayin' about it before, but don't reely think 'e'll get back afore we're finished."

If every cloud should have a silver lining, then, with each additional piece of information, the clouds slowly lifting from Euradice protracted brow now looked to be mingled with gold, dispersed by the softening rays of a similarly glorious effulgence. This one-way conversation had begun to lift her fallen spirit and replace it with one of a new intensity.

"It did seem unusually quiet when I came down," she said in a forcedly relaxed tone, hoping that Cook might be kept to chunter on a little longer.

"Mister Edward was up afore any of us, by the look on it. The note says not to worry 'bout the two up in the tower as they're fed and watered. Well, what with Mr Pale leavin' me to all the polishin' all mornin' I aren't 'ad no time for much anythin' else, I can assure you. Some of us 'ave routines to stick by, you see. These cats of yours ain't been fed, neither. I'll leave that to you, missus. I've done my part of a tidy buffet too, an' locked that in the ballroom out of arm's way. So now I'm goin' 'ome to change for the dancin' later. If I can lift a veiny leg arter all my sloggins."

Euradice clasped her equally veiny hand.

"I think you've done splendidly, Mrs Dains. I must confess, you are an inspiration to me."

Never was there a truer word spoken, and honest Cook took it at face value.

"Due thanks, I'm sure. But what I says I still stands by, an' I intend to tell Mr Edward so, as soon as 'e gets back."

Euradice looked reflective.

"Leave the cats to me. Most have gone back to sleep anyway. But you are right. Some of 'em do need a change of scene, and I have to concede that my aims for Brokehill may, perhaps, have been - er - a little too high. I've been lying in my bed doing a lot of thinking, Mrs Dains."

She had. But any such thoughts had been more unfruitful by far than any she'd been considering during the past two minutes.

"Glad to hear you talk a bit o' sense. P'raps the flu 'as given you more than enough time for a rethink."

"Yess. A change would do me some good, I believe. I fear you are right about the cats. They must be disbanded. Nothing good has come from keeping them cooped up to no avail. I should like to contribute to Mrs Pale's special day, if I may. In fact, I should like to offer two of the younger ones as a gift to Mrs Pale and her unfortunate sister-in-law. If the gesture is viewed as acceptable, that is."

She looked about as contrite as a felon who, having apparently seen the error of his ways, was keeping any lingering preference for them very much to himself. The teeth of her impressionable youth had been cut upon all the City Mile spivs, swindlers and mountebanks she had come across from her courting days. To lie between them now did no more than put such admirable tutelage to good use. Cook, though, had been looking down at her gloves, which she now flexed while weighing up what was being proposed.

"Hmm. Can't see no 'arm in givin' some of them little uns an 'ome. Bring 'em up. A few heys an' chains might cheer you up a bit, too."

"I used to jive at the Hammersmith *Palais* in my younger days. Bit out of touch with anything else."

"Oh, well, come up for a spot o' socialisin' an' a drink or two to get you back in touch, then. Your brother will be surprised an' no mistake when e' sees

230

the change in you."

Euradice positively flushed at the thought of this prospective spiritual conversion and tried hard to keep her eyes from reverting to the bag on the table.

"I'm sure you'll not feel so ill-used after tonight, either, Mrs Dains," she lied with an attractive and well-rehearsed lightness of voice.

"Used up I am already. Anyways, I can't stand here all day, as time's gettin' on. Six o' clock we've planned for, so I'm off. Else I'll never get back to open up for 'em all."

With that Cook squeezed her generous frame through the door and was gone.

Euradice, alone again, began to rat-a-tat the rim of the cup with her spoon with a coolness of mind that would have floored a polygraph had she been wired up to one at that particular moment. Options and intrigue. The opposition were only as good as the weakest link in the chain. A babbling bladder of a woman! This was the chance to snap it, a chance that wouldn't come again quite so conveniently. A golden opportunity, if ever there was one. There always had been more than one way to rob a bank. Horses for courses. A rôle for Mr Quills and those boys of his, and then, oh yes, *then*, something for her and those other predators to smile about later. She tried out a grateful smile several times with the help of the retro mirror, and followed it with a ready-made sneer by no means so weakly executed, before she rose with new vigour to prepare the gleaming dishes for three hungry cats.

Analogous to the fiery course of the famous comet once tracked from the balcony of the Brokehill ballroom, the dazzling reputation of Mr Quills had long ago reached its zenith and was now seen to be heading steadily into observable decline. There was a strong suspicion, too, that, unlike the comet, its captivating display of bravado might not be coming round again in a hurry, but go sputtering off into permanent oblivion. Not even all the distinguished stripes of a Bengal tiger could presently have inspired his 'boys' out of the irreducible tedium that lay as a pall over everyone in the outhouse. Like a pacemaker dropping away from a field of front runners, Mr Quills's generally racy enthusiasm was all too rapidly beginning to go on the wane. It was not helped by the fact that dinner-time no longer provided the former succulent offcuts from the roasted bone, and had not, for that matter, delivered much else since. Though no clock-watcher himself, his partner Cubshaw's natural sense of punctuality pained him more than usual on this Saturday afternoon as he consulted it through the half-open door of the kitchen. At Mr Quills' insistence he made another test of the air inside. Both showed up very badly in his estimation.

"Gone four, sir, and there's not a scrap in sight," he said, at pains to maintain an unassuming air over the plight they found themselves in.

"Come, come, man. Not even an opened can of anything?"

"Can, sir?"

"Surely a bit of biscuit or something?"

"Not a smidgeon, sir. Of anything, I assure you."

"Then things are looking decidedly odd, Cubshaw. Anyway, how do you know the woman was here with Cook at lunchtime, if you were asleep?"

"Cos Arty boy was watching," an unexpected voice shouted back from further up the room. "This door and the other from the kitchen were locked, in case you're wondering," said Gus, throwing his ragged glance at the nearest door, but remaining motionless.

"And where has that - hum - precious fellow disappeared to now?" asked the little General.

Cubshaw realised he was going to need all the long-suffering and philosophical tact he could muster.

"Out, sir, I believe. With - ahem! - Scrounger and the Nameless One. They left through the kitchen ages ago. I don't wish to sound like a stuck record, but though provisions have drastically subsided into what I would term as - ahem – less than ration levels, at least we do have a roof over our heads."

"So you've reminded me on and off. And is it all we can do? To sleep, Cubshaw?"

"Sleep is a great suppressor of hunger, sir, in its way," returned his friend delicately.

"Dang me, man, if I can put up with any more of all this carry-on. Where *is* the woman? Why did *they* get to go afield and not any of us?"

Mr Quills looked down at himself, from his dust-laden paws to the dullness of his once-sleek trim, and felt as if he'd been no better than roughing it in some back alley dustbin with little more than an increasingly grubby dignity left to lose. Boswick, on the other hand, felt he had nothing left to lose in making his own comments known.

"If you must know, they had a five-star nosh-up with a gallon or so of the gold top to wash it down. Just don't ask *me* why! Such is life!" he railed in a distant voice.

Gus added his usual sneer and hoped the facts hurt. They did. Immensely. No breakfast and, now, no lunch. The way it looked, no supper was about to become a not so illogical assumption to make. In the absence of anything to do or eat the youngsters had tired themselves out from aimless games of flip and spin and were still asleep on the rugs where they had eventually fallen in a heap. Cubshaw could only sigh at the unruly state things had reached and returned to his place beside his dumbfounded companion who, for once, was lost for any further words on the whole business. To sleep or to watch the door was all there was worth doing. Another half-hour of pondering went by.

"I mean, what *have* we done to deserve this?" came the final response of delayed thought processes on the part of Mr Quills.

"It's quite possibly what we haven't done, sir," said Cubshaw through closed eyes.

"And to think we used to enjoy such memorable week-ends!" was all Mr Quills could say to console himself, duly closing his own to remember them all the better. Having taken the events (or rather, non-events) of the day so badly, he was simply left with what he truly believed he did the best. To rally. Keep the juices of optimism flowing, even if the gastric ones could not just now be stimulated. If rallying be the food of optimism - shoulder on! Let's hear it for the boys! Emboldened by these stimulating thoughts, he stood up and was about to open his mouth when an unexpected clatter of the door opened it for him - in no little amazement.

Standing on the threshold stood a portly old woman wearing a long, crumpled gown cut like an outsize tablecloth and dotted with various pink birds of paradise perched at every angle but the correct one. Beside her, a gangly man with a greasy fringe of blackish hair lurched sideways, pointing an unsteady finger in the general direction of the cats, who had all awoken with a start. A third person was jumping up and down and trying hard to push a way between the pair. A slightly fuddled Cook was dumpily decked out in an overblown dress of dark green with garish pink ribbons sprouting from fat bare arms and topped off with an equally globular setting of pearl necklace. To Mr Quills it looked like a scene from one of the pantomimes he'd seen put on at her Ladyship's. An excess of rouge and powder that only lacked a bucket or two with a hole.

"Alright, alright. You've 'ad your bit o' fun. Now you'd better get up there with the rest on 'em. Afore th' lady gets down to pick th' ones she wants. A right c'llection, aren't they, though?"

The woman addressed had her own more immediate

matters to attend to.

"Lor, don't you lean on me like that, you great slope of a lulu. An' don't think you can drink me under th' table so's you won't 'ave to count the steps and the change-overs proper."

She pushed her partner aside and made some space for Mrs Dains, hiccupping behind her hand at the same time. That practical woman, sensing that the evening was beginning to show, turned on the light.

"Mrs Pale's sherry 'as made you worse for wear, I do b'lieve, Vera. P'raps a bite to eat an' a nice drop of hot tea or a coffee will settle you better."

She took her friend's arm and held on as if they were about to weave through a routine together.

"Now I looks at 'em, it don't seem as they've eaten a morsel between 'em. Or swallowed a good drink of - of - somethin' tingly," stated Vera tipsily, clutching Cook's wrist with her other hand. The tall man drooped his head like an overwrought tulip caught in a fierce gale. He had tried to count the number of cats scattered about, but lost his focus (as well as his fingers) after three blurry attempts.

"Wat she doin', then? 'Bout to be baggin' a gaggle o' bad ratters, is she? Spare a babby or two, an' chuck the rest into a lake or up river. Dredge the Dadge an' it'd spew out a few moggy skellies, I'd wager. Ain't doin' it tonight, by any chance, is she?"

"The only drowndin' you'll see is you in your drink, an' you won't see much o' that neither if you carry on wi' such devilment talk, you lean old goat, you!"

Cook's cheeks were puffing and shining as glazed as

Chelsea buns straight out of a hot oven. The man girned a gargoyle's face and poked another gruesome corkscrew of a finger at Cubshaw before the women pulled him away. He staggered out into the kitchen and sat down on a chair to teehee like a naughty, inebriated child. Cook twisted her pearl string and felt foolishly bad for having allowed the couple a preview of the poor creatures. Mr Quills kept an accusing and unblinking eye on her, which made her feel guilty and hurt for all the mixed feelings she had had about tolerating them. She shut the door and ushered the equally sozzled Vera back to the table.

"She ent goin' t' do nothin' of the sort. Not to these little uns, if I can help it. If we've made a sort of a peace, then, we should try an' keep it that way."

Cook's sense of moral obligation and tenderness hadn't altogether deserted her during this early start to the evening's fun. She might let her hair down with a tipple or two, but not her heart. She'd leave the kitchen light on for them before she left with her friends.

"I'll make sure there's some chicken an' bits of ham for all on 'em when we're finished dancin' an' eatin' ourselves out of house an' hardship. We'd better get up to th' others, Vera. With an arm each we'll get him onto that dance floor just 'bout in one piece, I reckon."

As the footsteps retreated, Mr Quills cushioned his deflated chest across folded paws in a study of grave misgiving. There were some strange customers in this house and their unsavoury remarks were unsettling to say the least. He turned wearily to Cubshaw.

"Do you think she's capable of murder, then?"

"That woman might well be capable of anything in desperate situations, I do believe, sir. However, whether she's finally arrived at this particular edge, I wouldn't like to say. We can only hope her present behaviour is merely a lapse from the - er - conventional state of things"

"Nothing's normal on this evidence. It would be one explanation as to why we're being starved - to death, man. "

Cubshaw was about to remark that truth was very often stranger than fiction, when the door spun wide again and three more familiar faces barged their way into the outhouse with all the swaggering unison of the renown musketeers. As the Amber Eye strode past, Gus leapt to his feet and stood his ground to demand answers all round.

"You all look very pleased with yourselves." He certainly sounded more than comparatively disgusted with his lot. "Well? So, what game is going on here?"

The Amber Eye stopped and whispered in his ear in his mysterious, ashen tone.

"Birds. And nest eggs, my friend," before continuing to his personal chair, grinning, just as mysteriously, to himself.

"Bin up to th' old disused barn at th' back, along of Artichoke, 'ere," added Scrounger as he followed quickly behind. "The lady was 'avin' a snoop around while the old un's not at 'ome."

Arturo seemed delighted with the developments of

the day and was deliberately slow to enter or to acknowledge the others as he squirmed inside, licking his lips tenderly.

"Bin limberin' up, so to speak, lads. More derrin'-dos on their way, if I read things right," said Scrounger, showing more than the usual amount of torn ear as he made himself comfortable. "For most of us," he added with a dire wink.

The others looked at him subdued more from curiosity than by the oppression of present hunger. That he did read things correctly was soon made clear with another more familiar bang of the door. The mistress of her Remodelled Army came in with two large, empty shopping bags under her arm. Cubshaw shut his eyes in a horror of disbelief as Mr Quills dug his once-noble, now nibbled claws into the cushion by way of indignant protest. To no avail. Euradice took him by the scruff of the neck and, on brandishing an equally large brush, combed as much dust and hidden grime from his coat as half a dozen purposeful strokes could reasonably accomplish. Before he could lower himself into making a fruitless dash for safety, she repeated the action for the grim-faced Cubshaw and dropped him, along with his distraught general, inside one of the bags. The limp sisal handles were tied together into an over-complicated knot and the bag left to stand on the floor like a week's full shopping. She then turned her attention to the other bag and gave it a systematic plump.

"And now for the offerings," she said, quickly doing

the same for the three youngsters, now wide-awake and wide-eyed from all the commotion. Gus and Boswick, sitting further in the shadows, were seemingly overlooked, and thus, to their combined relief, spared a similar fate. Too startled to run, they watched warily as the younger cats were carefully dropped, one by one, into the other bag before the handles were similarly tied thereafter. Scrabbling for air, it was only now that Cubshaw noticed what the woman was wearing. A thick, swirling skirt and a heavy sweater. And gloves. All in black. She beamed and dusted her hands in her usual symbol of self-satisfaction. She pointed darkly at Arturo and his co-workers.

"Phase two begins here. So keep on the alert for my return. Just be ready to go over the top!"

The old terminology was not lost on Arturo, but this time he looked pleased and no less eager for more action. Heaving the bags off the floor his mistress swung round and pulled the door to behind her as best she could. It was now past six. And up they went, each prized offering striving for a clearer view, as she climbed the stairs without variation to her normal pace, which was medium fast. For time, like her objective, was a very precious thing. Three of the smaller heads clung to the sides of their bag, bobbing and ducking at every turn as it weaved to and fro like a funfair roller coaster on its journey up to the north wing peak. In the left hand bag Cubshaw made a very good impression of a balloon spotter by balancing his toes on the neck of a distraught Mr Quills as he gave up his uncomfortable struggle to gain substantially more of the breathing space than was available.

"So where are we now, Cubshaw?" gasped the little general, after a minute's silence. The bumpy ride was as stuffy as it was unnerving.

"It appears we are on course for the ballroom, sir, if my sense of direction from a previously aborted visit is anything to go by."

"Seems an interminably long way to meet our end. Like being driven pell-mell through a maze of streets, Swiftly to hell in a handcart, and all that."

"Tumbrel, sir. You always were rather taken by those historical volumes of her Ladyship's. If anything, it's more to hell in a handbag in our case."

As they reached the ballroom a drone of hearty chatter, interspersed by high-pitched laughter and an occasional scream, could be heard coming from within. Euradice stopped and knocked tamely at the door, then, lowering a bag, opened it herself, before anyone had any chance to shout 'come in'. All of a sudden her burdens felt remarkably heavy, and she looked distinctly weakened by the task of having dragged them all the way upstairs in her present condition. A pair of freshly rouged lips began moving towards her in due sympathy.

"Ah, yus missus. 'Twas back-breakin' enough shiftin' my Norman up them steep stairs. Mrs Dains'll vouch for that, an' she do 'ave some strong arms of 'er own an' all."

"You do go on with such nonsense, Vera. Give th' lady them two chairs at th' end there."

Tucked in resplendently at the top of a long table, Cook's face shone as rosily as the well-polished surface of the wood she had lately buffed up. Mr Pale, who, with Mrs Pale at his side, had been in the process of toasting their guests with nothing stronger than iced lemonade, gave Euradice an odd stare as he made a space for the chairs. Dressed in a Sunday suit two or three sizes too large, he took the hand of his beloved wife of fifty years, as she stood up with difficulty in a rosebud dress that appeared to be two or three sizes too unspeakably small.

"As I was saying, being a man of few words, and which can be said in no time at all, fifty years seems to me to be just as short and as sweet. Too short for the love we have enjoyed in this our place. Cheers to my dearest and to all them who have sailed - and continue to sail - with us here at Brokehill." He included Euradice in a bold bow as she sat expressionless with one of the bags on her lap. "And, ladees and gen'lemen, may it ever be so."

All clapped heartily. There followed a small cheer from the ladies opposite as Mavis Marcomb unsuccessfully prevented the drooping Norman from burying his head in her side plate with a paper napkin for a pillow. Cook took up a bottle of Mr Pale's home-made elderberry wine, several of which had been provided for this especial occasion.

"Methinks a glass of this would do very nicely, as we needs to eat somethin' afore any dancin' is begun. Leastways, I do, considerin' as I 'ave worked meself into a famishment most of this day."

The bottle was opened and glasses went all round. Cook almost forgot her visitor as the first mouthful gave her a sharp smack. Then she remembered the cats.

"Let me introduce you all to the lady who 'as just come up with a surprise or two for us. You may bene-fit, too, Mavis Marcomb, if them inquisitive eyes of yours keep to their proper place. Mr Edward's sister, may you be welcome among friends and relatives of Mr an' Mrs Pale. So you may as well take 'em out now, if you like, missus. A glass of the wine will perk you up a bit yourself, too."

"Yerss, we likes to see the babbies 'fore ye thinks of taking 'em off to a dark an' lonely place whar they gets to be wor - wor - warter babbies."

It was the only barely coherent sentence likely to emerge from tall Norman's slurred and slow-witted mouth for the rest of the evening. Euradice took a full glass and sipped it graciously before giving her audience a fractured smile. She took out the three cats and presented them in profile to the curious onlookers. Her sales talk had been in full flow by the time both sides of the table had taken careful notice. The youngsters blinked rapidly against the bright light overhead before staring avidly at the serving platters of chicken drumsticks and portions of pork and ham pie laid out in a pile at the centre of the table. The company. especially the women, made positive noises with looks of sympathy in their appreciation. Euradice put on her equally gracious smile and consulted her watch from the corner of a cunning eye. With a sly toss of courage coursing down her bejewelled throat she untied the other bag beside her, then went on sipping and biding her most valuable time.

*　　　　　*　　　　　*

"Dunno why you've dragged me all the way down here."

The questioner glared up at the ponderous purple shadows that were gathered around him with a distinct lack of appreciation. Boswick edged forward until his whiskered cheek rubbed sensitively against an untried door.

"Better than my eyes, when I'm like this."

He made a sensitive dab at them, then turned nervously to his reluctant companion. Each waited for the other to make the next move.

"Well, go on! If you want to go in, go in."

The patch of Down Under reared a fraction, with a good deal of Pacific impatience showing with the indecision.

"It's probably shut, anyway. Most of 'em are locked, and as for the rest, well, it's as good as makes no difference. Covered or not. Empty. It's the same old story."

Boswick tried shaking the gloom from his charcoal head a few times and looked despairingly to the ceiling, desperately in need of some silent support.

"Now I know why a flea never jumps on you, Gus. It's the negative vibes you give off. Look, we may be damned if we do, or damned if we don't, but if you can just quit throwing in objections every five minutes, then perhaps, just perhaps, we can pull something off for a change. Just be thankful she had her hands full and didn't shut *our* door. We can use this chance to our advantage."

Ungrateful for this curt psychiatric assessment of himself, Gus turned and kept half a sullen eye on the top step of the short flight they had just descended. He didn't do emotion or elation, just frustration. He heard another muffled reminder of voices, voices up there having a fair old time, he'd bet on it. With plenty to eat.

"Alright, show me the goodies, Bossy, and I'm with you all the way," he said resignedly by way of a muted encouragement.

Boswick blinked the moisture of uncertainty from his unfocused eyes like a squeeze of a lemon and applied a fresh nudge to the door with more than usual force. It opened slowly.

"Well, how about that! It may be our turn tonight, after all. It stands to reason, if there's food up there. Let's face it, they won't be able to resist the possibilities that presents. I have this gut feeling we'll find a rat or two sniffing around in here. A dead rat would go a long way in proving we're no bit-part players simply to be ignored. We can turn the corner, you'll see."

"I do see - straight ahead." said Gus. "Though getting a severed head between your teeth might be a messy business in this dark."

"Ok, thanks for the slate," replied the would-be assassin in a coarse whisper, "let's just cut the misery, Gus. You make sure *your* marbles are sharp and go for it."

If the darkness outside had been predictable, the one inside was not. The permanence of night seemed to be mulled with a glow of some impermanent, ethereal light. An oak dining table, similar to the one in the room above, declared its generous length with a soft, sheeny parallel ray of understated reflection. And there was something more.

"Hang on a second. What's *she* doing here?"

Gus checked his partner and steered him to one side. His words were as incisive as his keenly-receptive eyes. Boswick flinched and blinked dumbly. A "who?" and a "where?" came in shorter breaths, as he looked high and low about him - everywhere bar the end of the table straight ahead. If there are ghostly footsteps that wander through passages, and apparitions that glide through walls, then, perhaps there are others that do neither. Those that linger in the choicest place and have no need to roam the evening hours afar.

"Over there, you blindbod!" Gus hissed, redirecting Boswick's head to the spot with the lightest of taps. "I thought you said she'd gone off out for the day. Of all of the places we had to pick, we had to go and pick this one. Now what?"

Boswick merely gave an uninspiring chuckle of surprise. Gus expressed his unalloyed annoyance with a silent puff from his speckled cheeks, and followed it up with the usual, though in this instance, unseen jeer to himself. For over there lay a thing of beauty: whose sleeping head spread a mournful canopy of long, wavy black curls over gently folded arms. The unopened, unseeing eyes were veiled perhaps by still subtler ghosts - the kind that peered from the windows of a haunted soul. Boswick was determined to remain upbeat and take this strange scenario in his stride. He patted steadily at the thick, patterned rug on which they stood, as though checking out the quality of the weave. A thread was, nevertheless, loosened by a nervous retraction.

"Yes, well, we mustn't start pressing any panic buttons too soon. Patience is our key, Gus. At least she hasn't noticed we're here."

"Oh, right, then." Gus ran a moisturising tongue around his pursed, dried lips. "I've waited all day for grub which never came my way, and now you're asking me to do pretty much the same for half the night. P'raps *you* haven't noticed - she's asleep. All this pussyfooting around of ours comes to nothing if her forty winks turns into a hundred or more."

The darkness around her seemed to have ingrained every detail of the room, with every possible sound soaked away into its insulation. Save for the wispy hue which hung about the girl's head like a fantasy of a headdress. Intuitively sensing that this scheme of theirs wasn't looking too bright, Gus couldn't resist having one more dig at its all-too-apparent craziness.

"Maybe she's not going to the shindig upstairs. Or maybe some of these rats we're after will simply turn up and join her here. Y' know, wave around a few stubs of candle of their own. The sort of taunt you'd expect from 'em for all the support they've enjoyed so far. Catch us if you can, an' all that!"

He spat what little he'd saved up into a dark region behind him.

Beware for what you whisper -
whether in jest or in disgust!

For with the snatch of a careless word and the blink of a mocking eye, the hazy glow of the room dissolves. And in its place, shredding the dark with its bewitching flow, a helter-skelter of soft light slowly wraps around the motionless figure like the silken ribbon of a rhythmic gymnast. With the *pas seul* of a maiden's foot she begins to float, as in a sea dream, dancing in mournful circles along the fluorescent table. Her dark eyes, sometimes mischievous, and sometimes malign, are always mysterious: where betrayal and despair are both locked away - like love's unposted letters - never to be read. Certainly not by other eyes tonight. Least of all by those of straying cats who stare back as guilty witnesses of something that perhaps they ought not to be seeing. But they go unnoticed. For the maiden dances to another audience, one whose reciprocal shadows clap their approval in a magic lantern of ghostly applause upon the wall opposite. Yet if one pair of cat's eyes are left to spin like a top, the other's have thankfully proved themselves not only to be doubly discriminating but, thankfully, supremely scotopic.

"Look!"

Gus nudged Boswick firmly in the ribs and pointed with horror to the floor below where the girl had been sitting. Something grisly was crawling up the table leg like a train of rustling black crinoline. Boswick, rigid in the blaze of a trance, mechanically lowered his head a few degrees to gaze upon a sequence of seductive movements that ebbed and flowed between the folds of the girl's sweeping skirt. Greyish contours of ears, backs and tails could be clearly traced within the silvery footlights of her invisible dancing feet.

"Rats!" whispered Gus hoarsely, digging his claws into the carpet at his own feet. "But wrong rats!" Wrong time! Wrong place! And wrong girl, too! he might have added.

"Look at their eyes!"

Frustration's anger seemed to have momentarily distilled his own wretched fear down to its last drop. The whole place was a cock-eyed carnival, one he wished he'd never been forced to set foot in it. The visible walls flickered more madly than ever as the dance began to speed up into a dervisher's delight. A silent shadowy scraping of violins, with a see-sawing of bows, arms, necks and elbows, began rising faster, faster, faster in a frenzied reel of screechless, speechless accompaniment. The dark eyes of the mesmerising dancer were now deathly closed. Gus again poked his partner-in-failure urgently in the ribs, as if to wake him further from his stupor. The action seemed to work sufficiently for a few seconds as

Boswick peered ever more intently with a rekindled state of alarm.

"Eyes? They - they - don't have any, do they? They seem to be -"

Robotic comforters. Minute hollows of skull-socketed nothingness had become her glitter-free guides.

"Exactly! Blind as bats! And so will we be, if we don't get out of here in a hurry!"

A crescendo of silent strings soared to the ceiling before the phantasm, as suddenly and abruptly as the music, ceased. The room was dark once more, and all else was gone without a trace. Gus, with his ears prickling uncontrollably, took his cue and swung out a telling scoop of a paw to bowl Boswick heavily backwards towards the door. And, in a few bounds of blind panic, they, too, were gone without a trace. To slink back down into an outhouse: with their bellies still empty, but with their heads mightily full - of food for thought.

★   ★   ★

"Where are we Cubshaw?"

Mr Quills wriggled free from his insufferable position and breathed more easily again.

"On a chair, sir."

"Yes, yes, man. I can see that. But *where* are we?"

"I think, if you care to look up and screw an eye, you may observe from the plaster embellishments along the coving and the finely-tiered chandelier over there - that we have reached our destination - er - which is indeed the ballroom, sir.

"A tasteful enough place to meet our end, at any rate, don't you think? So, where are the boys, Cubshaw?"

"Please, sir, I would rather you didn't keep harping on that supremely depressing aspect of your - "

The reply was brusquely cut short as a bony hand suddenly lifted him up firmly by the nape of the neck and dumped him without further ado onto the table, where he skidded about like a first-time skater unable to keep his feet. Before he'd even had time to look at the space vacated, Mr Quills very quickly joined him in his humiliation. Euradice got hold of each of them by the scruff and propped them on the table in the manner of an impatient auctioneer laying out a pair of battered Steiff teddies for prospective bidders.

"Of course, if any of you here would prefer an older, more mature specimen - see here. These two have a -um- more sedate disposition, one which some of us take to more easily. A *very* trustworthy combination."

Cubshaw seemed to bridle at the word 'specimen'. Mr Quills, ignoring the roughness of his handler, saw to his horror that two of their boys were being ominously held up for inspection - by the dark stranger and the woman in the red war paint. Only Squealy had not yet been selected by anyone and he only had eyes for one thing (or rather, a number of things) as he moved, unsteadily, but surely, towards the plates.

251

"Look, Cubshaw. Those people again. Is this some kind of ceremony I see before me? Can't we do something to save Squealy from their clutches!"

But his second-in-command had already made a quicker inspection, as he beheld the distracting selection of cooked meats and pies spread out before him like some timely mirage. Cook, alert to the danger at once, shouted as Squealy closed in on the drumsticks. There was a commotion as somebody reacted and stuck out a hand to push the plate back up the table, as luck would have it, straight into the path of a startled Mr Quills. The pile of chicken came to a halt right under his nose, with as many leg-ends pointing up and beckoning to him as he could ever have dared to imagine in his recent dreams.

"Do my eyes deceive me, Cubshaw? Or is this some kind of gruesome trick?"

"I don't think you'll find it's intended for our general consumption, sir, and, if I were you, I would strongly resist the urge to - "

For a second time he found himself unable to complete a warning sentence, before Mr Quills had instinctively pressed his paws into the front row of chicken thighs. The hesitation of disbelief was just enough for Euradice to make her move. She might have waited much longer for the chance to create a diversion, but this one was going to be as good as any other. With the perfect excuse presenting itself on a plate, as it were, she had every reason to hope her starving shock troops would play the part designed for them. On contriving a look of genuine alarm, she brought her arm down to the edge of the plate and, in the pretence of trying to shake off Mr Quills' tenuous grip on it, gave the plate one almighty shove, trusting to the work of the well-polished table to complete her wicked aim.

No shoved two pence coin ever flew with such high-speed accuracy. But not before Cubshaw had taken a despairing leap aboard to land on top of the pile with great aplomb. The extra weight seemed to make no difference, however, and with Mr Quills still clinging on at the end they sped down the table like a two-man bobsleigh. Before any of the guests could intervene, the plate had shunted into the pies, scattering several of them into several laps, as well as launching plenty of glasses of wine into high, undrinkable space. A spray of the best elderberry fizzled into Mavis Marcomb's nose, which made her cry, gasp and sneeze all in one go. Squealy corkscrewed and spun out of the way - just in time to punch his airborne paws through a generous chocolate gateau handily placed to break his fall The sandwiches were next to go, before the conveyor belt of disaster reached its end and a composite cascade of egg and cress, pies, Cubshaw, Mr Quills and the chicken descended on Cook as she sat frozen in a state of shock. Her chair tilted and swayed, before gravity finally opted for an indecorous landing. The buffet flew about in all directions, leaving only the little general and his subordinate at its epicentre, sprawled in a heap across her stomach on the empty plate. Diggles jerked free and chased after a drumstick which had bounced away from the mêlée, off on a journey of its own. Bedlam reigned before anyone else could get to their feet. Euradice's reactions were, needless to say, by far the fastest, as she darted straight to the scene of the crash and made a grab for the cats. She saw the handbag lying unscathed beside the chair, and, in a few more deft moments, she was up and away. And so was the key to the cellar she craved.

There was only one bag returning this time, and the journey back was to be a fast and bumpy one. Not that this was any more of a distraction for its tempest-tossed passengers within.

"Splendid texture to this meat, don't you think, Cubshaw?"

His companion found it awkward to make any eye contact under the present jaw-dropping circumstance and went on chewing with a greater degree of discrimination before making a reply.

"If you're referring to the pie, sir, it is indeed exceptional. It is encased in a formidable lining of jelly to make it a gastronomic delight."

He felt another unseen piece of pie, or perhaps a leg, prodding against his left shoulder as the bag went into a sharp turn and began to go through the bumpy motions of descent.

"No, I'm referring to these chicken thighs," said Mr Quills, munching on without letup.

"Legs, sir. Can't say I've come to one of them yet, though. We're now heading downwards, in case you hadn't noticed."

"What exactly was all that about, Cubshaw? I mean

the idea of washing her hands of us, then, next thing, we're eating supper inside a shopping bag. Really!"

Mr Quills located another meaty portion and, assuming it wasn't his partner's, began attacking it as ferociously as any last meal he might have on earth. Cubshaw braced himself, mentally counting, as the jolts increased in their regularity.

"I have a sneaking suspicion that we were rather being led up the garden path," he said at last. "I don't wish to be alarmist, sir, but she pushed that plate for all it was worth."

"Humph! If you're suggesting this whole business was staged, I take it she didn't leave the boys behind? Eh?"

Mr Quills stopped eating and tried to catch Cubshaw's eye, but he was facing the wrong way and another violent swerve made it even worse. His subordinate swallowed a stub of pork.

"Who knows? If she has decided to cut her losses, she may have. We were out of that door in a flash, though I'm certain she locked it behind her. She had no intention of overstaying her welcome."

"What! Do you mean they're up there with those people? And why is she in such a devil of a hurry?"

"Probably. Cook will deal with it. She's been very just with us, to be frank. We must take the rough with the smooth, sir. As we always have. As to the hasty departure - your guess is as good as mine."

The rocking ceased. Having survived the smooth, they quickly found themselves back in the rough, as the bag came to land with a thud and toppled onto its side. There was a sound of sharp activity followed by a sharper voice of command before the door slammed and the disoriented duo stumbled out into the familiar weak light of the outhouse. Two pairs of eyes greeted them with astonishment as the substantial remains of the uneaten buffet all but fell out alongside them. Gus and Boswick stared enviously at Cubshaw as he straightened himself and lent Mr Quills a broad arm. They looked around, but found themselves otherwise alone. Boswick licked his lips and pointed to the door.

"They've gone with her. Off like a bad wind."

The little general looked through the slatted glass into the kitchen with consternation written deeply into his face: "For the last time, Cubshaw. Why them?"

Cubshaw pondered for a few moments in order to select his words carefully. Sometimes a listener would understand much more by what was left unsaid.

"I've given it some consideration - from her point of view, that is. It is a kind of demarcation line, sir. They didn't cost her a penny. So, if her fortune is about to change, it - er –rather looks like money for old rope, as it were."

"Malarkey!" Mr Quills shifted his stance. "And making the rest of us look like a rather expensive extravagance. Is that it?".

"I don't know about that, sir," said Cubshaw, eyeing all three of them grimly, "she may, after all, just as easily end up hanging herself with it."

As a word of encouragement it was also as wry a

256

piece of prophecy as could have been foretold.

"So, what've you been up to, meantime, to deserve all this grub?" was all Gus could manage by way of response. Cubshaw regained his composure and stared back before rolling a few chicken legs towards him and Boswick.

"Fraternising with the enemy, if you must know. But you're both welcome to dine on what's left - if you can stomach it."

★   ★   ★

Night had fallen. So, too, had the angel of light with her dark minions in tow. At least for now the eagles were prepared to gather to the hand that fed them; to cut their teeth afresh - on the fleeing flesh of rat. A trembling hand unlocked and slowly descended into another kind of night, though neither were nearly so deep as the darkness of the angel's own soul. A night where a torch, like the waning moon on a sea of impenetrable waves, touched only the surface with a tarnished reflection of its own shallow desire.

Euradice soon began prompting Arturo with an impatient foot as he dithered half-way down the stairs. Scrounger went on ahead, screwing up his nose on passing the spot of his previous painful encounter, while the Amber Eye slunk to the rear, an invisible iron fist floating in a glove of velvet black. The torch flashed up and down, criss-crossing in uncertainty as they reached the bottom. Euradice coughed for the first time since the morning, as the vile fumes of turps

257

and paint grew overpowering. Nothing but a few boxes of tools and all manner of screws and other oddities. There were idle rows of paint pots and a rusted, greenish drum of machine oil to disappoint her in the restricted plane of the light. She had never set foot in the place since that time her mother caught her gargling the half-empty bottles of champagne she had pinched from Jack's awful wedding reception. Better to have been drunk down here as well as anywhere. Soon she'd be drunk with a new exultation. No half measures for her this time. This was the final resting place, alright. Had to be. Where the grime and dust of all the vile and pathetic past had been spirited away. Brokehill's rotten, rotting history decaying in a rattish miasma all of its own. Ugh! Fill it up. Seal it up. No way back for either the rat or the tat! Then the concrete and the clay beneath her feet would never crumble. Not like in the song. That was the way it was meant to be. And let the dead bury their dead.

Arturo wound his tail about the dark edges of her skirt, not quite knowing who to follow first. Euradice looked up and noticed a bare, dusty bulb hanging, shriven like a cursed fig; but no switch. Let there be no more light from you forever more beyond this night! Funny how all those sinister bits she most loved in the old sermons were coming up from an otherwise inarticulate heart. Modernization? Why labour on a gavotte, if you hated dancing? And she more than hated this house right now.

"Don't get under my feet, Arty. Shoo!" Her tone became fiercer. "Over there is your best chance to do some real damage. Now you're in here - seize the ruddy day!"

She flashed the beam again wildly along the walls. God knows what was there that hadn't seen the light of day for many a long year. Cycle frames, a gigantic roller used to flatten the croquet lawn through the sweat of pre-war summers. More of those apple things, and no end of blasted wooden crates, by the look of it. Empty or full? Lots more junk must have been stashed here after Dad died. Edward was always Mummy's boy after that. The true baron of Brokehill she called him. Nothing had to be thrown away. Oh, no. No. Ensconcing himself like some scholarly monk in his tower of strength, and holding up the future with it. Hah! And all she had ever got was a bloody pittance! She swore the words angrily under her breath and hoped her dearly departed heard it. Or the rats. Or the cats. Or anyone who ought to know. She wondered why time always seemed to beat her to everything. Hickory-dickory-dock. Only it was the devil himself running up her clock. To drag her down to this. This damned vault. She lowered the torch to skim it aimlessly over a gravestone floor of submerged secrets.

The Amber Eye and the lesser reddish one passed on, slowly and surely, to comb the dark recesses together. As though expertly negotiating a minefield, they listened for every click or scrape, real or imagined, that might check their stealthy advance. In and out of crate stacks the cat shapes came and went: mini-submarines gliding past rocks in the ocean. But the current of the night, racing along with the time, was flowing against Euradice's uncertain footsteps. Where to begin? To begin a search of a lifetime. Her arm slackened as the torch fell from an unclenched hand. And in a moment the night had blotted out all things. Arturo joined forces with Scrounger down the middle as they both waited for the light - a light which never came. Instead, something cracked in the darkness ahead and caused their hackles to rise and freeze upon their necks A monolithic figure, swaying and swaying – to tear the gloom asunder as it fell to the ground with a splintering crash. There was a shriek as the tall guard disintegrated, and a myriad of unseen poles and staves clanged against an overturned bucket as it rolled away. The cats dived for cover as some of the wooden shafts hit the ground and rebounded back up with unerring force, tripping and trapping them in their frightened flight. Euradice reeled back like a drunkard groping for support, before finally collapsing onto a low crate behind her. Her whole world had begun to fly off in a spin. Then, just as suddenly, it was all over. And on came a light.

"Sorry to have to frighten you like that. But even if you weren't expecting us, we have most certainly been expecting you."

It was Edward, or at least Edward's voice. Blinded by a light much brighter than her own, she had to readjust her focus for several seconds. But there he was, sitting astride a packing case, bathed in a halo of lamplight - with something in his lap whose gleams and reflections only added to the intensity of such a sequestered and sepulchral setting. He drew out a hand and snapped his fingers briskly.

"Right, you two. You can come out now."

From behind the remaining upright sentinel both Harriet and the bloodhound emerged with a look of relieved triumph. She patted the dog, as he sat down to survey his handiwork, or rather, the damage. All the poles were strewn about like a giant throw of mah-jong. So much for the wooden top. No fun for snooping cats, though, either, he thought. Mr Brimble waited for some reaction from his hapless and speechless sister, but there was none. She sat, open-mouthed, like Dracula's daughter, raddled and uncomfortably exposed, all her dreams having turned to dust in an instant. He moved the lamp to one side and looked down for a moment where the object he cradled seemed to hover like the jewel of earth in space. He spoke once again, this time in a calmer tone than before, even as their eyes met in the brightening of the musty gloom.

"This is what you've been searching for, Euradice, isn't it? Now you've found it. But not quite in the way you would have preferred. A thousand turns of the hour-glass might not have brought you any closer were it not for Mrs Dains and the modern convenience of a mobile phone," here he stroked his chin, "and not forgetting to mention a cat or two. Indeed, from our point of view, the intensity of the darkness down here might just as well have been broad daylight."

The irony of someone saying such a thing with

the light of his world radiating between them was not lost on her. There was no sign of her two cats, now cowering in some concealed spot to nurse tenderer ones of their own. But if vengeance was a dish best served cold, nothing could conceal the claim of the third one as it took advantage of the lull: to hurtle forward with the force of a black torpedo and plunge through the gap vacated by the fallen warrior. A venomous smile formed over the face of Euradice as she watched the Amber Eye (lately the apple of her own) slashing at the curtain's folds with a demon's delight until it was rent apart. He burst through into the tunnel with a fiery speed that, for once, caught the staunch old bloodhound out of position. Three human shadows swam together on the ceiling in the uncanny light, but no one moved an inch.

"What's have you got in there?"

Euradice found her voice at last as the upper hand seemed, in a moment, to have been regained. Her brother looked so provokingly relaxed despite his defences having just been unexpectedly breached.

"Not now, Euradice. Another day, perhaps. I was hoping no blood was going to be spilled tonight. But if he has a brain, as well as a good eye, he'll think twice and come on out. Like your good self."

Cooper stuck his head through the shredded curtain and barked loudly twice. Inside the tunnel the amber eyes grew larger and more wary as the descent levelled and a strong glare ahead became more apparent. A bark did not deter his insatiable desire to know what was down there. He followed its curve until the light revealed the presence of what could only be described as angelic in its appearance. Brilliantly lit by a semi-circle of flames, it wielded, however, no sword. Only a pink tongue and a cheerful grin of jade-green eyes as it got to its feet in recognition.

"Well, fency our paths crossin' agin in a plaice loike this. It's bin dull dry as a reg'lar billabong till yew turned up. Still, yew c'n jest turn arawnd and skip beck up agin, if yer please. 'Cos th' roawd ends roight here, chum."

The black cat remembered the rumble on the stairs and did not look anything like as cheerful for doing so. An arc of large candles burned before the end wall, shielding it with its powerful incandescence, as the backdrop of Prince's shadow rose fantastically above it like a yeti emerging from a snowstorm. The Amber Eye glittered with rage and swiped at the air as though his paws were flame-proof.

"Yore playin' with foire, mate. One more step an' oi'll jes' hev t' yenk yew owver it. "

A black paw jabbed viciously through the barrier and struck the glistening cream of the cat across his shoulder. But the attacker did not reckon with the move that followed, as Prince threw all his weight into the next attempt, to tug him unceremoniously into the flaming arc. With a scream and a jerk the not-so-amber-eye broke away, rolling free of the hot wax, as it seared his toes and the fur along his forehead. To flee back up the tunnel as fast as his scorched and heated heels would allow him. Two minutes later DH met the winner, as he sauntered back to the top and peered through the curtain. The dog looked well satisfied. The cellar had been cleared of the opposition and both master and mistress were ready to leave at once. Prince, ignoring his sore spot, studied the damage roundabout the floor by the light of his master's lamp.

"They're gone," murmured the dog as the two of them followed its departing glow, "that is, we let 'em go. And I don't think they'll want any more tonight after the shock treatment we've provided for 'em. When he plays his hunch he's dead on the ball and won't give way. I see you've got a cut there. Mebbe there's a bit of a wolf in you, after all."

Prince noticed it for the first time and licked at a smudge of red along the outside of his right shoulder.

"Aw, all in th' loine of dewty, as they say. End th" cendleloights did their bit, too. Sow, all's well that inds well."

DH nodded obliquely as he shuffled up the stairs.

"Don't know about that, though. I've something of an idea there's more to play for yet."

DH kept nodding forensically, but said nothing else all the way back. Having appropriated the keys, and duly released the party-goers from the ballroom, the much smaller party reached the tower where Mr Brimble kicked off his shoes and flopped back into his armchair, tired but relieved. The others sat before the fire, waiting for the final comments they felt sure would conclude the whole miserable affair. Harriet raked the fire, then sat down on the rug cradling the hourglass protectively, till its array of tourmalines began winking in appreciation of their new-found resting place. The old man smiled at his menagerie with pride, then began to look more serious by clearing his throat and sitting forward. He relaxed his hunched shoulders, wiped his forehead and laid the palms of his hands over the small table in front of him. He then pointed to his left palm with a turn of his right thumb. There was a quiet conviction in his voice as his right palm changed into a fist.

"One away game today deserves another, I think. I've made up my mind to do it. We're going to have a game of our own. To settle the score - once and for all. The game to end all games."

Silence reigned save for the gentle snap and crackle of fresh logs, before DH turned sharply to Prince in a whisper.

"See what I told you. He's made his decision. And believe you me, if I understand him right, you'll never see another match like it as long as you live, my friend."

"What!"

The master of Brokehill Manor went on quietly sipping his tea in anticipation of the response. Which wasn't slow arriving

"But arter all that woman's done! An' there's me encouragin' her like a fairy godmother. Phooff! There ain't no changin' some people's evil intentions, Mr Edward. All down t' pure greed."

Mr Brimble offered Cook a regrettable nod of his head and waited for further condemnation. Why, she could recall any number of personal flashbacks from the distant past which, as far as she was concerned, told their own sad and disparaging story.

"She never did love th' life 'ere, if I remember rightly. I mean, to come turnin' up out of the blue like this, without so much as a by-your-leave, disruptin' everythin' with some crackpot scheme. An' then to be given another chance - to wipe us all off th' map! Oh! I just hope you know what you're doin', sir."

Mrs Dains seemed to have summed up succinctly how the case stood, and its possible outcome, however outrageous to her feelings, could not be argued against. Even the Grand Disorder of Cats, now reassembled once more under their despotic owner's care and keeping, seemed to realise they had been let off the hook as they snoozed the night's events out of their collective system behind a closed door. The old man felt an explanation was in order and carefully considered his next words.

"Well, yes, but she is my sister, Mrs Dains. And perhaps it's been a long time coming. This is a last throw of the dice, as it were. Why not let her take the hourglass, you might say, to leave us alone in peace. But this is much more than simply a family heirloom. It's very presence is bound up with the spirit of Brokehill. The two things cannot in any way be viewed as mutually exclusive. Together they are priceless, and to sacrifice the one will diminish both to very little purpose, if freedom is denied. You allow the world bargain for that which becomes worthless. That's what this fight is about, for those who cherish it dearly. So, you see, it's right that they should make that throw. Perhaps it appears to be a ridiculous test with so much at stake, I know. But, then, for these least ones to keep hold on it successfully, naturally preserves the status quo for the next inheritor of the house."

"Miss Harriet, I presume," said Cook in earnest. "Well, all I know is that I've never heard the like of it. Football runnin' in this family is one thing, but I don't see how any game can ever be played between a few rats an' these here, hard-put-upon cats. If I live to witness this strange an' perculiar specticle, Mr Edward, I do 'ope your dice is - how d' they call it?"

"Loaded, Mrs Dains?"

"You seem to 'ave great reliance and trust in this arrangement, so I 'ope there's a trick or two left in you. Not that I c'n envisage *you* havin' to resort to doin' anythin' under'and, mind."

"I am a fair judge of what is possible and have the greatest confidence in the opposition - to the cats, I mean. Though I'm no Pied Piper, you understand. And the only trick I've pulled so far was the one to discover at which table my sister wished to eat. You gave her the chance and the choice to do one thing or the other, just as I asked you to. And, regrettably, the poorer choice was taken. It was a pity the evening ended the way it did. However, I intend to make it up to Mr Pale and his wife when this is issue is resolved. And I'm grateful that you have agreed to stay on for us. You would be sorely missed."

Cook looked barely placated, though her loyalty, fortunately, ran somewhat deeper.

"I really thought she would be so, so - oh, more fool me for wishin' for what some people don't honestly appreciate. How to be 'appy. Them poor cats!"

"They may have been an unwanted nuisance, yet I am not heartless enough to have no interest in their welfare. If Euradice intends to cut her losses instead, then homes can be found for them. Well, for most, at any rate. The trouble is, she has always inclined herself more to independence than to any kind of interdependence."

Mrs Dains gave Mr Brimble an apprehensive shrug and poured a strong mug of the tea for herself.

"If she ain't mistress of Brokehill by then. An' if she was to win this - this here - game," she could hardly bring herself to say the word, "where will *your* home be then, might I ask?"

"Oh, I could be sitting in the tower and watching the New World Order take shape beneath my feet, Mrs Dains, and living to regret the changes, I suppose."

"Hmph! Not you. You couldn't bear it. Neither could Miss Harriet. Or 'er mother either, come to that. I fear it'd be the end of Brokehill as we knows it."

"Well, the die is cast. I think the offer is certain to be accepted when my sister has got her head round the idea. For her it's all or nothing, you understand. But for the rightful winner a precedent will thereby be fully established."

The insertion of this legal term had a sort of elegant correctness about it to Mr Brimble's way of thinking, seeming, as it did, to put a seal on everything.

"For all our sakes, I only 'ope you're right."

With these final words on the subject Mrs Dains sighed and, stirring her tea, left the unnatural morning's peace to run along on its equally unsettling and, as yet, unsettled course.

★   ★   ★

It wasn't until Mr Brimble returned to the tower that he realised there were a number of logistics to sort out, as well as somebody else's head, on the matter. Like Cook, Harriet had her own reservations about the prospect of such a match as this going ahead. She sat, for once, in the old man's leather chair, her elbows lodged firmly between the brass studs which dented its broad arms. Whether for quite practical

269

reasons or because she thought he had already lost the plot and, therefore, his status, was not certain. But if her temper was tetchy, buffing the silver and gold of the hour-glass to a finer sheen was one way of mellowing the rougher edges of her mood.

"It was worth doing, grandfather. See how the rims shine like the glass. And those marks around the base aren't scratches or anything. I think it's some kind of inscription in squiggly writing. I'm still working on it."

She buffed away at the area fastidiously before placing the glistening object gently next to the reproduction Jules Rimet lampstand. She could not imagine such an established symbol of freedom ending up anywhere else. Thus the concept of bitter rivals sorting it out on the pitch where a winner would literally be taking all became a frightening prospect, one that dominated any sense of impending excitement.

"I suppose you're thinking: the bigger they come ... you know ... well, I do hope you are thinking along those lines, grandfather."

Before he sat down Mr Brimble lifted Prince from his comfort zone onto the opposite arm of his grand-daughter's chair to demonstrate how he viewed the matter.

"Take this cat as a species of the opponent. He reveals both agility and alertness."

Exhibit A provided a glossy yawn for his admirers and tried to get himself comfortable again as best he could on all fours. Harriet ruffled the curls on his neck and forgave him at once. Heroics didn't come every day, and he had nothing to prove to her after his bravery of the previous night.

"It's not always what it says on the tin with them," insisted Harriet, turning from one rather ornamental shape with jade eyes to another with many more pairs of blue ones.

"Ah! But there you're wrong!" exclaimed her grandfather gleefully. "You see, cats are athletic creatures, but only when they want to be. They will answer to no one. Will you, my lad?"

Prince, after all he'd put up with in that tunnel, looked across with an expression of hurt in an otherwise enlightened face. Mr Brimble had to make a hasty correction to his claim.

"Of course, there are exceptions, but these cats below, as we have seen, don't work as a team. A dog will say *'when ?'*, you understand, whereas a cat only asks *'why ?'* Then again, our black rats are a different breed to rats in general. Over the years I believe their free-for-all game has evolved into a much more street-wise affair. A love affair helped on, no doubt, by the advent of televised matches. And there are plenty more of them to choose from these days." His eyes had the timer's glint in them. "There's nothing superfluous about their state of play. Degrees of sophistication have kept them moving along with the spirit of their Arena - and the sporting times."

"So, maybe teamwork and ability with the ball will compensate for speed and size, is that it?"

"Yes, I think so. With that more noble reason to

survive - which should enable them to generate a more unstoppable desire to win. I rest my case."

"But the rats are not used to a grass surface, are they? Besides, there's the horrible possibility of the cats taking matters into their own hands. They won't simply be after goals, if you ask me."

"I don't think so, with all that's at stake. What happens after the game is quite another thing. Having observed them for some time, I don't think we've anything to fear from the majority. But I have some protective measures in mind regarding the exceptions - win or lose. Hmm, on second thoughts, disregard that '*or*', if I were you, my dear."

Harriet gave the hour-glass another aggressive polish and, like Cook before her, hoped its shine was not about to be tarnished by those undeserving of it.

From the moment the game was announced Cooper (DH) had dubbed it the 'Freedom Final' and had been relishing his part in bringing it about all morning. Both sides had to be vetted and given a bit of a team talk. For preparation's sake. Let 'em know what was expected. Fundamental rules to go over, and all that sort of thing. Trickier job with the cats, so best to get it out of the way first. Prince wouldn't be assisting him, so he planned to make his points from the outhouse doorway as unambiguously as possible, and leave 'em to fight over the details amongst their logger-headed selves. He strode into the kitchen and braced himself for the reception. A few heads spotted him coming and put the rest of the outhouse on high alert. Only the Amber Eye appeared to be tight shut on this occasion.

"These is private quarters, if it's all th' same t' you," rasped Scrounger, not in the best of moods with most of the bruises on his limbs still aching tenderly from the night before.

DH nodded his acceptance of this notable fact and made a quick count of the participants available. Just as the governor had described it. A Great Rump, if ever there was one.

"All present and correct, I take it. Just to clarify what's been put forward. Ten of you there ought to be. For the game in general its incorrect, but it'll do for us. Ten-a-side is what the governor has settled for."

Gus, steamed up as usual, got in the first reaction.

"Listen, you. Whatever barmy army of rats you care to drag out into the big, wide yonder - they're gonners. Take it as done. They wanna come out and play? We'll play. Crush 'em like grapes, we will."

Phew! It might be claptrap, but at least he talked a good game. Only hope it stayed as talk. If this lot got wound up and sprang their coils, then what? DH stood his ground to let them know he was having none of it.

"It's good to talk. But all you've got to make sure of is that your predatory instincts don't get the better of you. As things stand, I'm refereeing this. Neutral, you can be sure."

A loud cackle came from the back as Boswick decided to add his own less than generous remarks to the instructions being delivered to their door.

"Wah! Ho! Only thing you'll be needing is a clean pair of heels when it's over - if it gets that far."

DH held his ground.

"Enough of this. Game is: ten versus ten, and fifteen minutes each way, and no handballs penalised unless your upright and it's deliberate, therefore being beyond the spirit of fair play. If we're level after that, well, then, an extra five minutes each way. Happy with that?"

Mr Quills sat nearest to the door as the rules were rolled off in a quick-fire, no-nonsense manner. His star had since risen a fraction with his boys and his response came, naturally, with them in mind.

"Hum - excuse me. As you are to be the - er - adjudicator on this - hum - field of conflict, we should appreciate suitable practice with an appropriate ball."

DH squinted down at the bravely inflated chest.

"Oh, yes. A sensible comment at last. Almost forgot. Here's some to be going on with. Till this Saturday, then. Kick-off, in case you need reminding, which I don't suppose you do, is four o' clock on the dot. West wing lawn."

With that the bloodhound flicked at a string from a small plastic bag wrapped tight as a sausage skin and hanging below his neck. Three off-white fives balls bounced nicely inside for the cats grouped at the front. Having drowned their sorrows in a lunch of more pitiful leftovers, none were in an especially playful, or inquisitive, mood.

"If anything else comes up, your mistress will be

the first to know. So, as they say elsewhere - g'day to you, fellas."

As he turned, the thought of several sets of claws raining down like daggers of resentment against his broad shoulders was dismissed at once as he padded off for the second half of the job in hand. Which was across to the scene of yesterday's misadventures - the old ballroom. The return journey upstairs was made with greater deliberation and with far deeper thought than when he had first started out. His handling of the cats had gone off without too much ado, but with the rats he was going to have to be a good deal more motivating, if not more circumspect, for a number of valid reasons. One: for them this proposition (for that's what it was) might be viewed as a challenge too far. They had survived for nearly two months with the governor's help and that of his able assistants. Now they were being asked to play a game which, they might well argue, was, as of last night, already won. Two: the playing conditions would certainly be something new to them. When he and the governor had collected the timer they had interrupted a game in progress. One thing to see 'em zipping about with a ball at their feet. It was quite another to watch 'em clippin' it about with all the control and skill to make a dog's eyes really water. But being on a lawn in broad daylight was going to be quite a contrast to their regular world of stone and candlelight. And three: well, against any other team of rats they would fancy themselves. But the opposition here were cats. Sworn enemies, with their own agenda to fulfil, and a few sizes bigger to boot. Tough points to overcome. He had good reason to choose this venue for a meeting, since his acute eye had spotted some curious visitors on the scene when he and the governor had inspected the room earlier that morning. The Pales and their friends had been released from their temporal prison with much apologising and the promise of another do in the future. Now, having both both sets of keys, the governor had decided to carry out a spot of furniture rearranging of his own. Thus, with the door being left ajar for the further addition of another table and more chairs, he was fairly hopeful of quickly finding one of the little so-and-sos in order to state his case concisely.

He crept in softly, listening, ear to the ground,. for the tell-tale scurrying of feet caught unawares by his sudden arrival. But a brief inspection above ground level quickly provided him with all the evidence he required. Two lithe and compact figures were currently absorbed in a reckless race to see how far they could slide down the length of Cook's well-polished table. Made his job all the more easier. They came skidding to a halt just as DH leapt onto a chair half-way down to grunt his applause for these boisterous skills.

"Nice work when you can find it. Don't you both go skipping off now, 'cause we need to talk," grunted DH again.

Despite the suddenness of the interruption, neither of them seemed especially eager to leave the scene.

"You got us anything nice to eat today, then? We're

famished," said the one nearest to him, as he eyed DH gracelessly up and down.

"I ain't come all this way just to feed you. Were you the two here earlier this morning?"

"Probably. Who wants to know? Must say you're a fast mover for someone carrying quite a bit of bulk," answered the other in similar fashion. "Almost took us by surprise, you did."

"Cheeky pair, both of you. Enjoying a touch more freedom now, are we? I'd like to know what you saw last night. Don't you tell me you missed the fun. Out with it."

"Well, we have to admit the ballroom's a top place to train in. We come here for sprints, dribbling routines and a bit of movement off the ball. That sort of thing. A lot of it on this table, where it's narrow and testing. But since Cookie started polishing away at it, those work-outs aren't so easy to do. Too slippery."

The speaker stopped as his partner nudged him with a whisper.

"Oh, yes. Well, the party was in full swing and we did more or less see what happened. The lady got everything whipped into a right old state and made away with Cook's keys. Piece of daylight robbery, if ever there was one." He gazed up to the chandelier and chuckled. "Cats tumbling about and plenty of mouthfuls as the food goes flying everywhere."

His partner, deciding to spin his own line on things, took up the story.

"We had to warn the Arena about impending

trouble, so one of us shot off to tell the scouts. The rest you know. Mind you, we thought the wall of fire was a neat trick, and Cream Tart did ok, as well."

"So you play a bit, do you?" asked DH, ignoring the flippant description of his comrade in arms, though he'd already seen enough of the rats to know what they were capable of. He turned his large head back to the first speaker. "And you are?"

"Name's Nobs. He's Hobs. Of course. Competitive at everything, we are. Even on this slide. Top strikers in the main team. Or rather would be, if the tactics weren't so negative and predictable. I bet you don't play much."

DH had begun to warm to the brazen little upstarts.

"Try me," he said drily. "If you've as much nerve as that pal of yours who we were bringing on nicely until he caught the late bus home. There's gratitude for you. I suppose watching the game on a certain person's telly wouldn't be unknown to you now, would it?

Hobs offered an embarrassed grin that promptly gave away another penchant of their secret lifestyles.

"Olly's on the mend, though he's not played in the team since he got back," said Nobs, to change the subject.

"Oh! He's alive and not kicking, is he?"

"Of course he is. You didn't think he was the ghost of Christmas Past, did you? This house is haunted enough without needing his help."

The twins high-fived at this and enjoyed their joke on Olly. DH twitched a wrinkle above his left eye.

"You've been influenced by too many fairy stories, you have. What would you know about any haunting in here? "

"Enough. There's a girl who walks at the window. She was dancing girl who died in the room below. Didn't you know?"

"A bit. But don't you go filling your heads with any of those old tales. Superstition, my lads. Just concern yourself with getting this Olly match fit. A *super sub* would fit the bill, if it comes to it. Where does he play?"

"Midfielder, as a rule. Not the same without him, is it, Hobs?" said his not-so-shy fellow striker.

"I'll tell you what won't be the same. Something your friend was very eager to share with us. And that's where our little chat comes in, my merry lads."

Hobs gave Nobs the sort of nervous look reserved only for when they were reading each other's mind.

"I'm not here to make any demands of you lot. You're free to choose what you do. As you always have been. But things have come to a mighty pass, and we need to see where everyone stands, if you get my meaning. The governor's been the great Protector of all of you. Not just with convenient parcels recently dropped on your doorstep, so to speak. This great game of ours runs in the family, as well you know. But what keeps it all ticking over is the gift of freedom. Don't ask me how it works, I'm not that forensic, but if you lose your grip on this timer that's been sitting in your Arena goodness knows how many a long year, then you lose what the governors from the past have fought for. Whether they were fights on the battlefield or on the playing field."

There was a long silence before a response was forthcoming. But not from either of the twins.

"Well spoken. I see I have arrived at a crucial moment. What is it you wish us to do?"

The twins seemed to shrink back, as the calm, authoritative voice fell crisply upon the stillness of the great room around them. Brown eyes, dignified, yet resilient, sought out those of the master's spokesman with all the intensity of a practised mind-reader as their owner balanced on the tip of a chair arm and waited.

"Blow me, if it's not another one I never saw coming. And who might you be, now, for an untimely eavesdropper?" asked DH, peering down the table to size up the diminutive and serious-eyed newcomer. He looked in turn at Hobs and Nobs, quickly working out the answer for himself before anyone of them could explain anything.

"Ah, yes, now let me guess. You would be the one they call the Captain. Am I right or am I right?"

Greybands jumped onto the table and returned his look with the same penetrating steadiness as before.

"I am the Captain. And I think I know what you wish us to do. Please go on."

The bloodhound shifted his position heavily, as the unflinching stance of the Captain made him feel a little uneasy after the engaging exchange he'd had with the younger pair. He needed to reassert himself smartish, and his eyes began to focus elsewhere for a measure of inspiration. Motes of unfiltered dust captured and exposed within a ray of afternoon sun as it crept its low course between the arched columns of the west window. Boring a hole like a blood orange into the adjacent rosewood panelling ahead of him. The portrait of Miss Aurora Jane Belmont partly in deep shadow. Another next to her. Dancing girls, alright! Finally his eyes alighted back on the Captain.

"Well, Boss Rat, if you think you're in charge of this unruly rabble of a squad, you had better start now! A proposition is all very well, but if you value the Arena and the governor's good guidance, you had better concentrate your mind as well as them nifty feet of yours on the most important game of your poor lives. Win the timer, and you and I, with all the good folk of Brokehill, will surely live to fight another day!"

★　　　　★　　　　★

Mr Brimble paced to the window and back again but could still see no sign of a parked van. There was another jingle on the phone.

"Where are you now? Remember, enough of that plastic mesh for both of them. That's seven feet by four each. Better in whole pieces to save time cutting and joining. Is it potatoes or collies?"

"I don't think it matters a lot, grandfather. Rory's just got back from the sellers. We've got plenty of what's wanted. I had it all written down."

"Good. Mr Pale says we can assemble it all in the morning. I'm feeling quite excited, you know."

"Yes, I can tell. Mum wants me to stay home tonight and help her in the kitchen. She wants *me* to make cook's glorious Crundle pudding, while she's doing a lasagne or something. Can you imagine that! Me and her cooking *together* in the kitchen! I think it will help me take my mind off tomorrow, grandfather. Rory says he'll bring me over early. I just hope this – hang on! – Rory's trying to say something ..."

The phone went dead before her voice returned with a gasp: "Grandfather! Rory wants to come and watch the match! And – and – it looks like mum wants to come, too!"

★   ★   ★

Saturday saw a beginning of March that came shining with a slice of fortune to favour the brave. Bathed in the warmth of an afternoon sun, the lawn, manicured and greensward smooth, was set to become another of those deceptive field of dreams where there never was an unlucky loser whose nightmare might just be shorter than the day was long. Mr Pale shook his head over the proceedings, but nevertheless continued to mark only the pitch in preference to any of the grandiose words of victory that Euradice had been loudly auguring (when anybody was in earshot) all through the week. Being of a philosophical turn of mind, he had decided that what would be would be, and if his foreknowledge ran any deeper than the discarded pitchforks and broom handles trussed up in the cellar, then he certainly wasn't about to let on.

Preparations, though, clearly revealed this to be no ordinary Saturday. How could it be, as the master of Brokehill kept reminding the others throughout the morning. When the theatre of a cup final awaited them! A stage on which neither of its players could, by any stretch of imagination, be viewed as ordinary, either. Cup Final breakfast was, however, enjoyed by no one (not even Euradice in her lonely room) save for the master whose hearty eating went along without any apparent tremble of the hand as he lifted his own cup. Cup Final lunch went much the same way as the breakfast, with Mr Brimble chatting away merrily to a subdued Mr Pale about the simple layout of the pitch and the area where everyone coming would be standing. Indeed, no Cup Final would be complete without its interesting collection of spectators, and apart from his daughter and her curious boyfriend, there was a suggestion that Cook had invited her friend Vera along with that gangling husband of hers, Norman the Poacher. Mr Pale had also hinted at the presence of dear Mrs Pale, but after last week's miseries her attendance was by no means seen as a certainty.

Soon enough, with the hall clock showing three-thirty and gone, and the sun still shining its encouragement, a van came slowly up the lane and rumbled to a halt. Out from the shadow of the lines of trees stepped Harriet with Rory beside her carrying a bundle under his arm. Behind them, after a brief delay, another figure emerged, coming up with both hands deep in the pockets of her faded, embroidered denims. Mr Brimble sighed deeply as he stood in welcome at the gate. Rory grinned as they neared and pointed out the 'Scotland The Brave' sweatshirt he was wearing under his jumper. Harriet, too, was all smiles. The third figure caught her up and linked arms. At last, the game, perhaps like another there to be won, finally seemed to be on.

Whether it was winnable was quite another matter to referee Cooper (DH), even if his governor's confidence continued to be a mite infectious. The kitchen had been closed off discreetly, and he waited by the top step of the opened cellar door. There was no sound from the stairwell's depths, but, had he been stationed earlier at the mouth of the tunnel itself, his spirit might have been lifted by the distant ricocheting of a fives ball being whacked hard against the walls of the Arena in a defiant final practice session before the team readied themselves to come to the surface. Finally, to his great relief, he heard an unmistakeable, clicking patter of small feet steadily wending their way up from the darkness below. Into the light: a line of noble-hearted rats coming up behind the intense brown eyes of their leader without ever once lifting their own. On reaching the top step Greybands hesitated, allowing DH a moment to welcome the arrival of the team. They came through the door, one by one, and waited patiently, adjusting their eyes to the brightness of the hallway like resistance fighters unsure as to whether their game was finally up or the war finally over. DH's big head steadily lowered to meet that of the Captain's, then drew him aside. He looked him over with the greatest of concerned sympathy.

"Glad you could make it, Captain," he said quietly. "You don't need to worry about the opposition for the moment. They're going out the other way. Now, it's not incumbent on me to say anything by way of advice to you. In fact, as the ref, it's highly improper. But since this ain't a regular game, I don't want any disadvantages spilling over onto the pitch."

Greybands looked down at the pale green smoothness of the hall carpet and nodded his humble acceptance of the offer.

"Far be it from me to tell you lot how to play your game, but you need to go out there with a strategy in mind to cope with the unexpected. These cats are big and fast compared to you, but they ain't a team as you are. They will be chasing after the ball into all manner of dead ends and difficulties without thinking of each other when they should. You may play them off the park with all your skills, but I wouldn't recommend it, however. I suggest you to keep your strikers back a bit more. As another line of defence, as needs be. Don't leave 'em isolated where they'll get roughed up if they're too far forward. Keep passing the ball about, keep the opposition running after it. But not too much, in case they get frustrated and things get out of hand and take a nasty turn. Hope not, but it's just possible. Every so often you must punt the ball upfield. You'll get it back quickly enough. This way, if you keep your part of the park well congested, then, you may keep the game nice and steady and all square till the second half. Maybe in the last five minutes or so you can go hell for leather and nick us a goal. The grass is flat and dry, so don't try mixing it and get yourselves bowled over by too many reckless tackles. Injuries means loss of personnel. They're big 'uns, so keep it pinging. That's about it. If it's anything to go by, my governor, out there with his family, is quietly confidant. We're relying on you to do your stuff. But a fair dose of discipline you will well and truly need."

DH eyed them all, but noticed particularly the bowed heads of the twins and nodded to them, as they looked up. Greybands considered what had been said and checked over his men for DH's benefit before replying.

"Georgio, goalie. Roly, Jed, Lief and myself in defence. Yes. Maxie, Herbert, Cedric, Norbert in the middle. Yes. Billy up front. Yes." Then he looked up.

"I agree, a conservative system will be best today. We shall do our utmost - and, of course, our very best."

He did not falter.

DH moved forward to the front door which had likewise been left open: "Somebody else just outside is waiting to escort you onto the pitch. Talk about giving a team talk! Hope I've not said too much. Anyway, it's time to go. So, if you want to make our eyes water again, play up! And may the best team win it!"

With that the bloodhound gave a short, snorting bark and shouldered his way out through the door. The rats of Brokehill waited behind, taking in a few deep breaths as they watched and counted the seconds ticking by above on the very old and very non partisan clock.

Meanwhile, as the hall maintained its dignified, though apprehensive silence, not so far away the latest clash of egos was filling the outhouse with a familiar stock in trade in insults and ignorance. At this crucial hour it was the Amber Eye who was holding court. Poised at the edge of the lumpy chair, he seemed ready to spring upon any objector and throttle him into submission, if it was so required. Despite the livid line of scorch marks that decorated the back of his neck, a mysterious aura still hung about the eyes just enough to make his presence a menacing one. But for some, it was not nearly enough. Boswick, inevitably, was one of them.

"Just what makes you so sure it will be so-o-o, so different this time? I mean, every time, you and that henchman of yours have done what *you* wanted, you've returned with more injuries than you care to mention."

"Yeah. Not to mention the worse ones affecting your reputations," added Gus, the other dyed-in-the-wood sceptic.

The Amber Eye burned with an incendiary of iris before deciding that a suitable application of doused, hot ashes were better than mere words.

"I will tell you why, you half-wits." His breath grew low and ominous. "It's staring you in the *face*."

The hiss on 'face' was as long and as scalding as kettle steam. Nobody dared to look him directly in the eye.

"There will be no walls of stone, no darkness, where

287

they can hide this time. For once they are face to face - revealed - before our very eyes."

The poise and pause for effect he elicited would have gained the praise of Matthew Hopkins.

"No, please. No interruptions, I beg of you."

Beg? Please? It would be the other way round long before he'd finished.

"We must keep our part of the bargain, for we are an honourable race, my friends. But remember, we are also – catss."

The defining word fell with a fang-bared sibilance; as a jolting reminder of an all too unsubtle difference his audience dare not ignore.

"We must run them down to exhaustion. When they see the fire in our eyes they will be terrified. No raised paws or claws being allowed, except mine, of course, we must throw them about in the tackles. A few hard knocks will leave them demoralised. Thus shall they be overcome. Then we move in for the kill. To smash in the goals - and finish it. Finish them thereafter - from the face of the earth!"

More fierce sibilance concluded this tactically terrifying tirade. But the small print had not gone unnoticed by Arturo and he made sure he got in the first response.

"Hey! Wait a minute! What do you mean by 'except mine' in the bit about the handling?"

"Ah, now. You see, 'e's goin' in goal." explained Scrounger quickly, as his mouthpiece. "So nothin'll get past 'im, see. Gus an' Bossy will take charge of defence, like, while me an' you go up front to attack 'em. Give 'em a real sixes an' sevens time of it, so t' ' speak. The rest c'n keep up a few distractions of their own."

In typical arrogance, the final formation had been left till the eleventh hour. But it was all cut and dried. Mr Quills looked at Cubshaw without a word. Scrounger, standing nearest to Arturo, whispered in his ear as the others digested the line-up without a murmur.

"The rest are sort of ciphers. Run around an' get in their own - as well as the others – way, is about it."

Arturo nodded an agreement, but felt something had been missed somewhere. They had flung themselves around for little less than a week to get used to the bounce and flight of these confounded balls, but no one had said anything about actually coping with the opposition until now. As if they were an irrelevance. There was something that worried him about this game. He didn't enjoy the irresistible and nagging thought that this team of theirs, knocked together so casually and with such overweening confidence, might just be heading nowhere - except to the cleaners. He had to say what was in his mind before it was too late. In the kitchen, the clock struck quarter to four. These misgivings had resurfaced just in time, but was it time enough? The silence offered him one late chance to unburden himself..

"Look, has it occurred to anyone here why it is we are being roped into playing a football match to settle our differences? The stakes being so high and all that, why would they set up such a thing?"

"P'raps the old 'un feels sorry for us all of a sudden

an' wishes to give us a fair crack at 'em," grinned Scrounger facetiously.

Arturo wasn't to be deflected.

"Listen. Nothing's done by half here. How do we know whether or not these rats can play a bit? How come these little balls just came out of nowhere? Think about it, you lot. Why was that tunnel so well defended? Then maybe you'll come to the same conclusion as I do. Which is that these rats probably know how to play the game. What's more, they're quite possibly able to give back pretty much as good as they get. We can't just go out and chase 'em off the park, not with an audience present. No chance. We've got to play *their* game. That's the stupid deal we're stuck with."

As a dressing-room gee-up it was a non-starter, but the facts had to be faced and the game had to be won. Good and proper. Arturo screwed up his nose in doubt and looked around.

"Look, as it stands, they ain't goin' t' score or anythin'. We c'n play 'em off th' park. Wot wiv 'im bein' in goal an' the other two biggies moppin' up at the back," said Scrounger, dismissive of any such reasoned argument.

"Would that be our sweat or their blood?" jeered Gus with a sneer forming on his questioning face. "Thing is this – tell me who's gonna score for us?"

The Amber Eye looked down coldly this time round and addressed them all in such a way as to put a slammer on the uncertainties surfacing.

"You've all patted and toyed with a ball of wool once

in your younger days, haven't you? Well, then, remember, the boot's on the other foot this time. Swipe it harder and, I tell you, this game *will* unravel before their very eyes."

The sound of Euradice stomping through the kitchen told them their time was up, and he jumped down. Arturo followed Scrounger at the rear of an exuberant file, still deeply unsure of the situation they were heading into, and as to whether a different kind of skein wasn't about to unravel around their springy heels to trip them up - and turn into a flimsier own goal for them instead.

From either side of the house the teams filed out onto a famous, historic lawn, where the former masters of Brokehill had, at various times, either entertained or fought for supremacy with either their guests or their foes. In that respect nothing had changed. The motley group of visitors (who had, unnaturally, gotten in without so much as a ticket) now straddled the touchline at the rear of which, a few yards off, a topiary wall of box hedge stood as a barrier between a thriving herb garden and a small pool. First onto the pitch came the Rats, ushered out by Prince, with Captain Greybands following at the head of his valiant team. The Cats gradually tumbled into view in an unruly straggle of twos and threes, limbering up here and there with a sprightly leap, ushered forward, rather than led out, by the taut-lipped manageress and mistress of their sorrows. If not exactly one for all, then better for it to be all for one - or else. Thus was the impression given. Mr

Quills nodded to his opposite number as they met in the middle, but got nothing in return. Last, but by no means least, came the Amber Eye, who threw a mightily vengeful glare at Prince and DH as he passed by at more than double an arm's length. Arturo directed his pointy nose to the rats and studied them closely, as they flipped a few balls up and down in the warm- up. It was the nearest he'd ever got to one. If they were on a hiding to nothing they certainly weren't showing it.

It is all the build-up and razzmatazz that makes a Cup Final the great occasion it is - until the teams come out and spoil it all. Or so it has been said. The cats may have come out to do some spoiling of their own, but as far as the master of Brokehill was concerned nothing and no one was going to spoil his day. He pretended not to notice the anxious glances coming from Cook, as she stood beside her friend Vera and her wide-eyed husband. The rats, it seemed, were gaining the attention of everyone. Mr Brimble took out a silver whistle and then turned to the figure who stood next to him.

"Well, what do you think of our Brokehill team, then, Claire?"

""Really amazing, Dad. I always thought you only coached the village team. Rory thinks they'd be mean little nippers to get under your feet."

He paused as he looked at her long auburn hair with the glitzy hair clips on each side spangled in the lowering rays of the sun. The fringed, silk scarf tied loosely with a girlish knot. The Cheyenne boots from America. Her arm was locked in Harriet's and more auburn hair as they both waited for the start. Like mother like daughter. Claire bit her lip and laughed, holding onto the daughter all the more tightly. The air around them had begun to stir a fraction in the lateness of the afternoon.

"Wow! It's a long time since I've laid eyes on dear Aunt Radish over there. That is her, isn't it?"

The nearest and dearest of aunts was pacing to and fro behind the west wing goal where any number of taunts with a long, threatening forefinger were mistakenly believed to be the most effective and motivating of methods for getting the right result. Claire watched these antics with far less incredulity than her daughter did beside her.

"No change there, then. You've got to admit, Dad, she's still a rough, tough act to follow. Always was a misery waiting for a disaster to happen, in my book."

Mr Brimble liked being called Dad again. It was a pleasant alternative to Grandfather, at any rate. Concerning his sister he said nothing. Wily managers remained unruffled. Today, as he surveyed the scene, no thought of disaster could possibly enter *his* head. The setting was somehow almost as surreal as it was serene: pale orange nets, barely ruffled by the waft of a breeze, draped across soft emerald turf neatly enshrined with low, white painted goalposts. And here stood his Claire, carefree and smiling. Saturday's sun could surely never be turned into a Sunday's rain. Having just heard his name mentioned, Rory turned his quick-witted attention to his girlfriend's father.

The old man gave him a good-natured pat on the arm and pointed to where the rats were congregating.

"Aye. A tell ye wart, A dinna see how them carts are gonna score. A reely dohn't. Reckon thum rarts kin keck a ba', too. Noo doot aboot it. Maite burst ma nets, wha knaws. Gort sum speed, too, a thenk."

Mr Brimble had rediscovered a fresh twinkle in his eye. The Scots always did have a soft spot for tricky talent. Trouble was, it generally came south. Except for goalkeepers, anyway.

"None of your timorous beasties, here, Rory! No B-team this - unless under the name of Brokehill."

Rory caught on and chuckled mischievously.

"Aye, all well an' gud! Th' tim'rous beasties are th' carts a reckon, whale yon teeny uns are moor th' Bremners an' th' Baxters, a'right."

Mr Brimble gave the word as DH got up from the touchline and scampered to the middle, the teams staying in the halves where they had grouped. The bloodhound barked for both sets of players to get into some semblance of order and waited for the whistle to be blown. Cats were towards the river (hidden by bushes and a trellised fence) and Rats faced the west wing. No one moved except for Euradice who stalked behind her goal still muttering fierce imprecations to the Amber Eye if anything should dare to go wrong. He, in turn, began pacing up and down the goal without needing a better excuse to work up an acceptable head of steam. The master of Brokehill met his sister's eyes with a glance as he raised his arm. Their moment of truth had arrived. A new fives ball was thrown into the middle, where DH trapped it neatly with one huge paw. There followed a bit of clapping, with an exceptionally loud cheer from Norman the Poacher, before the acute interest resumed in suspended silence. Then the governor's hand went up and the whistle made its shrill signal. The game was off and away.

With the rats having the privilege of kicking off first, Captain Greybands kept the order going to keep the passing to no more than a couple of yards and to keep it brisk. The back four each got an early touch and moved the ball cleanly towards their midfielders. Scrounger and Arturo hopped about in two minds as the ball ping-ponged back and forth between the swift-moving opposition. Mr Quills found the whole business a little too street-wise for him, but couldn't help having a secret admiration for these nimble chaps and considered whether they might not also excel at something more sedately noble - like crown bowls - if they would but put their minds to it. Cubshaw became surprisingly energetic whenever the ball came over to his side, though such well-meaning resourcefulness never got him any nearer to actually touching it. Eventually, as planned, it was Hobs who, resisting the urge to dribble through the massed ranks of cats ahead of him, belted the ball high upfield instead towards the confines of the ever-alert Amber Eye. Stationed at the edge of his area, he pounced on it before rolling it out to Gus with a warning for him not to loose it in a hurry. Despite a lack of ability in some areas, the cats tried using their pace to create a bit of danger whenever they regained possession, as they frequently did, according to the plan. One mad dash took Diggles sprinting past three defenders until he lost control of the bounce and kneed it haplessly over the by-line near the corner. Scrounger hollered a choice word or two, but the irrepressible flyer skidded slap bang into the fence without hearing the reproof. The rats resisted an appropriate reaction by keeping a decidedly straight face. As referee, DH had very little to do while practically no direct challenges were being made, and a glance across revealed ten minutes had already gone as two upright palms of the governor's were spread open for his benefit. It was at this stage of the game that Arturo began to work out what the rats' superior tactics were all about. When the ball reached him next he swatted it high over the heads of the spectators and watched it bounce through an opening in the hedge behind them. The whistle went and DH halted play before bounding off to retrieve it. Scrounger looked on incredulous at the move before he sidled over to his fellow forward.

"Oi! Th' goal's over 'ere, in case you've lost your sense of direction all of a sudden."

"I know. We need to talk before they restart the game," said Arturo, keeping his voice low and holding a paw over his mouth. "You see, I *was* right about these rats. They certainly *can* play. And they're better organised to do it how they want. So why are they staying mainly in their own half and just giving the ball away after ever so many passes?

"P'raps they're savin' all their puff f' later on, arter

all, we cats c'n cover more ground."

It was a plausible, yet insufficient answer for Arturo.

"Yes, but don't you see? This way they're making us feel as though we're doing ok. So no one gets too frustrated and starts knocking them about in a temper. Right? Then they simply wait for us to give 'em the ball back - which we're tending to do quickly enough – and start all over again. This way they can keep the mood sweet *and* go on avoiding any body contact. We haven't got within two yards of 'em yet, have we? If they can keep it all going like this into the second half they may eventually try for a goal - after we've run out of *our* own puff chasing them around."

It was an impressive piece of analysis and Scrounger didn't mind admitting it.

"Y' know, yore 'ead's screwed on tight, Arty. An' wot 'xactly, then, do you suggest we 'ave t' do t' counteract it?"

"We're too spread out at the front. We need to crowd and rush them more, so that when one of them gets the ball at least *two* of us are onto them. Perhaps then we can throw them off their stride before they can get rid of it and catch them on the back foot with our own pace."

"Ah, an' with th' ball at our feet, so t' speak, headin' goalwards, nat'rally. Hello, an' here comes the ball agin."

Scrounger glanced back at his own goal and duly nodded an acceptance to Arturo.

"We'll see wot 'e says at 'alf-time. 'E's a bit jumpy in front o' them sticks. But th' lady wants t' keep 'im

297

there, I reckon. Maybe you an' me can put 'em more than a little off their stride. Maybe an accidental stamp of th' foot would do it. In other words - a nobble."

"So they would end up a player short."

Arturo stroked his pointy nose, as his partner of foul play smirked and winked behind a raised paw of his own. The game quickly restarted, finishing shortly after in much the same way it had begun. The whistle for half-time blew - with the score remaining goalless.

The spectacle had so far been entertaining in its novelty and, considering the tremendous importance that was hanging on the outcome of this game, the master of Brokehill evinced none of the usual tension normally to be found at cup finals. He chatted away to Rory for all the world as if he hadn't a care in it. His sister was gathering her team around her like no mother hen would ever do with her own chicks and giving them the usual blast - to stick with it or else. The rats, meanwhile, huddled in their goalmouth to listen to the calmer thoughts of the Captain. It was to be more of the same, depending on how taxing they found the turf. And, of course, the intermittent speed of the enemy. After ten minutes the shackles might or might not come off. Without Oliver, they would be looking for something special from one of the Twins. He had hoped that young fellow might be induced to play his part, but the team had to stay focused regardless. Look at their eyes. Catch them napping. Cat napping. It got a brief laugh and kept them all positive. In an interval during which no refreshment had been provided, Mr Quills allowed his observant eye to rest upon Cook. She was doling out a steaming mixture from a large flask into some polystyrene cups which had been passed among the guests. By this time the sun was slipping behind the high, bare elms and had begun to squint through the branches.

"This air is bracing, Cubshaw," he said, stretching the stiffness from the muscles of his hind legs, "you can almost taste it."

"Oxtail, sir. Soup, that is," came the astute, albeit puffed, reply of his worthy friend.

"We shall have to win this thing, if we're ever to be fed, I suppose. Can't say my heart's in it, though. Maybe I'm going soft."

He sighed, plumped up his chest and, with it, a bit of his remaining dignity as he looked about him for the boys. But something else gave him cause for concern.

"What are No-name and the other two conferring over now, do you think?"

Like the witches in Macbeth the three of them were huddled together in the goalmouth - where any brew being stirred was, after all the fruitless toil of the first half, more than likely to be only one of trouble. Cubshaw appeared to be disconcerted on seeing this.

"Judging from what we know already, I would say they are probably inadvertently engineering our ultimate downfall, sir. If fate and past events are anything to go by."

"Hum. As I see it, the way these chaps are playing, perhaps they won't be needing any extra help from us, Cubshaw."

The teams stayed well apart, as DH got them to

skirt either side of the touchlines and reassemble at new ends for the second half. Then the battle began again. If the new plan was now to rush and harry the opposition into losing the ball, the rats certainly had other ideas of their own. And they wasted no time in showing the less wilier cats what they were really up against.

The emerging pattern was much the same as before, but with one big difference. The rats' middle quartet picked up their pace considerably, and, when it came to the final clearance, the ball was lifted straight into touch. This enabled Messrs Hobs, Nobs, Maxie and Cedric to earn a breather, since the cats were clumsily slow in fetching the ball and deciding where the kick-in should go. Sidesteps and shuffles were out, and crisper, split-second, angular passes were now clearly the order of the day. If they had anticipated the move of the cats to close down space, then the new methods worked a treat in keeping their bodies, as well as the ball, well away from them. Euradice and the Amber Eye seethed as they pounded the turf in stationary unison, one with her foot and the other with a massive back leg. Scrounger's plan was getting harder to execute by the minute but he didn't seem too bothered. At the next roll out, he sauntered back to the goal area for a few choice and equanimous words about the current situation.

"Look, as it is, they can't keep this up much longer. They're still mostly sittin' inside their own 'alf, so you're 'avin' it easy. So's Gus an' Bossy. I'm bankin' on th' extra-time bit. By then, they'll be a busted flush.

They're wound up an' runnin' like clockwork for now - till their batteries run out o' juice. Then we c'n all run 'em down, afore we gets to chasin' 'em into th' river."

He grinned easily. The Amber Eye straightened and bonked the ball once against an ear rip.

"Make sure you do it, then," he snarled, throwing the ball out to Boswick without looking away, "or the grin will be all you have left."

The seconds ticked away with no change to the tempo, although Scrounger's opinion looked to be well founded by the time the final whistle blew. The cats had remained awkward enough in their own endeavours, and it had stayed goalless. But at a cost. Mr Brimble looked casually at his watch without seeming to cast a glance towards an entirely wearied outfield of rats upon whom the grassy surface had taken its toll.

"We'd better begin extra-time right away, I think, while the light's still reasonable," was all he could say.

Harriet looked in earnest at the rats and tried to hide a sense of mounting anxiety as she began scanning the perimeter of the whole lawn. She hadn't slept much due to all the worry, and big, dark rings had begun to show up around her eyes. However, with her arm still locked inside her mother's, she was reluctant to move. Her mother wished she could help.

"There's so many cats out there. Did you say he was cream in colour? I can't see anything moving over there, Harry."

"He's gorgeous, mum. With big curls and big green

eyes. Grandfather got him from a doctor who came from Australia. A flying doctor. He's a Persian. A Brisbane tom. He led the team out, so he must be about here somewhere."

She so wanted everything to remain the way it was. Yet, for all she knew, in the next ten or so minutes that happiness might be sorely dented. Irreparably. Forever. She failed to catch her grandfather's evasive eye; and there was still no sign of Prince anywhere.

The teams remained the same way as the whistle started extra-time. The rats were quickly back into action, but not having been allowed any rest had left them more sluggish and uncoordinated than before. Hobs took to humping the ball straight to Mr Quills or Cubshaw whose combined lack of control made a blindfolded juggler with too many balls seem positively capable. Captain told him off despite its effectiveness in wasting precious seconds of the cats' time. That there is a right time as well as a wrong time for everything, even in a game of football, cannot be gainsaid; but what happened next was quite possibly the moment when fate, as Cubshaw had recently described it, lent a hand. Someone booted the ball high near to the touchline where Maxie stood wide on the right. As he trapped the ball he stumbled and lost its whereabouts for two vital seconds, giving Arturo time enough to charge forward. Maxie dithered and, turning too late, found himself jolted off his feet by the hammer blow of an unseen leg coming the other way. Scrounger slid to a halt. DH galloped to the scene where the right-wing rat had landed. Out cold.

"Aw, sorry 'bout that. 'E didn't see me comin'. Loose ball, see. Wot a pity."

Scrounger looked to the heavens for forgiveness as he picked himself up. Or rather in thanks.

"Well, perhaps I can give you the benefit of the doubt on that one," said DH, as a movement beyond the touchline distracted him sufficiently for his mood to brighten in an instant. Familiar cream curls revealed themselves to be nudging forward a small, dark figure from the shadow of a darker evergreen bush. "I suppose you do know that a substitute is allowed on for an injured party?" said DH, quickly recomposing himself with an air of authority.

Arturo showed a look of perplexed dismay at hearing this.

"What! Do you mean they can use another player?"

DH knew their tricks too well, but also knew the rats were tiring and needed a short-term boost to get them through the last five minutes for any chance of snatching the game from the fire.

"That's about it. I never thought to mention it before, since there's only ten of you to start with. But, if you've no objection, and I can't think why you should have, all's being fair in love and war ... "

"Let Lumpalong 'ave it 'is way, Arty. It don't signify," said Scrounger, hiding the truth with another fixed grin, knowing more desperate measures could now be on the cards. There was a signalling snort and the whistle blew again.

"There! See! There he is!" Harriet clutched at her

303

mother's arm, as her beloved cream cat came into full view on the other side of the lawn. As the players trudged round on opposite sides to opposite ends for the last time, Prince was urging Olly to give it the best shot he could to see them through.

"Naw, Oi'm naw ixpert loike yerself. But you can't forgit yer skills owvernoight. Yew ain't jes maykin' up th' nambers. Besides, yew've plenty in the tenk t' last yew foive odd minutes, mate. So, you git yerself on. Yore what's knawn es an impect player - to chaynge the course of the metch!"

Standing nearest for the restart, Arturo heard the closing words of the incitement and was unable to resist one of his own.

"*You're* a fine one for changing courses! A fine traitor *you've* turned out to be!"

Prince leaned forward and cocked an ear, ready as ever for a slick riposte.

"Plenty of wind buildin' up hereabowts. Was it trainer ya sed, mate? 'Cos if ya did, Oi'll take it as a compliment, an' naw mistayke!"

Olly quietly acknowledged he'd always been in the wrong place at the wrong time and that this might be the last time it really mattered to change all that. To the relief of his team, he stepped out into his best position: in the middle of a reshuffled pack.

To say his speed pulverised the cats' back four would be to misinterpret what happened next. But in the following four minutes a renewed sense of their destiny made his surging runs very dangerous. Only the desperate leaps of stricken cats at crucial moments delayed the final killer pass that looked likely to be coming.

"Them little varmints are leavin' the babbies an' the rest of 'em t' be drownded in th' sack, now!" shouted Norman the Poacher, whose former attributes of patience and silence might have been better suited to the present occasion instead of the morbid spout of verbal disparagements he was more eager to display.

Cook warned him at once.

"I do wish you'd stop goin' down that track, if you please, Norm,"

She hardly dared to look as the flurry of fur swerved back and forth like skaters on a rink of green ice. But it was a gripping finale, all the same. Mr Brimble and Rory checked their watches almost simultaneously. Then the older man gave a mysterious hand signal to Mr Pale, who departed the scene at once. Gaining some rare possession, there was just time for the cats to make one full-scale advance, as they tried to break through by sheer force of numbers. But Boswick messed up the sequence of passes and, slow to run back, left a gaping hole in the defence. Nobs was onto it in a flash and finished the counter-attack by cutting inside a beleaguered Gus and sending over a raking cross which Lief, a rat replica of big Norman if ever there was one, should have met like an express train. But the Amber Eye came out like one himself to put him off the ball as it flew over their heads. Coming in late on the blind side Hobs tried to sneak it inside the post, but it skimmed over his foot and squirted behind to safety.

All eyes closed. Ooh! So near ... and yet so far! Euradice blew her top, and the referee blew out his cheeks - as the governor blew the final whistle. 0-0! It was still all square.

The master of Brokehill sought out his sister, as she stood alone in folded-arm defiance behind the cats' goal. The teams had fallen back on either side of DH, who now strictly marshalled the middle line accompanied by Prince.

"Hah! And now what?" said Euradice, getting in the first of the inevitable exchanges.

"I suppose you'll want to toss a coin for the winner. Double-headed, is it?"

Her brother ignored this remark and stated the case as to how a result could be obtained.

"We could do things the old-fashioned way and have a replay. But I hardly think it's right under the circumstances, and since you detest the old ways, I fear we shall have to resort to a scaled-down version of the modern method."

"Which is?" Her face said everything.

"The penalty shoot-out. Not something I regard as always appropriate when it comes to cup finals. But, perhaps, wholly fitting in our case. Holding your nerve. A touch of the OK-Coral, eh?"

She looked at the cats and then at the rats, slumped and exhausted, who, having had most of the ball, hadn't yet managed to put it in the net. Pooh! Foolish man. So be it! Mr Brimble nodded, and DH called the captains together. The distinct possibility of this happening had thoughtfully been anticipated, and

DH was ready to detail the arrangements made for it.

"Right, lads! West wing goal. Best of three kicks it is. First two by the forwards, then the third one to be nominated. Winner takes - er – all."

He closed the wrinkles over his eyes as the reality of what was at stake hit home to him like never before. But he didn't let them see it. He feigned the removal of a mote from one of them and rubbed at it fairly rapidly. Yet the jade eyes beside him understood it perfectly. The eyes of Captain Greybands and his opposite, Mr Quills, also shared an understanding of their own as they faced each other across the line. Win or lose, it was the moment their boys would become men. You could be magnanimous in victory, yet not so proud in defeat. It wasn't just about prominent positions, or abominable cats versus indomitable rats, even. A captain was not one forever, as Greybands and Mr Quills well knew in their staunch hearts. Neither spoke a word. There was no need. DH regained his grip on things and barked an order.

"Rats of Brokehill!" he yelled, uttering the identifying name with emphasis, "over on the right, there! And you lot can stay hereabouts!"

He pointed the cats in the direction where the governor and his family were standing. That would give 'em something to think about. Who they were up against. It would also later prove to be a shrewd move. Having watched the rats take the game by the scruff of the neck from the opposite touchline, Prince ambled past the grouping cats with the hiss of traitor sounding into his indifferent ear till he reached the family side, where he got a warmer reception from his mistress and her delightful mother. Mr Brimble faithfully believed that a happier ending could not be denied these true and loyal supporters of Brokehill manor. Not now. He turned and asked Rory to toss a coin, if he had one on him, and then turned to face Euradice once more.

"You call. It's just to decide who goes first."

"Rats tails!" cried his sister with a vengeance.

Rory flipped a fifty-pence piece. Heads it was. Cats had first kick.

Georgio had been a goalie for a long time but had never faced anything like this before. And probably hoped he never would again. Thees could only 'appen een Eengland, he said to himself as he walked slowly to the goal. Silent faces watched him from the designated area as he checked his position and braced himself. Greybands had whispered the single word "Arena!" in order for each loyal member of the team to keep that vision fixed firmly before him. Scrounger had been miffed by the failure to gain an advantage in extra-time and was determined for once not only score, but to knock somebody's flippin' block off in the process. Hit it hard and take the midget with it. Easy as birds. With the ball already on the spot, he backed away, spun round and hit it, just as he'd intended, hard at the head of the fearful goalkeeper. Too hard and too fast and too true the ball slammed off the side of Georgio's head as he made a reflex dive to his right. It ricocheted from the inside of the post to whack him hard between his ears once more as he landed. He hadn't seen it coming, and neither did he see it going, as it spooned off him straight back into the net. 1-0 to the Cats. A couple of the younger players dragged him away before the rest gathered round trying to restore him to his senses. Scrounger swaggered back to where Arturo waited his turn and chose this key moment to impart another of his intimate and self-possessed disclosures.

"Look, I ain't about t' capitulate, though there ain't no tellin' wot'll 'appen with 'im when 'e gets 'eadstrong. Or 'er, f' that matter. 'Cos if anythin' goes, shall we say, pear-shaped, she's liable t' cut an' run an' leave most of us adrift. Then agin, if she get's control of this ole place, most of us will be an irrelevance. Seen it before. So, I'm ready t' fly, if I must. Like that ole chant goes: Kay sirrah, sirrah. What will be, will be."

The first penalty for the rats was left to the capable feet of Billy Battle. Billy had not seen too much of the ball during the game, although he'd sat deep and plugged away obediently as agreed in the game plan. He took only a couple of steps back as the Amber Eye spread himself across the goal as expansively as he could. Not that it was an easy shot, but that it was a placement stroked more gently than it might have been, gave the Amber Eye plenty of time to corkscrew in mid-air as he headed the wrong way. To the heart-stopping relief of the cats he stretched out an elongated fist to swat the ball well clear. The Battler, avoiding their eyes of jubilation, turned and walked away from the scene without a word. Next up for the cats' number two kick was Arturo. The face in goal was also a number two - the sole volunteer replacement, in this instance - the fearless little Jed.

"Go on, Arty! Another nail in their coffin! It's where you always wanted to be. Now get this one in! There's nothing to miss! Bang it!"

His mistress screwed up her features into all the long-standing aggression that he had become well used to seeing. Maybe some semblance of a smile would return to that hard face, so long as he didn't screw up. He saw through the net to the buttoned up raincoat, to the piercing eyes whose fiery condition had no need of support from the lowering sun as they glinted venally above the crossbar. Was this where he'd always wanted to be? Whose nail was this really for? Suddenly he wasn't so sure if he wanted to spend the rest of his days, either here or at a seaside flat, as some second or third-rate stooge cat. Do your natural duty. You must. He clenched his eyes ... que sera, sera ... what will be, will be ... and blazed the ball wildly over the bar, missing his mistress by a hard yard.

"You complete idiot of a pinched-nosed piece of pointlessness!" she yelled into his face, each word flung out as a chosen stone for every bone in his skimpy frame.

Arturo warded them off with a satisfied indifference and wheeled away, smiling to himself. There was no time for further recriminations, because the rats had Cedric ready for their chance to level it. His great fault, if he had one, was of never being certain which

310

side to aim for in these situations. And it is in moments such as these that a wavering, two-minded failing is so cruelly revealed for what it is. A bottle. The Amber Eye saw precisely where the ball was heading and palmed it away disdainfully as it arrived far too close to him in its hashed execution. He had hardly had to move his body. Cedric, on the other hand, crouched in anguish and put his muddled head between his knees. Ye -ess! The cats were back in the hunt! And Euradice knew who she wanted next for the last kick.

The final penalty-taker had not yet been decided upon by Mr Quills, but even as he was about to open his mouth he was unceremoniously barged aside, as the Amber Eye, emboldened by his two triumphant stops in the shoot-out, made his dominating way to the penalty spot.

"This one's mine. The pleasure of the coup de grâce is to be all mine," his voice snarled in an undisguised tone of murderous intent. "This one to finish it! They can't come back from this!"

Arturo's miss was not entirely wasted on Jed in that he had been able to judge how fast the ball travelled through the air and was thus all the better prepared to respond to the trajectory of the thunderbolt that was certain to be coming his way next. He stood again between the posts and winked bravely at a groggy-looking Georgio before staring back down, locking onto the ball waiting on its spot. He had not taken up this art for nothing. Euradice chanced to look up to the dark, black stones that rose above her in the heady realisation that they were but one net-searing strike away from her grasp. Not to mention, of course, the hour-glass of her obsession. She clenched her fists, as the Amber Eye thundered in to thrash the ball towards what to him appeared more than ever to be a virtually empty net. As Jed said afterwards, everything seemed to be moving in slow motion from the moment the clunking foot made contact with the ball and he had in an instant launched himself in the right direction. As it floated above his head, he jack-knifed into a backflip, sticking out his nose as far as he could for the faintest of touches, enough to wobble the ball out of its devastating flight path. It lifted a fraction and zoomed narrowly over the bar with barely a half inch to spare. As in all things miraculous the save was over in a flash. But for those who missed it, a ball landing cheerfully on a flowerbed instead of in the back of the net was proof enough of its occurrence. The strong did not have the battle.

Euradice was as speechless as the Amber Eye was disbelieving. Harriet was one who had shut her eyes, and she now opened them to the shrill yells of relief from those about her. A tight-knit circle of rats jiggered in delight. The game, somehow, was still on! One final penalty was left, and its taker was also perfectly ready. A sense of something dramatic was unfolding, something almost intangibly sublime, especially to those who had witnessed knife-edge moments like this before. Rory leaned down to test the reaction of the cats, as they milled about the touchline, trying to escape the radar of their mistress's anger. But her sights were fixed upon a group of rats whose calmness would come to define the stark difference between the takers of these final shots. The line between glory and ignominy, however fine, was still a line. To an untrained eye, separating the wheat from the chaff was no easy task. Euradice was only practised in deception - deluding self-deception – where straggling trees loomed forever large without so much as a wood in sight. Rory scratched his chin and chuckled with a notion of expectancy.

"They look reel tense, a fancy. Them twa carts yonder, they dinna b'lieve the big yin c'n pull sumthin' oot o' th' barg."

Mr Brimble said nothing and made no attempt to observe closely any of the faces around him. Could skill and know-how be neutralised by sheer size and power? Perhaps. But, then, this had been a highly unusual match where any number of relevant factors might prevent the purists' choice from winning. The history of football was full of stories of that kind, and it was all of a lame excuse if you ended up being on the losing side. Something more than just an ability to score or to defend was needed when it was all as cliff-hangingly close to the wire as it was right now. Nerve. The identity of the chosen taker was well-known to him. The bands along his back were the marks of generations past who had kept freedom's flame burning brightly long before his time arrived. The present Captain was no less a true upholder, and a cool customer he was, too, by the look of him, as he made his unflappable way to the penalty spot. A worthy inheritor of the dignity and strength which had been passed on by his predecessors. He was the living proof of Mr Brimble's theory of belief being invincible. And knowing that his master's eyes were upon him, Greybands was ready to give as good a demonstration of it as you would ever get. The cool, brown eyes aimed steadily through and beyond the object blocking his path as he visualised the ball as being already home and dry. He turned to Olly and gave him a look of firm assurance that the right decision had been taken. It was his responsibility. This one was definitely for him. Which way? Where? The roaring fire had since become more of a simmer of uncertainty in the belly of an Amber Eye whose dominating presence no longer struck the same fear. The lawn held its breath as the ball was fired. The big cat dived one way, but the deceptive kick, all coolness and craft, flew straight and true, dissecting the goal through its centre with Euradice behind as its target. In!! Rats had levelled the score! 1-1!

The lawn duly erupted with a roar louder than before as momentary astonishment purified itself into an undiluted feeling of real hope. Mr Brimble allowed himself to squeeze Cook's right hand and his grand-daughter's left, as they in turn showed their unbridled joy by hugging the ladies next to each of them. He then raised a hand and posted DH and Prince as cover for the rats' positions. Euradice stood drained and ashen, her arms motionlessly folded, as the control she'd envisaged two minutes ago looked to be doing some fairly formidable folding of its own

314

around her. Saying nothing, she gave Claire a dirty look. Her niece shook her auburn head slowly and returned it with a disgusted look of her own. Mr Brimble, meanwhile, stepped forward, took the ball from the net and placed it back on the spot.

"Now comes what is termed as sudden death, Euradice," said her brother as he faced her without emotion. "First one to miss - loses - all. Sudden death, you see."

Greater emphasis was placed on the negatives than on the mortal word.

"Aye, thart's th' rools an' aboot how it stands, missus," agreed Rory, giving her a mock salute. "So ye'd better peck yer best maun, if ye have onyone on 'em left. Exceptin' yerself, ye unnerstand."

The cats had slumped visibly, as though having to take another kick might be asking too much of their erratic abilities. Scrounger, though, was in no doubt that Boswick had more than enough snap in him for this and pushed him forward. Little Jed trotted back into the limelight, slightly unsure if he could pull off his trick for the second time, although his face, at least, was giving nothing away. As he began taking a few deep breaths, Greybands mouthed him a whisper of hope. 'We shall not fear'. But fear was the one thing the Amber Eye was not about to let get the better of the Cats. He reasserted his authority with a steam hammer of a shove into Gus' back.

"There's our man for the job! Boswick nearly cost us a goal. With those eyes, I wouldn't trust *him* with a beach ball!"

But Scrounger was equally adamant and told Boswick to get on with it. Miracles didn't happen twice. Gus, however, took one look at the Amber Eye and needed no second asking. In full obedience to both their mentors, the squabbling pair began a furious stint of pushing and shoving of their own to get to the ball first.

"Gerroff! You can't find your own eyeballs! This one's mine!"

"No! You get out of my way, you cat ass, or I'll kick you out of it!"

The stand-off reached a vigorous level of resistance as they locked arms in the embarrassing battle to take the kick. Little Jed watched in amazement, as they staggered nearer and nearer to the ball. Mr Quills shouted in alarm, but too late. A foot swung sideways and clipped the ball with the gentlest of force. Whoever it was that made first contact was hard to say, as both cats lurched apart and fell on their backs at the same time. It bobbled into the goalmouth where Jed stopped it with the lightest of touches and picked it up. He wore an expression of goggling disbelief. There was a silence followed by an unearthly shriek as the two cats rolled onto their stomachs to witness the evaporation of their dream. Euradice gripped the crossbar for support and split her nails, as they dug into the painted wood. Greybands was first to move by yanking Jed out of the firing line and back into their protective circle where he finally dropped the precious ball. The tall figure of a man gave an order and pointed insistently towards the empty goalmouth.

The Amber Eye, steaming with furious resentment, marched alone to the goal as though to a place of execution and waited. And waited. Waited for the deathblow now loaded and sprung back like a bullet in a pinball machine. For the taker was taking his time. And for the taker, it was more than just the privilege extended to the last man standing. More than just a personal act of sweet revenge. Around him familiar faces, animal and human, were tense with anticipation, waiting for the cry of victory that would mean different things to different people - in his case the realisation of a dream - but nothing less than the whispering cry of freedom. The cool air mingled with the distant echoes of centuries as they reverberated against the dark, sun-struck stones. Olly sized up the goalmouth with its small matter of the keeper.

Many a dream stranger than this had been fulfilled, and since he had rehearsed this moment many times, it didn't seem so strange any more. He had almost no need to look upon the goal or take several strides back before turning his attention to that one final obstacle between him and true freedom: the evil of the unforgettable Amber Eye. The past and future might reel away like frames of an endless lifetime - but the dream was now, and the present was to be no shot in the dark. The whispers that knew so many things had ceased, and his mind was empty save for what his eyes remembered. No further words needed to be said, no visions needed to be seen. His shoulder twinged. Then came the moment of recognition as the cat-with-no-name greeted him with a curled lip of ebony.

Of hatred's heart. A hiss of boiling water spurted forth in one large, single drop.

"You!"

His ashes were about to be blown away for good - whichever way he or any one else looked at it. Olly ran in and answered him in the only way he could: striking the fearful blow to drain the lifeblood from the Goliath in the goalmouth. The aim was true. Lowering his shoulder, it was a dipper and a swerver of a shot. As it had always been. Past the despair of the Amber Eye. Almost past the stricken eyes of the would-be mistress. Till the ball was embedded in the top right-hand corner of the net. It was all over. 2-1! Rats had won! Then came a long, shrill whistle. Then it was sheer pandemonium.

The final whistle signalled the start of an unusual display. A procession of candles were lighted up, seemingly without hand, one by one, along the lower and upper windows of the west wing. Shadowy figures could be seen shuffling the length of each of the darkening rooms where the curtains had been swept apart, the yellow dots multiplying in their dark bluish interiors like pinpricks of galactic lamplight. If the battlement stones had come crashing down all around her, Euradice could not have fled the scene with a more dexterous a dash than she did as the whistle blew. Her game was up and her whole world was falling apart around her ears. But such a rapid departure was nothing compared to the vanishing act accomplished by Scrounger and the Amber Eye. Their game, too, was irrefutably up, but they were the first back into gear. They charged headlong through a forest of legs and darted away through the gap in the hedge beyond. Gus and Boswick had decided on the same course, but found the route promptly blocked by Rory and Norman the Poacher, crouching on the touchline like slip fielders in bad light. Undaunted, both cats executed a sidestep more nimble than anything they had done during the game and fled along the path that led back to the outhouse. Mr Quills, looking from Cubshaw to his three dumbstruck youngsters, then, finally, to the tight circle of rats, dallied in two minds on what to do. The circle was guarded by DH, who had remained at the rats' side, both unmoved and unmoveable, as the final whistle went.

"The boys, Cubshaw! Keep 'em close! It seems to be every man for himself now we've fallen short. You were right about the game being up for us. I have to say, though, I thought the rats were formidable in every department."

Cubshaw ducked nervously, as a yard or two away a pair of jade eyes sought him out. The three younger cats formed a small circle of their own with their defenceless eyes riveted to the ground.

"As I said earlier, our downward spiral was inevitable. No-name had more hot air in him than her Ladyship's tropical greenhouse ever had. With his unfortunate propensity for getting out of his own puff. We could make a run for it, sir, but our boys are rather done in, and done for, I fear."

Cubshaw was proven correct in this opinion also,

as several pairs of arms came down and hemmed them in all at once. By then, it was too late – and there was nowhere to run.

The candles had frightened the life out of Arturo, coming on like that - life that was needed by his frozen limbs to jerk him back into action. In all the confusion no one had singled him out or had made a grab for him, certainly not his frenetic mistress, who was presently nowhere to be seen. He thought a voice shouted at him and he tore off in the direction chosen by Gus and Boswick, since it was the line of least resistance. He nearly ran into Mr Pale coming up the path with a small box in his grasp, but, ignored yet again, he scuttered away and broke into a wary trot as he turned the corner. Then he saw it. The black saloon, drawn up and ready to go. His mistress was slamming a rear door in a strop of anger when her eagle eye caught sight of him on the path. She raised her fist and motioned with her other hand.

"So! There you are, you prune head! Get in, because I am about to go - right now!"

Euradice waited by the open door, hovering gauntly like a charged-up bouncer outside a busy nightclub. Arturo stood and waited also. Suddenly,, from out of the shadow of the stable door two darting shapes, thinking quite the opposite, flung themselves across the back seat in a blur of diving tails With the bells of defeat still clanging in her ears, Euradice looked on with alarm as they fought for space, scuffing at the plush leather seats where a few bags had been injudiciously placed. She glared pointedly from one cat to the other, though no amount of objection was going to shift either Gus or Boswick from their chosen place.

Arturo watched the panic station with a mixture of consternation and mild amusement, still in two minds, before he heard himself addressed by a different voice. It was coming from behind a tree next to the stable. A torn ear craned round its sinewy bole.

"Hey! Pssst! Why don't you come wiv us? It's th' life you deserve. She's got wot she deserves - them two squabblers. Just do yerself a favour. Old haunts. Thameside. Well? We ain't got all night."

Arturo's mind went off at a tangent as he waited, too consumed to go over all his fears once more. Perhaps a fear of the unknown was a much lesser evil than he had imagined, more notional than real. No meow had ever passed his lips, not since the time when she used to smile and say they sounded like the seagulls on the nearby shore. When she smiled he hadn't felt lonely, and when she went out he could always listen quietly to the slopping music of the waves, as they gushed back and forth below the window before sending him to sleep. Only scowlers were landlocked, but he wanted to learn how to smile again – alone. There were always the rivers - winding and winding - to always make a life seem longer.

"Well, how long are you going to remain a waste of space! I'm not stopping a minute more. So, you'd better get a move on - *now!*"

He straightened, took one last look at those bothersome, angry eyes ahead of him, hesitated for a split second, then chose life by scampering across to the tree where he vanished - for good. Or perhaps for bad. A scapegoat, a scapecat, to carry the sins of his mistress away into the wilderness for ever and a day. Euradice shrugged and slammed the door before struggling into the driving seat. She paused to glance through the mirror at all that remained to her. The quarrelling between her disenchanting pair of refugees was over for now, as they occupied themselves in vigorously licking a variety of scratch marks to soothe their battered spirits. Brokehill and its environs, however, received not so much as a bat of an eyelid as their mistress wrenched at the ignition and sped away with a gutsy roar which articulated pretty well the pent-up rage of her silent fury.

The scene of triumph left behind was, as to be expected, the very antithesis of her rapid departure. Instead of the long shadows of the elms, the rats, now tranquil and expectant, beheld row upon row of candles, their stuttering flames glimmering against the windows like a congregation of angels' wings. The circle of rats had broken up, with various individuals in continuous hugs of congratulation, by the time DH stepped back to allow the governor a bit of their attention. Mr Brimble went down on one knee, as if in solemn reverence, and gently placed the hourglass on the ground in front of Captain Greybands with a sense of gratitude not easily translatable into mere words. He tilted it in his hands to make the silvery sand of time trickle and sparkle in the embers of the setting sun. Like all things good are meant to be, the presentation was kept simple.

"This symbol of your freedom you have won for all the right reasons. Your heads did not drop when all looked lost. They never shall, as I - as we - well know. So then, to the Rats of Brokehill!"

He'd said more than enough. He stood back to let them look upon, and be allured by, the ever-changing, never-changing gleams, as twilight fell besotted and entwined by the spiritual tears of a house of stars.

"Have we won it?" asked little Jed, touching the smoothness of the pedestals, as they winked back the last of the sun to his bewitched and bewildered smile. The others crowded round him and laughed in a delirious, electrifying dance of victory,, the flecks of earth and bits of grass sticking to their hair beginning to be attracted by the pulling power of the blue-black stones studded around the top and bottom of this most intricate of trophies.

" 'Cos if we have, I'm feeling tired right now, and, if nobody minds, I should rather like to go home again!"

A Time For Peace   Chapter 10

Home. Home is where the heart is. Or should be. And if many more than two are beating at the same time and in the same place, then it can only be the best of homes possible. Where the gentle hum of conversation and occasional laughter fills and spills about the room like those proverbial apples of gold tumbling from a generous basket. For the long shadows of Saturday evening sun has turned into a Sunday morning glory and, since the time is both right and bright, whatever words are spoken here are bound to be soothing to someone or other. Gold is fairly appropriate, and not so rare, either, for a room that's full of it. Where rays of sunlight gild objects and warm faces in such a way as to makes the presence and purpose of a flaming fire seem almost superfluous. But, as always, a fire there is. The tower may be cramped, but the hearts of those here are by no means cramped towards each other. So it is good to talk. Except to one member of this little gathering.

A wrinkled eye looks smartly around before deciding to go back to sleep. What's all the fuss about? They didn't know him like he did. Said they were going to win, didn't he? To keep the peace. Well then, let a dog enjoy his bit of peace. You always put your money on the best team to do it. A safe bet's a safe bet, and he knows a winner when he sees one. So what, if the governor had put his whole way of life on it?

Great managers take bold decisions. Mind you, it had been a close run thing. Hard enough at the best of times to get any uninterrupted kip around here, though. Not much chance of that today with another nipper grabbing all the attention. One's enough, though he's an exception, he is. He'll keep his pea green eyes on this tearaway and say a few choice words when needed, no doubt. Never short of a phrase, he ain't. Would've been an asset to the agency, only they never considered cats. More's the pity. He brought the best out of our friend the supersub, at any rate. Made us all go to bed happy in the end. Bet that lot are sleeping it off well after waltzing up and down that pitch, doing laps of honour round and round the timer. With those twins staring at the candles, rabbiting on about the dancing girl. Ridiculous pair. Still, they earned a bit of praise from the Captain for keeping it nice and restrained. A cucumber if ever there was one, him. Forensic? Definitely. Whorr! Now it seems this lot are staying on for a Sunday roast, so I'll just have to put up with all of it. Blow me if they're not going off again! A woman's voice, followed by two or more laughing. Perhaps he wouldn't have it any other way, mind, this being the best of times. So long as they left him alone with a bone and a bit of Yorkshire dipped in the gravy. No real need to smell that. To keep his big heart beating by the fire.

"You don't believe a word I'm saying, do you. I can see you don't."

His matter-of-fact voice of calm confession had

been interrupted by a loud and extremely wide-eyed gasp of incredulity. The master of Brokehill Manor expressively widened his own in the ensuing silence in an endeavour to prove he wasn't having her on. The fire licked the underside of a fresh log as an adroit poker was applied. He went on nodding insistently as though to verify its truthfulness as he sat down, then broke into a smile aimed solely at the two women sitting side by side on the carpet. There was a third woman sitting in the leather chair, who was adding a nod or two of her own but with a good deal more gravity. The penny seemed to drop, as Claire covered her face with her hands, lost her balance and fell backwards, laughing in astonishment. Harriet looked on highly amused as an agile, pert-faced cat, startled by the movement, seized the chance it had been waiting for and leapt out of the comfortable lap of the third woman. Clinging, lightweight feet trembled unsteadily with tension as they landed on Claire's stomach. A new game. She lay back to catch her breath. Both were too much to take in at once.

"Of all people, you do amaze me, Dad. The *entire* house?" she said at last.

Her father nodded again. So did Harriet. His daughter lifted herself upright, clasping the cat skilfully to her before it could spy out the land and take another springy leap elsewhere. She looked from the cat to her father and back again, wondering who had the greater sense of misadventure.

"All you've worked and struggled to keep. It would all have disappeared - in a flash. That's if those rats hadn't produced a flash in the pan of their own," she said with a passion.

Her father knotted his eyebrows as he sought to get things back into perspective. His mood grew a little more demanding of fairness and understanding.

"Claire, I think you can cut a bit more slack for the rats than that. You saw it for yourself. They showed belief and great courage in overcoming what was, even to me, an unknown quantity. As rats go, they were no underdogs."

DH Cooper might have twitched a sullen ear, but nobody was looking.

"Yes, they were terrific, Dad," she conceded, using another of her favourite words, but meaning it quite sincerely this time, "and yet to risk everything for *her.* That awful aunt whose name I can't bring myself to mention."

"I know, I know. We've been over that already. You might consider it to have been a risk, but it was to show the value I put on freedom. To preserve the sort of peace that we're enjoying now. You see, I'm no skinflint, and these ambassadors of mine just happen to be sporting ones in the grand tradition of the great game. So I feel indebted and vindicated. I suppose, when you come to think about it, all the Brimbles have taken certain risks at various times in their chequered lives." He stopped to give her an audacious smile. "I took a risk with your mother, you know."

Claire twitched her nose and brought the struggling cat up close to her face: "Umm. And look what you got. I've made such a real mess of *my* life, haven't I?

"No. There's always time left to turn things around. If the rats can prove that point, you can. So can we all."

His daughter sat up and placed the invincible Diggles next to Jade Eyes for safekeeping, then put an affectionate arm round her own daughter. Her father was adamant.

"Whatever I have tried to do for Harriet, I have done for you, too. If there was any risk, it was taken with you in mind. And I don't say that to blow my own trumpet. The result makes me glad you're both here today!"

He looked from the one to the indistinguishable other.

"My home will always be yours. For both of you."

Claire nudged her daughter and brightened.

I suppose we do like this risk-taking, no-nonsense Dad, don't we?"

Harriet assented readily. Mr Brimble sat back and winked broadly at Rory, the one other member of this close-knit group. Rory asserted with a wide, gummy grin of his own.

"Do you, indeed. Maybe some of the enduring power of the hourglass has rubbed off on me at last," he said, jerking his thumb to the window ledge behind him.

There the object of desire continued to pulsate in a dazzle of blue and gold, swallowing and spewing out streams of sunbeams as they poured in from the window as though drawn by an unseen magnet. Claire got up and side-stepped her way to the chair occupied by her father to sit girlishly along the narrow arm. He felt her light touch, as his daughter observed closer to hand the shimmering that wavered like a patina of charged electrum around its upper and lower filigreed rims.

"It is, if I may use the expression, fabulously old, and I thought it was time to keep it at the highest point of the house rather than the lowest. For a while."

His daughter tapped the scroll of the arm before locking her own inside her father's.

"Maybe you're good for each other. You're old and fabulous, too. Or you will be, if you keep us all on the edge of our seats like this."

It is in such moments that new hope and trust are formed. Until now, Rory had remained tactfully anonymous, but the studied look on his face had been changing as often as the hourglass itself as he stroked pensively on an unshaven chin.

"Aye, thar's mony a slip 'twixt cup an' lep, as th' saying goes. Yer sester seems t' have hard plenty o' those. How'd she know aboot the bauble bein' here, then?"

Mr Brimble, alerted by the proverb, found in it a suitable link to throw as much light on the affair as any reflected by the relic in question.

"It was, in fact, another slip which set me on the track of my sister's devious scheme. A slip of paper, to be precise. I guessed DH had discovered it by some mysterious act of good fortune and, being the instinctive detective he is, left the evidence where I

329

could not fail to miss it."

"And? What did it say?" Claire gripped his arm as though the intrigue was becoming a classic case of 'Whodunnit'.

"Well, there was a London address and a diagram which I recognised at once to be that of the hourglass. How she had been able to draw this from memory with all its component parts and a rough measurement added, I did wonder. I remembered leaving her in here to her own devices one morning about a month or so after her arrival, so she certainly would have had the opportunity to search around for the glass. Then I took out an old pre-war photo album of when we were children. I hunted through until I found the pages where my father had displayed the hourglass for the only time I can recall. Most of them were taken by an archaeologist friend to whom he'd accidentally let slip about its existence. He was interested in seeing the tourmalines, as I dimly recall. There was a photo of me with this man's arm around my shoulder, which my father must have taken, I think. Then another where my father, me and my sister were sitting behind a close-up of the hourglass. I remember her crying when my father eventually removed it, and he made sure she never saw it again. It was this picture that was missing. So she hadn't found the hourglass itself, but the next most useful thing to be getting on with. Of course, she never believed I would somehow discover its loss."

"Whart did ya do wi' th' slip o' pippa?" prompted Rory.

"Ah, well, I rang the number and had a very pleasant chat with an antiquarian who cheerfully admitted having received the photograph in question. I asked him whether he was aware that it was in fact around seventy years old. Really? He had guessed it was old and wondered why the picture wasn't simply an up-to-date colour print. A woman had made a valuation enquiry – but without having enclosed any correspondence address with the photo when it arrived. Just a mobile number. All very unconventional, he agreed. He stated that working solely from a picture was not ideal and it might take quite a while before any conclusions could be reached on it. He would be in touch, but she would need to be patient in the mean time. I then revealed that the photograph had been stolen, and that the woman in question was an imposter, likely to be of criminal intent. That she was being monitored. Strong words, but all very true, of course."

Claire laughed irreverently at this.

"I told him not to worry, but that his services wouldn't be required any longer. I asked him to return it to me, and gave him the missing address he needed. Which he has. End of story. I think I handled it rather well, all things considered. If my sister's desire had not gone any further, she would have been welcome to keep it. But now she has nothing with which to console herself."

Cook had been listening with the others, her admiration for Mr Edward knowing no bounds, seeing as how he'd been one step ahead of everything

331

and everyone.

"From start to finish, always anticipatin' her moves, so to speak, sir. An' her never knowin' 'ow the pretty thing was all bound up with them rats arter all."

Then she remembered the dinner.

"I best be gone to see what it's doin'. An' in case them boys of mine 'ave quite failed to get the better of themselves. Still, they are a stately pair who love their nook in the kitchen. Now I don't 'ave to put up with no more o' them catcalls which as near drove me to a madness".

She was about to go, but, catching her breath, was unable to resist a further comment about the new inmates.

"Arter breakfast this mornin' they slipped out very quiet, an' I found 'em later in the library under the French windows. Sittin' in the sun an' lookin' to be snoozin' at first, till I saw they 'ad their eyes openin' now an' agin like they were chattin' to each other."

"Do they have names, Mrs Dains?" asked Harriet as she looked down at the young cat which her mother had adopted since the night before.

"Well, talk about slips o' paper. That woman left me a crumpled one when she first brought 'em in. She never cared for their names. These two are - well, I calls 'em Quills an' Cubby. They look at me a bit funny when they hears that, though they don't seem to mind the meals I make 'em. The old 'ouse seems to 'ave its compensations, if you know what I mean. Now as to these others, I got t' know 'em from callin' an' callin' 'em till I was in a frazzle. This one's Diggles, as you know, an' the others were Squeals, who Mrs Pale says she were fated to 'ave arter bein' squirted by 'im with the insides of a chocolate cake, an' Sabre, who now crosses swords with Vera unless that Norman comes to pop 'im in a bag which I don't reckon she'll allow." She drew a deep breath. "Anyway, I'll best get on down. If you really are 'appy to eat in the kitchen, sir? Or p'raps you'd rather - "

"We wouldn't think of eating anywhere else, Mrs Dains. We'll be down around one-ish."

"I can't tell you 'ow relieved I am to see the last o' that woman, so's I can get on in peace besides."

With that she bustled out more lighter of heart than the coming of Spring could ever have made her.

"And so say all of us," agreed Claire as she leaned over to kiss her father on the cheek and gather the latest member of the family into her arms once more.

"She simmed to harve loozer wretten all oover 'er," added Rory. "Lake a bad 'un."

"Which reminds me," said Mr Brimble with a beam. "It looks like I'll be having a crop of my rare apples ready by this year or next. And I should like it if you'd help me market them, Rory. They'll probably turn out to be a very distinguished variety - sweet and golden, I hope - namely, the Brokehill Honeytops!"

Claire looked from the settled array of family across to the solitary cat sitting luxuriously by the fire. She knitted her brow and shook her own generous tresses.

"When I think of her storming off like that, all ready to go, win or lose, well, it could almost make you feel ashamed to be a Brimble!"

Harriet sat back with a wide, contented smile of surprise on her face and stroked Prince's gleaming back. It was by far the best thing she'd heard anyone say all morning.

★   ★   ★

As mornings go it was the best one he had known for a long, long time. The whispers were as silent as the air was still. He no longer needed the dreams of sleep to hold him fast. For the dream was indeed real. And he had done it. Where never such a great crowd of sleeping rats were ever seen strewn across the Arena, as an unusually fat candle burned in the middle of the centre circle. Hobs and Nobs, with the smiling face of Billy Battle between them. And not a ball in sight in their lambent field of dreams. He had never seen that before. Nor this. The lawn with its two orange nets framed in white - the sole remains of yesterday's memories. The second coming. Yesterday's reality had become a blur. Just the taking of a kick, while the rest was ... well, nowhere. Like a candle soon extinguished by the wind. All that mattered was freedom, the timelessness of pure freedom. He saw the ball, the very same ball, still embedded in the west wing net. A symbol of the reality that time had not forgotten. Where their freedom had become an undisputed fact. No number of imaginative 'ifs' or 'buts' could ever change the result of yesterday. It was history now. Whether he liked it or not, he was a part of that history. Unerasable history. And the stuff of legends.

There had been no roar of a crowd, only a hushed silence when the kick was taken. Almost without any need of careful aim. To embed it - deep in the net where it now still stood. If your name was on it, it was on it, Billy had said. He shook it free and carried it to the halfway-line, before dropping it on the centre spot. To take one more accurate, yet much gentler, shot. The river ran on indifferently, as two excitable birds went on with their daily quarrel upon a branch high in the elms, without ever noticing the unerring journey of the ball, as it finally crept undefended into the opposite net. He raised his eyes to the blue sky and whispered. He had stepped inside another world, a world he had always known existed, but one which he had never really known before. For the purist of freedoms. Just to play the game - the game that would go on forever. And he had no need to hear the words of the inscription written beneath the gift of the hourglass, as it sat in the tower window watching over this wide, wide world :

' *For Time Hath No Consequence*
≈ *And Leadeth Me To Nowhere* '

Lightning Source UK Ltd.
Milton Keynes UK
09 March 2011

168933UK00001B/3/P